Terribly Charming

Jenni Archibald

This book is a work of fiction. Any resemblance to persons living or dead is coincidental. All scenarios, conversations, incidents, interactions and personalities are drawn from the author's imagination and are not to be construed as real in any way. If you see a striking similarity in yourself or others, realize that it is to the credit of the author to have hit upon human nature so accurately. If you see a resemblance between yourself and the evil enchanters, you may want to consider a reformation.

ISBN-13:
978-0692488843 (Super Jala Publications)

ISBN-10:
0692488847

To my mom and dad, who taught me to love books

Chapter 1

It was long past dark by the time I rode up to the castle gates. I had been gone for a little over a week and I was tired, dusty and so hungry I could have eaten a feast made for giants and still asked for seconds. I reined in my mare, Rowena, and then paused. The sound of slightly muffled shrieks of rage filled the otherwise quiet courtyard. It was coming from inside the castle and I recognized the voice even though it was pitched much higher in decibel than when I'd last heard it.

The shrieking continued, increasing in volume and intensity even though it was traveling through stone walls thicker than the tails of Miraysian dragons. My men glanced at me and I sighed. We all knew what it meant.

"Sounds like the Princess Mia," said one of my guards.

"It *is* the Princess Mia," I said, dismounting. I pulled my maps from the saddlebags and turned Rowena over to a waiting servant. Walking to one of the side doors, I pulled it open and looked cautiously inside. The screeching increased in volume now that it was no longer blocked by thick stone walls. I inched into the alcove leading to the main hall and peered around a large potted plant.

Princess Mia stood before Ron, her entire frame trembling with the force of her anger. "And to think," she shrilled, "that I gave you a chance to wed me, *me*, the Princess of Rynora, when I could have any king, emperor, or tyrant, from the sea east to the western shores!"

Ron shrugged, which is one of the worst responses he could have given to an arrogant little speech like that. Sure enough, Mia shrieked with rage and flew at him, her fingers curled into sharp little claws of wrath. I watched with interest, thinking that this one might actually manage to do some damage, but alas, two castle guards caught her and held her back.

"I give you full leave," said Ron haughtily, "to seek your kings, your emperors *and* your tyrants. As for me, I'm finished with you." He brushed clumps of dirt off the front of his tunic and stepped over a small pile of broken pottery and mangled plants. I grinned. The feistier ones usually threw things.

The guards delivered Mia into the hands of her entourage, who stood by the main entrance with bags packed and departure planned. Ron was nothing if not organized. I waited until the doors closed behind them before emerging from my hiding place, my ears still ringing slightly from Mia's piercing shriek.

"Princess Mia was a record for you," I said by way of greeting, setting my maps onto a side table. "I expected you to move on *at least* a week ago."

Ron didn't look surprised by either my sudden appearance or my quick summation of the recent drama. "If you must know, Maxine, I only prolonged it because I knew she would be louder than the others."

"The longer you wait with a girl like her, the worse you make it for yourself." I settled into one of the hall chairs and kicked my legs out in front of me. "Where are Mother and Father? Don't tell me they slept through that unholy tantrum."

"They are at Aunt Marge's for the summer celebration. I thought you were with them." Ron sat beside me, his posture perfectly erect as though he were at tea with visiting dignitaries instead of relaxing beside his sister after a long day.

"I was mapping those swamps in the lower quarter of Veiland," I said. "It was a bit messier than I expected." I studied the toe of my mud-encrusted boot, partially obscured by my bedraggled skirt. I hadn't seen a mirror in days and knew the sight wouldn't be pretty. I sighed and continued, "But a swamp is infinitely preferable to this castle when you're disengaging yourself from the latest princess."

He bristled. "Would you prefer that I *married* Mia? You saw what she's like."

"I would've preferred that you not get engaged to her in the first place."

Ron assumed his I-Am-the-Crown-Prince look, which involved looking down at me with his eyebrows raised and his mouth pursed up like he'd just bitten into a lemon. "I am the Crown Prince," he intoned. "As such, it is my duty to seek the hand of a suitable maiden to be my future queen."

I rolled my eyes. "Well, *I* am the Crown Prince's younger sister, and it is my duty to tell him when he's behaving like a Royal Idiot."

"I take exception to that."

"I figured you would." We were silent for a moment, each thinking our own thoughts. Mine were fairly dark ones. People are always asking me if I know how lucky I am to have Prince Charming, *the* Prince Charming, as my older brother. I suppose it's easy for others to look at my life and assume, wrongly, that it's a piece of cake. They think that just because I have a wonderful, almost universally adored brother, that I must be the happiest girl alive. None of them understand that my brother is currently a bigger thorn in my side than my unruly red hair or the princess training classes that mother still insists I attend.

Ronald Alastair Charming the First was born with eyes the color of the sky on a spring morning and shining golden hair the color of, well, gold. He's the perfect prince: handsome,

4

strong, brave and bold, with a deep voice and a way with poetry. The problem isn't so much that he's ideal, it's that he is *more* than ideal. His personal motto seems to be to live up to everything a prince has ever been expected to be in every possible way. Quite frankly, it's nauseating.

He wasn't always like this. Not too long ago he was a fairly typical guy, still universally adored, of course, but overall down to earth and comfortable to be around. He even slouched in his chair every so often. Then my parents got this "fabulous" idea to have a ball and invite all of the kingdom's eligible females. They had been scheming and plotting to find Ron a wife and must have decided that a ball was as good a way as any to get things rolling.

The night of the ball, I spent the greater portion of that particular evening in the kitchens, where no one cared if I tripped or otherwise made a fool of myself like I usually do. Because of this, the drama unfolding in the ballroom was not discovered by me until Ron came rushing in to where I sat shading in the mountain ranges on my latest map. He was holding this impossibly tiny glass slipper and babbling something about the stroke of midnight. Apparently he'd just met the love of his life and she took off before he could get her address. …Or even her name, for that matter.

It took us awhile to find said love of life, given that all we had to go on was her shoe, but eventually we did and a wedding was promptly scheduled. It looked like Prince Charming and his future bride, the overwhelmingly sweet Cinderella, were going to live happily ever after, if you'll pardon me from using such a sappy expression.

Then, for no reason that I've yet been able to discover, the wedding was canceled. Cinderella returned home to her terrifying stepmother and Ron sank into a moody abyss that lasted for several months. He refused to go anywhere and would hardly reply to even the simplest of questions.

So imagine my surprise when, early one morning, I went out to the stables and found Ron there saddling up his favorite horse. This was unusual enough given his absolute lack of activity in the last few weeks, but what was truly bizarre was that his once golden hair was now a deep raven black.

"Ron, your hair!" I exclaimed. "It's black!"

He turned to glare at me and my mouth fell open when I saw that his eyes were a shade of green never before found in the natural world.

"I'm amazed at your powers of observation," he sneered, pushing a lock of ebony hair off of his forehead. Unfortunately for him, this left behind a smear of brown the origin of which I did not want to contemplate. We were in a stable, after all.

"What in the name of trolls did you do to yourself?" I demanded.

"If you must know," he said snootily. "I am going to rescue a princess out in Loustershire. She's trapped in a tower."

"What does rescuing a princess have to do with completely changing how you look?"

He flashed me a smile that had a hard edge to it. It was a look that I'd never seen on my brother's face before. "Rumor has it that the princess of Loustershire fancies fellows with black hair and green eyes." He swung himself into the saddle and galloped away without another word. As I stood there watching him ride off into the sunrise, I had a premonition that the perfect prince was about to become a perfect headache.

Chapter 2

Of course I was right; I usually am. Ron came home a few days later with a girl named Rapunzel, a princess with a lot of hair and very little brains. I had a hard time swallowing her story, which she delivered with wide eyes and a trembling voice to my parents. She claimed that a witch had trapped her in a tower, but it's more likely that Rapunzel bribed the old lady to lock her up so a handsome rescuer would save her. It wasn't her brightest move since her method of rescue involved having Ron climb up the side of the tower using *her hair* as the rope. Can you imagine how much that must have hurt?

In spite of Rapunzel's scheming, Ron ended their engagement after only a week, mostly because he couldn't stand waiting for her to fix the aforementioned hair every day. It took her hours to shampoo it and curl it and jab thousands of hair pins into it. When he realized that he faced an unnerving future involving an untold amount of bad hair days and clogged bathtub drains, he sent her packing.

Then he got engaged to Snow White, whom he found in a forest looking all cute, asleep in a glass case. Now the part of this story that's fake (in my opinion) is that when Ron found her, she was sleeping all delicately with her makeup and hair arranged perfectly. See, if her story really were true, she would have had her hair going every which way and no makeup at all since it was the dwarfs that supposedly put her in that case, and as everyone who knows anything knows, dwarfs are good at a lot of things, but hair and makeup are *not* among them.

Snow White didn't have a chance with Ron once they had been around each other for a few weeks. All she wanted to do was have him kneel at her feet admiring her beauty all day. I suspect that he would have rather had it be the other way around, but whatever the case, he got restless and bored, and off he went on another quest.

During all of this, Ron kept changing the color of his hair and the color of his eyes to accommodate the inclinations of every girl he rescued. Talk about embarrassing. Every time I saw him striding through the castle with a new hair color I wanted to sink into the floor.

No one seemed to care that Ron dyed his hair so often that it became brittle and straw-like; after all, what princess in her right mind is going to quibble when the perfect prince has split ends? And sometimes his eyes were a bit blood-shot, I guess because whatever spell the Royal Wizard used in order to change their color had a few unpleasant side effects. Still, the end result was that the pretty little princesses-in-generally-on-purpose distress got exactly what they wanted: a handsome prince who looked exactly like they'd always imagined, courtesy of a touch of artificial coloring.

Soon all of the kingdoms far and wide knew about the amazing and wonderful Prince Charming, and more and more princesses *somehow* got themselves embroiled into one helpless mess after another, all in the hopes that *The* Prince Charming would come to her rescue. I had already intercepted countless tear-stained letters from young ladies claiming to need rescuing from goblins, hags, dragons, and in one case, a house cat.

There were also a few letters indicating that if Ron didn't come marry them *immediately*, he was really going to regret it. These letters made me nervous, but when I tried to show them to Dad, he just shooed me out of his war chambers with a lot of scoffing noises. He also said (along with the scoffing noises), "No one is going to cause any trouble for your brother. You worry too much."

When I tried to show them to Mother, she was distracted because one of the queen bees in her hives was behaving strangely. I could tell that she wasn't really listening because when I read the part in one of the letters where it said, "and if you don't marry me, I will come to you and I will have your weak body crushed and thrown to the crocodiles," all she said was, "Well, dear, sometimes these things happen."

Sometimes these things happen?

Finally I read the letters to Ron. He listened patiently, as befits a perfect prince, but when I finished he only smiled and patted me on the head. Since he's only four years older than my fifteen years, I found this extremely irritating. I glared at him as he said, "Maxine. I am *Prince Charming*. I do not fear silly little females who send me 'scary' letters. Besides, I'm almost never home, so if this girl does come, I won't be here to worry about it." He wouldn't listen when I expressed concern for the rest of us being home when the 'silly female' came.

Realizing that no one else was going to do anything, I met with the palace Captain of the Guards and arranged an increase in security. But this had been going on for almost six months now, and as I sat in the Great Hall beside my oblivious brother (whose hair was currently a disturbing orange color and whose eyes were an odd shade of purple—Mia had unusual tastes), I realized that an increase in security just wasn't enough. At the rate Ron was going, he would propose to every single girl in every kingdom in the land. Given that a lot of these girls had rather powerful parents, it seemed like it might be a good idea to stop my brother before we were wiped off the map.

Chapter 3

I didn't sleep much that night, as I was busy going over what I needed to do. My plans included making a personal visit to the Royal Wizard, whose official title was "The Magnificent Wizard Marvelonius." I felt he was at least partially to blame in regards to the whole mess with Ron since he was the one who helped him change the color of his hair and eyes. The wizard had to have some idea of where Ron was heading next, and I planned to find out all I could.

Marvelonius had attended only a handful of the Charming family royal events during the twelve or so years of his employment in the Kingdom of Veiland. He tended to keep to himself, which is usually the way of things when it comes to wizards, so I didn't know him very well. My parents had hired him after the last three wizards died of old age in quick succession of each other. They figured that hiring a younger wizard would spare them from having to deal with another funeral and hiring process. Mother and Dad are very practical that way.

Early the next morning. I rode out towards the small wooded area where the so-called *magnificent* wizard lived. It was important to catch him unawares, as from what I had heard, he tended to not be at home if he knew visitors were coming.

"Hey, Max."

I'd been so deep in thought that the quiet voice was enough to make me yelp in surprise. Poor Rowena thought that we were under attack and she reared up on her hind legs, her eyes rolling in alarm. It took me a minute to calm her down, after which I narrowed a deadly glare at Connor Landon, my best friend and occasionally greatest irritant.

"Thanks a lot, Connor." I growled. "You scared me half to death!"

Connor is the adopted ward of my Aunt Marge. While she is the queen of the neighboring country of Laria, Connor himself is not of royal blood, which means that he isn't allowed to talk back to me on penalty of beheading.

Technically.

Of course, no one really takes the whole beheading threat literally anymore. It's left over from the days of my great, great, great grandfather King Maximilian the Menace, who beheaded his subjects for all sorts of trivial reasons. When I was eleven I memorized this list of archaic laws for use as leverage in my arguments with Connor. I'd needed all the help I could get.

I still do, actually.

"If you would prefer that I not say anything," said Connor, "even when you are about to trample me with your horse, I suppose I must submit to your wishes and die in silence." He scratched Rowena under her chin. "And for your information, I said hello three times. You just didn't hear me until you were right up to me. At least Rowena knew I was here, didn't you, sweetheart?" Rowena nickered, the hairy traitor.

"You did *not* say hello three times!" I protested.

"I did too. As you first cleared the hill, I said, 'Hello, Princess Maxine, where are you off to?' When you ignored me, I asked quite politely, 'Did you not hear me, you simpleton?' And finally I marched right up to you and said 'Hey, Max.' That's when you yelled at me."

I narrowed my eyes and drew myself up to my full five feet three inches. In the saddle this was obviously more impressive than it would have been if I'd been standing by Connor, who at seventeen is almost six feet tall. "I think that you've forgotten that you aren't allowed to show insolence to me. I could have you beheaded if you aren't careful."

He rolled his eyes. "How many times are you going to use the old, '*I'm going to behead you, I am a princess*,' line? Try for something a little more original, I beg of you." His voice as he had mimicked me had been high-pitched and nasally.

I kicked him with my boot. "I do *not* sound like that."

"'*I do not sound like that. I am going to have you beheaded. I am a princess.*'" He dodged out of the way of a second kick and grinned up at me. "Where are you off to, Your Royal Highness Princess Maxine?"

I was conscious of a secret relief as he teasingly regarded me. More and more often lately Connor had been acting strangely distant and formal. Although I tried to get him to joke around with me like he had when we were younger, he'd developed this troubling tendency to retreat into a secret world of his own.

Still, I wasn't sure how to answer his question. If he knew that I was planning on visiting the wizard alone, he would almost certainly try to stop me.

"I'm just out for a morning ride," I muttered. I admit that I'm not a good liar. Though this lie was perfectly believable, even I could tell from the sound of my voice that I was up to something.

Instead of answering right away, Connor studied me inscrutably. If you've never seen this expression on someone's face before, let me assure you that it is really annoying. It's as though they have all sorts of secret thoughts going through their mind, usually thoughts that you'd want to know about, but their face is completely blank.

"How interesting," he finally said.

"What? Don't you believe me?"

Instead of challenging me on it like he would have once done, he just shook his head. "It's not my place to question your activities. However, I feel compelled to remind you that you are a princess."

Like I might have forgotten. And anyway, wasn't he just giving me a hard time for always bringing that up? Suppressing a surge of irritation, I asked, "What's your point?"

"Princess Maxine, soon your parents will be looking for a suitable husband for you. Maybe you should stop wasting time wandering around every corner of your family's kingdoms with your maps. Maybe you should learn how to host balls and—I don't know—" Connor waved his hands impatiently, "Learn how to play a harp or something. What I mean is, maybe you ought to learn things that a proper princess would already know how to do."

"Just what is it that you're trying to say?" I demanded.

"I'm saying that I think it's time you grew up. I think that you need to stop behaving like a tomboy and learn how to be a lady." Connor looked away as he said this, his expression grim.

I could feel my face turning red like it always does when I'm really and truly furious. "Just because I map kingdoms doesn't mean that I am not a lady," I snapped. "I know everything there is to know about being a princess and I've found it to be an empty occupation. If I choose to fill my time with more meaningful pursuits than sitting around being silly and gossiping, it's no business of yours." I gathered up the reins and spurred Rowena forward.

"Wait, Max—" Connor called, but I didn't turn and I didn't stop.

Chapter 4

While it has been my observation that most wizards are strange and reclusive—it's almost like a job requirement—as soon as I rode into the clearing where the Wizard Marvelonius' cottage stood, I realized that in his case, he seemed to have the edge. All sorts of odd things were scattered around: large metallic objects, small colorful gadgets and other bits and pieces that I couldn't even begin to describe.

I dismounted and went to inspect a bizarre item that loosely resembled a chariot. It was a dull green color, with a window in front and back, and windows along the sides. There were four round black wheels made of some strange substance that yielded slightly under my finger when I pressed on it. I peered in the window and noticed another round wheel, much smaller and narrower, in front of one of the seats.

If this were a carriage, how did one harness the horses to pull it? And what were the strange symbols and knobs along the panel by the narrow wheel inside? I pulled the silver handle on the door and it opened easily. I was about to climb in so as to begin a more thorough inspection when a voice stopped me. "Princess Maxine! Hello there, my lady! Um, please do not enter that object, if you please!"

I turned to see Marvelonius approaching, his dark eyes narrowed. He was strangely attired in trousers of a faded blue shade and a tunic that seemed rather too short, ending inches below his waist rather than going to his knees as was the current style. I eyed Marvelonius' clean-shaven face, wondering that he wore no beard as is traditional among wizards. He *was* wearing an exceptionally fake smile, which did nothing to conceal the irritation in his eyes.

"Princess Maxine," he said. "What an unexpected pleasure to see you here, at my intentionally remote home, where I am only occasionally interrupted by decent people who never touch any of my things."

"What kind of carriage is this?" I asked, ignoring his sarcastic tone. "And how does one harness the horses to draw it?"

"That? You can't. I mean, it doesn't work," he said, looking guilty. "Nothing here does."

I glanced at him. "Doesn't work? How could any of it *work*? Everything here is inanimate." His mouth tightened into a thin line, which I figured meant that he wasn't going to answer me. I walked over to inspect another object: a wooden box with a glass front and a lot of dials and knobs on one side. The glass was slightly cracked and the wood was warped from being exposed too long to the elements. "What is the purpose of this?"

"Um. It doesn't have a purpose." He stepped in front of me, blocking my view. "Would you like some refreshments, Princess Maxine? Or maybe a nice potion? A little princess like you, maybe you have a young man whom you'd like to give a love potion to?"

I raised an eyebrow. "Are you implying that I would *need* a potion to get the attention of a young man?"

He blinked. "No, of course not—"

"Forget it," I said, putting up one hand. "Actually, I came to see you because I was wondering if I could ask you a few questions."

"Er. Certainly. Please, come inside. I have some nice tea and biscuits all ready."

I gave a last glance at the chariot and then followed him into his cottage. The inside of Marvelonius' cottage was also full of the most interesting objects imaginable. I was so busy staring at everything that I stumbled into something leaning against the wall just outside the front sitting room. It was another object with wheels, this time just two of them, one in front and one in back. It had a seat in between the wheels, and was made of a combination of shiny black and silver metal. I stared at it, fascinated.

"What is this?" I asked the wizard's fast disappearing back. It was obvious that he wanted to get this visit over with as quickly as possible.

"What? What are you asking?"

"This object. What's it for?" I ran my fingers over the smooth leather seat.

Marvelonius ran his hands through his spiky black hair, muttering to himself. It sounded suspiciously like cursing. Cursing in front of a princess would've made you liable to get your tongue chopped out in my great, great, great grandfather's day. What a pity that some laws have been set aside.

"Princess Maxine, what about that tea, eh? Wouldn't you rather have tea than look at boring, dusty objects of no interest?"

"Not really." I turned my back on him and continued to inspect the object. Something about it fascinated me. "It seems to be a riding machine of some kind," I mused. "This is the seat, you hold onto these handles, but how do you make it go?" I pulled it away from the wall. "It's pretty heavy," I commented, glancing at the wizard to see his reaction. He was watching me closely but to my surprise made no move to stop me. I fiddled with the various knobs and buttons until finally he made an irritated noise and stepped forward.

"Most people just ignore everything in here. All they want are their measly little potions and they don't care about anything else." He gave me a hard stare. "I'll show you how it works on one condition: that you promise me, on your honor, that you won't bother with anything else around here without my permission. Some of this stuff is pretty dangerous. Agreed?"

I didn't hesitate. "Yes, I promise."

Marvelonius looked into my eyes for a second before nodding. He pulled the machine away from me and wheeled it outside. I followed him, feeling a growing sense of anticipation that I didn't understand. There was something about this two-wheeled machine that gave me the same feeling I used to get as a child on my birthday: an almost fierce excitement.

Marv cleared his throat. "This is what's called a motorcycle. Technically, it's a Harley-Davidson Dyna Low Rider." He saw my blank look, shook his head, and continued. "It's an object used for travel in countries that you have never heard of and couldn't go to even if you had. Most people in this area don't pay much attention to my collection." He glared at me. "You just have an overdeveloped sense of curiosity."

I nodded. I would have agreed if he had told me I had two heads. I just wanted to find out how it worked.

"First," he said, eying me, "You might need to change your clothes."

I glanced down at my comfortable, well-worn dress. "What's wrong with this?" I asked.

Marvelonius ignored my comment, ushering me back into a small room in his cottage where he gave me a pair of trousers similar to the ones he was wearing, along with a loose, long-sleeved tunic. He left me to change with an order to hurry. Once dressed, I returned outside, enjoying the ease of movement made possible by the trousers. I knew Mother would have a heart attack if she saw what I was wearing. She hated my tired old gowns enough as it was.

Marvelonius put on a pair of dark spectacles and handed me a shiny black helmet similar to what knights wore. I pushed it down over my head and then clambered on behind him. I barely had time to get settled when a loud roaring sound filled the air. An instant later we were flying down the road, going a speed I had never thought possible.

"Yeeeehaaaah!" yelled Marvelonius as we took a corner at so tilted an angle that I thought for sure we were going to tip over. We didn't, and I laughed as he sped on at an even greater rate, the motorcycle roaring like a dragon. All too soon he came to a stop.

"That was fantastic!" I exclaimed.

He glanced back at me. "You want to try it?"

I gaped at him. "Try what?"

"Driving this thing," he said impatiently.

"By myself?"

"Sure."

"Are you serious?"

"You can ride a horse, can't you?"

"Of course. How do you think I got to your cottage?"

He ignored that. "Well, riding requires balance, which you obviously have, and as for guts," he grinned at me. "That remains to be seen." He instructed me on how to operate it, having me dismount so he could demonstrate. After showing me various parts of the machine, explaining their functions, and teaching me important words like "bike" and "rev," he got off and held it for me as I climbed on.

"Start out slow," he cautioned. "And if you crash, not even my magic can help you."

My heart was pounding but I felt wonderful, alive in a way that I had rarely felt before. I gently released the clutch, shifting my foot on the pedal as I'd been shown. The machine roared beneath me and I began to move in a small circle, one foot dragging in the dust. The wizard shouted instructions. "Get your foot up! And steer it in the direction you *want* to go, for pity's sake! No, not that way, you dunce, you're going to run into that tree!"

It took awhile but slowly I felt myself getting the hang of it. The absolute pleasure of controlling the machine, of flying along faster than I had ever gone before, thrilled me to the core. I finally came to a stop in front of the wizard and pulled off the helmet, laughing out loud for the sheer joy of it.

"That's it," he said, nodding with satisfaction. "You understand."

I climbed off the bike, putting down the kickstand like he'd shown me. Standing still felt strange after my rapid movement on the machine and I realized that I had better sit down or fall down. I sat in the grass at the side of the road and Marv came over and settled beside me.

After a moment of companionable silence I asked, "So how does this motorcycle work? How is it powered?"

Marv grinned. "The people who invented it use something called gasoline, but I modified it so it runs on plain old air. It's a lot more cost effective, let me tell you." He lay back on the grass and put his arms behind his head. "So, what did you want to ask me?"

"Oh yeah." I had forgotten about my original purpose in visiting the wizard. I picked a blade of grass and began tearing it to pieces. "It's about my brother."

He muttered something under his breath. I ignored him and continued. "I was wondering why you help him change the color of his eyes and hair. Don't you realize how much trouble he's been causing by charging around looking like every girl's dream?"

A soft snort made me look up. "Your brother's looks have nothing to do with his behavior," he said.

"Yes, they do! He thinks that he should look perfect and be perfect and help every girl who needs rescuing. And it all started with him changing the color of his hair."

Marvelonius shook his head. "Princess Maxine, think about it: Prince Charming would act that way even if he couldn't change how he looks. He just goes the extra mile and tries to make the princesses he rescues feel like their dreams have been fulfilled. In a way it's pretty thoughtful; he has to do a lot of investigating sometimes to find out what a princess likes, and it's a lot of work for him to change things around like he does."

"So you're on his side." I stood up to go.

"Hang on! You have a quick temper, don't you?"

I glared at him. "And don't you dare say that it goes along with my red hair like everyone else does."

"I wasn't going to."

"Good."

"Good."

We glared at each other for a minute and then he threw up his hands. "Alright, look, we're not getting anywhere. Do you have any other questions for me or shall we head back?"

"Yes, I do."

"Go ahead."

"Do you know what princess my brother is going to rescue next?"

"Do you think that I know everything?" Marvelonius demanded.

"I think that you know where my brother will be going."

"And why should I tell you, if I did know?"

"Because it's extremely important," I said. "My brother's behavior is causing problems that will have far-reaching consequences for this kingdom if someone doesn't stop him soon."

Marvelonius looked at me. "Alright," he said. "We'll go back to my cottage and I'll tell you what I know."

Chapter 5

In no time at all, we were back at his home. Marvelonius settled in a chair on his porch and waved for me to do the same. "Okay, here's what I know," he said, with the air of a man who wants to get things over with. "Your brother, the debonair Prince Charming, is off on a quest to rescue a princess who is further away and harder to reach than any other lady he's ever gone to the aid of before."

"I don't remember seeing any letters from princesses really far away. How'd he find out about this girl?"

Marvelonius shifted in his chair, not looking at me.

"Wait a minute. You told him, didn't you?" I accused.

"Look, are we going to quibble over measly details or are we going to get to the point?"

I folded my arms. "Go on."

"As I was saying, this particular damsel in distress is being held captive in a castle over the tops of the highest peaks to the east, where dangers lurk in every desperate shadow."

I made a scoffing noise. "How can shadows be desperate?" I asked.

He shot me an irritated look. "Your brother is going to rescue Princess Golden from the clutches of three malevolent beasts, their eyes glowing red, their fangs long and yellow, their claws sharp and deadly. They live beyond the Guarded Entrance to the Eastern Peaks."

"Oh, right. I know exactly where *that* is."

"I thought that you were the big map-maker of the Charming family," he said. "So I suggest that you put your skills to use."

It was harder to get information out of this guy than it was to get my brother to keep his hair the same color for three consecutive days. "Fine," I said. "Now let's talk about my quest."

Instantly I had his full attention. "Your what?"

"You know, my quest? The quest I'm going on to stop my brother from proposing to every girl in the land?"

Marvelonius shook his head. "Sorry, Princess. If I'd known that you had some crazy idea to go off and 'rescue' your brother, I never would have told you anything."

"What did you think I was asking you these questions for? An autobiography about life in a royal family? Of course I'm going to rescue my brother, and I'll do it with or without your information."

"Don't make me use a memory-erasing spell on you," he threatened.

"And don't make *me* angry. I'm liable to do things that I wouldn't ordinarily do."

He smirked. "Like what? Cry and stomp your feet? Pout in your tower room?"

"That's it." I stood up. "You are the rudest person I have ever met. And I think that you have forgotten that every princess is given one special gift at her birth."

He paused, a look of alarm flitting across his face. "I did kind of forget about that. So, uh. What gift were you given?"

I smiled. He had reason to be nervous. While most fairy godmother gifts were sweet and sugary, there were the occasional princesses who could transform themselves into fire-breathing dragons or had the ability to give entire villages a severe case of warts.

As a kid, I'd worked long and hard learning how to whistle so I could use my gift. When I finally mastered it, Mother and Dad made it a rule that I not whistle in the castle, or on the castle grounds. ...Or anywhere else.

Ever.

And while I didn't always obey the no-whistling decree, the unexpected perk of this rule is that not many people know about my ability, so when I do use it no one even realizes it was me.

"Don't worry," I told Marv. "I'll only make it last for a few days." Before he could respond, I pursed my lips and whistled. Then I whispered into his ear, "Three days." The Magnificent Wizard Marvelonius didn't even blink. He sat unmoving, staring at me without even a hair of his head shifting in the breeze.

I had always kind of thought that my fairy godmother, whoever she was, must be a bit batty giving me a gift of freezing living creatures instead of a beautiful singing voice or a heart of gold. Not that people were really *frozen*, of course, that was just the easiest way to describe the condition people ended up in when I whistled. What actually happened was that they stopped moving, almost like they were living statues. And I had the power to decide how long they stayed as statues, whether it was only for a minute or for days on end.

As I stepped back to survey my work, I had to hand it to my fairy godmother: for the first time in my life this little gift that she had given me had really come in handy. I suspected that it might prove useful again before my newly undertaken quest was through. In any case, right now the wizard was stuck; frozen for exactly three days. Hopefully that would be enough time for me to be well on my way.

I felt a guilty twinge as I left Marvelonius sitting stiff on his porch, his face frozen in a comical mixture of surprise and the beginnings of outrage. By the time he came free from my little game of statues, the outrage would no doubt have developed into a full-blown loss of temper. I hoped to be far away by then.

I led Rowena into the nearby stable and gave her enough hay to hold her over for the next few days. I also wrote the wizard a short note. It read:

The Magnificent Wizard Marvelonius

Dear Sir,

I regret to inform you that I was placed in the unavoidable position of having to borrow your motorcycle. I promise to take excellent care of it, and hope to be able to return it to you within the week, provided the windswept peaks to the east are easy to scale on this thing.

Thanks for teaching me to use it!

Sincerely,

The Royal Princess Maxine Cordelia Hazel Rose Charming

P.S. Rowena is in your stable. Be sure to feed her, will you?

It took me a minute to decide where to put the note so that Marv would be sure to see it. I finally decided to secure it to his forehead using a little dab of some glue that I found in a pot in his cottage. With that taken care of, I settled myself on the motorcycle and revved it up.

There was no time to waste. I had to get home, pack my bags, and then be ready to sneak out and follow my brother without anyone noticing. I also needed to consult a few maps on the off-chance Ron left without my being able to follow him. I had an idea of where the eastern peaks were and was confident that I could find my way there on my own if I had to, but it would be a lot easier to just follow him.

I made it back to the castle unseen. After hiding the motorcycle in a thick stand of trees I slipped inside, making it upstairs without a single encounter. Everything was going so smoothly; it was as though my plan to follow my brother on his quest was meant to be.

"Hold it right there, young lady!"

"Mother!" As she marched down the hall towards me, my thoughts were racing. Maybe I could pull this off, maybe she wouldn't suspect—

"What in the name of the Kingdom of Veiland are you wearing?"

Of all the rotten luck—I had forgotten about the trousers.

"I was just about to change. Give me a minute." I tried to slip into my room and close the door, but Mother stepped in the way.

"Maxine." She put her hands on her hips. "Please do not tell me that you forgot again. I could understand when you forgot about Great Aunt Emaline's birthday last month, I could even see that you might have forgotten about the summer celebration. But please, *please* tell me that you remembered your cousin Weldon's engagement ball tonight."

"Engagement ball? You mean to that girl who transformed him back from being a beast?"

Mother rubbed her forehead like she had a headache. "Everyone has been asking me all morning, 'Queen Charming, where is your lovely daughter?' And what do I tell them, Maxine? Do I admit that I rarely know where my lovely daughter is? Of course not! I say, 'Oh, she must still be at the castle, getting ready for the ball tonight. She wants to look her best, after all.' And I come here, hoping that it's true, hoping that for once you are concerning yourself with your appearance, *and what do I find?*"

I was pretty sure that there was no right answer to this question but I gave it a shot anyway. "That I'm almost ready?"

"Oh, not hardly." Mother pulled me into my room and closed the door.

Chapter 6

The following hour was one of the most harrowing that I have ever spent, even counting this one time when a wicked witch tried to get me to use her spinning wheel—one of the oldest tricks in the book, by the way. I had to tackle the old girl and hold her down until the guards came and took her away. That was pretty nerve wracking, but it was nothing compared to what I went through at Mother's hands. She came at me with curling devices for my hair and curling devices for my eyelashes. Then she came at me with corsets, girdles, silk gowns, and shoes with heels so high and narrow that I wondered if she were trying to cripple me. After poking and prodding, plucking, painting and perfuming, she proclaimed me "A Princess at Last."

Apparently creating A Princess at Last can wreak havoc on one's own looks: Mother's artfully arranged appearance was now wrinkled and smudged disgracefully. She rushed out, calling for her maids.

As soon as she was gone, I walked unsteadily in the high-heeled shoes to the mirror to see the results of this unique torture. An elegant stranger gazed back at me; her hair upswept into a lovely creation of shimmering copper curls with little sprays of white flowers. Her eyes were wide and staring; the curled lashes seeming to make them bigger than they already were. The gown, a light green silk with emeralds and diamonds interspersed on the neckline and sleeves, was softer and prettier than anything I had ever worn before.

I shook my head as though shaking off an enchantment. I had more important things to think about than silk gowns and new hairstyles. I grabbed my leather traveling bag and crammed the trousers and peasant blouse into it, along with my boots and a few maps. I threw in a cloak for the cool summer nights and then crammed in two objects that I never travel without: a silver jug and a sword. The jug has been handed down through the Charming family for years. I don't know where it originally came from but it is reputed to hold a never-ending supply of water (very handy when I map desert regions). As for the sword, my grandfather gave it to me when I was a girl and I'd discovered early on that no one ever seemed to see that I was wearing it until I drew it from its scabbard. Having a weapon that stays invisible until you need to use it is an extremely useful feature. Or at least, I imagined it would be. I had never had occasion to test this theory.

I shouldered my bag and threw open the door, wobbling a little on the heels of those wicked shoes. I managed one step out the door when a hand like the pincers of a lobster clamped around my upper arm. I sighed and turned to face my captor.

"Mother, what is going on?" I asked. Without answering, she pulled me along behind her as she marched down the stairs and outside to the waiting carriage. I was starting to feel a little nervous. "You've never bothered me with these girly things before. Why is it suddenly so important to you now?"

"Maxine, please. I do not see why you should be angry and suspicious merely because I brought out some of your natural beauty." She settled in the carriage and waited as I climbed in beside her. The footman closed the door behind me as I turned to face Mother. "It wounds me that my own daughter would feel so distrustfully towards me."

I reached for the door handle. "I think I'll just stay home," I said.

Mother signaled for the carriage to move forward, ruining my escape. I slumped back against the carriage seat as Mother began one of her lectures. "Now, Maxine, I do not want to overhear you talking about maps or swamps or any of the things that you usually talk about. After all, you are a lady, and we don't want to have anyone thinking that you know more than you should about...anything." She drew a small mirror out of her bag and studied her reflection. "Also, no more rough housing with your little cousins. They are too young to know better. You, on the other hand, should realize that pretending to be a horse and letting the children ride on your back, as you did at the last family affair, is not how a grown princess behaves."

I looked at her. "Mother, be honest with me: what are you up to?"

She didn't answer. Her eyes were dark with scheming, looking me over like I was a jar of honey she was thinking of selling. "Darling, you look lovely. You will be a credit to your country."

A credit to my country?

Fighting a feeling of increasing alarm, I asked, "Mother, I hate to ask this, but are you under a spell? Have you noticed any uncannily ugly women giving out apples? You haven't eaten any apples lately, have you?"

"Sweetheart, don't be ridiculous!" She shifted away from me and looked out the window.

I decided that the time for beating around the bush was at an end. I took a deep, fortifying breath. "Please, please tell me that you aren't planning anything drastic like trying to get me married off." She was silent. "Mother!"

"Yes, dear?" She turned from the window and blinked at me vaguely.

"Oh no, it's true, isn't it? You've got a crowd of princes all ready to meet me at this ball tonight, don't you?" I sat back, feeling like I was going to faint for the first time in my life. Unlike other princesses my age, almost all of whom were already married or engaged, I had been left alone when it came to matters of matrimony. I had assumed that my parents had forgotten about me and I'd been very careful to not say or do anything to remind them. Having them turn on me like this was a real shock to my system.

Mother's face hovered into view, her eyes wide and imploring. "Sweetie, I have something *very* important to tell you. Now, you must listen carefully." Just then the carriage rolled to a stop. A footman swung the door open with a well-trained flourish.

"Oh my, we're already here. What a shame. I will have to tell you later, darling."

When I didn't move, she began to climb over me to get out of the carriage. It was a sign that she was really flustered.

I grabbed her arm. "Mother, if you don't tell me whatever it is that you're not telling me, I swear to you by all of the fire-breathing dragons of Veiland that you will have to drag me kicking and screaming into that castle."

Mother's face blanched under her carefully applied powder. "Maxine! Now, there is no need to be so dramatic—"

I narrowed my eyes.

"Oh, all right! I'll tell you." She ordered the bewildered footman to close the carriage door. After we were restored to the relative privacy of the carriage, Mother looked down at her clasped hands and said, "Darling, when you were born, we were so happy. You were such a beautiful baby and we wanted the very best future for you." She glanced at me. "You might remember, dear, how we have a close alliance with the Kingdom of Treagal? You know, to the north by the sea?"

I looked at her blankly. I had heard of Treagal but I didn't remember anything about a close alliance.

Mother continued. "They have a son who was only two years old at the time of your birth, and we made an agreement between the two kingdoms—"

"Do you mean to tell me I am betrothed?" I was so shocked that I could hardly breathe, much less speak. It was fairly common for this to happen to a princess, I had just never expected that I would be one of them. "Why hasn't anyone ever told me?"

"Well, Maxine, your affianced has been out traveling for many years, doing a great deal of exploration by sea. And what with one thing or another, I suppose it just slipped our minds."

"*It slipped your mind* that you had me practically married off to some stranger when I was just a defenseless little baby?"

"And time passes so quickly…"

"So what now?" I managed to say. "I suppose he's here somewhere, waiting to meet me?"

She smiled at me uneasily.

Before I could decide between throttling my own mother or dying from the shock, the door to the carriage was thrown open and my father glared in at us. "What in the name of gnomes are you two doing? Planning on living in this carriage forever, are you?" Beyond him was a large crowd of people, all of them lined up on either side of a red velvet carpet.

"Oh dear," Mother said. "They're all waiting to see you, Maxine. You'd better get out now."

"What are you talking about?"

"Many of these people have come for your wedding as well as Weldon's. He's getting married this week, and you and darling Prince Torstein will be wed, um…next week."

"You've only now told her?" Father scowled at Mother.

"Oh, and I'm to blame? There have been fifteen long years with you having every opportunity, Richard!"

I was in a state of shock. Only by an extra sharp prod did Mother succeed in getting me out of the carriage. Immediately the people on either side of the carpet began to clap and cheer in the celebration of a wedding that everyone knew about except for the bride.

Mother appeared beside me and took my arm. "Smile, dear," she hissed.

I wasn't sure that I remembered how. Somehow or other we made it inside Uncle Phillip's castle where the crowds took on a more familiar appearance. It was my extended family.

"Maxine, darling," Aunt Regina, Uncle Phil's wife, and one scary lady, came swooping over. She kissed the air above both of my cheeks and gripped my shoulders until it hurt. "My dear, you *actually* look nice! I don't know what you did with her, Alanna, but whatever it was, keep it up." She smiled, every pearly tooth gleaming.

There's nothing like a verbal duel with an evil relative to restore one's mental acuity. Aunt Regina and I had been feuding for years. I smiled back at her and said, "Aunt Regina, may I return the compliment. I have admired those crow's feet around your eyes for some time now. I hope that when I'm your age I have such attractive wrinkles." It wasn't true, of course; no wrinkle would ever dare to venture onto Aunt Regina's face without her permission, but it was enough to get her to let go of me.

I rubbed my shoulders, trying to restore the flow of blood, while she glared at me. "One of these days, my girl," she began, when a welcome voice interrupted her.

"Regina, let's all have a cozy little chat later. I'm sure Maxine will love to catch up with you then."

I turned and met my Aunt Marge's twinkling eyes with undisguised relief. "Aunt Marge, am I glad to see you. You will never believe the horrible thing that Mother just told me—"

Aunt Marge shook her head almost imperceptibly before saying, "Maxine, may I present you to Prince Torstein of Treagal? Prince Torstein, this is our dear Maxine."

Time stopped.

Alright, I wish it had. Unfortunately, time has never once accommodated me, not when I've been trapped in endless hours of princess training classes, and certainly not now. I looked at my betrothed and my heart dropped. Dragon's scales, but did he have to be so unbelievably good-looking? Somehow that made it all that much worse.

"How pleased I am to see you, Princess Maxine," he said, bowing over my hand with elegant grace. He straightened and stood gazing down at me with amazing blue eyes. His dark brown hair gleamed in the light from the windows and when he smiled my heart did the funniest thing...

I came to my senses courtesy of a sharp jab to the ribs, credit: Aunt Marge's elbow. "Pleased to meet you too, Prince Totstain," I managed.

"Torstein, actually." He was still holding my hand.

"Pardon?"

"My name is *Torstein,* not Totstain."

"Oh. Right."

Mother stepped in, "Dear Maxine, perhaps you would like to rest a bit before tonight's celebrations?"

"Yes, Maxine, let's go upstairs for a bit." Aunt Marge took my arm. "We will see you this evening, Prince Torstein." After the usual bowing and curtseying protocol had been satisfied, I allowed Aunt Marge to lead me to the relative safety of the fourth floor.

Chapter 7

"You've got to help me, Aunt Marge. They're saying that I'm betrothed to that guy down there and that our wedding is scheduled for next week!" I was pacing frantically back and forth in front of the fireplace while Aunt Marge watched me from a comfortable chair nearby.

"I should have realized that no one told you about that."

"Clearly it's the most well-guarded secret in the Kingdom of Veiland," I said. "Except that I'm the only one who was kept in the dark."

"Well, it *was* recorded in the Charming Book of Royal Events, not that you ever bother with that sort of thing."

"The Book of Royal Events? They write engagements in that?" I was temporarily sidetracked. "So what have they done with Ron and all of his botched attempts—write, 'Oops, sorry, wrong again?'"

She smiled and shook her head. "All I know is that you've been promised to Prince Torstein since you were born."

"Yes, but don't you think that something this important might have come up at least once during the past fifteen years?" I demanded. "Something like, 'Maxine, don't track mud into the castle; by the way, you're engaged to be married to a man you've never met?'"

"I suspect that they were kind of avoiding the topic. You turned out to be a little more strong-willed than they expected. Then the Kingdom of Treagal became involved with their extensive overseas explorations, so communications slowed down a bit. Anyway, you have met Prince Torstein."

"What do you mean, I've met him?" I demanded, waving my hands over my head. "I distinctly remember *never* meeting him." I wasn't making a lot of sense, but it's difficult to make sense when your world is falling apart.

"You were six and he was eight. You lost your favorite toy boat out on the pond and he swam in and got it back for you. It was really quite sweet of him."

"Even if I did remember that, which I don't, rescuing a toy from the clutches of an evil pond hardly seems like grounds for marriage. If he had rescued me from a *dragon* at least, then all of the other important relationship matters would be inconsequential. You know, things like getting to know each other, falling in love, that kind of thing." I picked up a pillow and began to squeeze it mercilessly.

"Most girls would be delighted to find out that they were engaged to such a handsome prince." Aunt Marge looked amused.

"Then most girls are air-headed ninnys," I growled.

The door opened and Mother slipped into the room. "Anyone feeling like a wedding?" she trilled.

It was the last straw. I hurled the pillow at Mother's head. My aim was true but unfortunately she ducked just in time.

"I think that Maxine needs some time alone," Aunt Marge said with a significant look at Mother. They left, closing the door behind them.

There was no way that I was going to stay in this den of scheming relatives and good-looking fiancés if I could help it. I waited until I was sure that they were gone before slipping out of my room, my thoughts already absorbed in the route I would take to get out of the castle unseen. Because of this, I didn't see the individual seated on the floor until I was already stumbling over him. Only by a complicated combination of arm swinging and hopping did I manage to stay upright. Recovering, I turned and glared at the obstacle in disbelief.

"What are *you* doing here?" I demanded. "More specifically, what are you doing sitting on the floor right outside my room?"

Connor didn't look up from his card game. Straightening a card that I had kicked, he said, "I'm guarding to make sure that you don't sneak out."

"You? Why you?"

He gave a brief, mirthless laugh. "It was Queen Marge's idea. No one else would have imagined that you would be audacious enough to skip out on your fiancé. So she sent lucky me to make sure you don't *mysteriously* disappear."

I paused. Although I was still angry with him, I had to ask. "Connor, did *you* know that my parents had a wedding planned for me next week?"

Connor looked intently at the ten of spades he held. "No. I found out when I got here today and saw your fabulous prince."

I felt a rush of relief so powerful it surprised me. At least Connor hadn't been hiding things from me like everyone else. "Good to know. Well, I'd better get going."

Connor looked up. "I can't let you--" He stopped. "Wow." He gazed at me wordlessly. Connor had never seen me dressed up like a princess before, mostly because I never *had* dressed up like a princess before—at least, not to this extent. Either way, as the long moment of silence extended, I began to find his speechless state a bit insulting.

"What?" I asked. "Is it so amazing that I'm nicely dressed for once?" I turned and started down the long hall towards the back stairs.

Connor scrambled to his feet and caught my arm from behind. "Sorry, Max, but you're not going anywhere. I was told that if you disappeared, I would be held personally responsible. Queen Marge gave me permission to take whatever drastic measures necessary."

I glared up at him. "Like what?"

"Don't challenge me on this. Just go to your room and stay there like a good girl."

Good girl, huh? Now there's incentive to be the exact opposite. My eyes grew wide as I stared over his shoulder. I gasped.

"What?" Connor looked behind him, his grip on my arm loosening.

I yanked my arm away, hoisted my skirts up a bit, and bolted down the hall. Unfortunately, bolting in high heels is not very effective. I risked a glance behind to see where Connor was and saw him much closer than I had expected, running with an expression of grim determination. There was no way that I could outrun him, with or without the shoes.

Whirling around, I put up my hands in a signal of surrender, realizing a second too late that I shouldn't have stopped right in his path. The next instant I was thrown backward as he landed on me. Then there was a ringing silence as I lay gasping and trying to get some air back into my lungs.

"Max, are you alright?" Connor's anxious-sounding voice floated somewhere above me and I opened my eyes, fully prepared to deliver a speech about the consequences of tackling royalty. I was startled to find Connor's face inches from mine as he gazed down at me with a worried look. As I watched, his gaze softened and filled with a warmth that caused me to lose my breath again, this time for an entirely different reason. His eyes had little flecks of gold in them. I had never noticed that before.

"You smell…" he murmured.

If you are ever lost in the incredible eyes of your erstwhile best friend and he says, 'You smell,' it sort of shatters the mood, you know?

"Yeah, well, you're squashing me." Even as I said it, though, I caught the rest of what he said, which startled me so much that I stopped squirming. By then it was too late; the strange spell that we'd been in was over. He scrambled to his feet, pulling me up with him, and without a word towed me back to my room.

"Please, Maxine, just stay in there." Connor's voice was strained and he wouldn't look at me as he pulled the door closed behind him. The rest of his sentence echoed in my ears. *"You smell…enchanting."* Connor had never said anything like that to me before. It was so unlike him, I had no idea what to make of it.

My mind was whirling so much that it took me a minute to realize that I was now a prisoner. I went over to the window and looked out. I was on the fourth floor of Uncle Phil and Aunt Regina's enormous castle. According to reports I'd heard, princesses sometimes tore up sheets and knotted them together to create a ladder of sorts to climb down when they were trapped in high places. It's surprising how resourceful princesses can be when they don't have the hope of some noble prince coming along to rescue them.

The irony of my situation was that I was trying to get *away* from the noble prince. Since it's generally an accepted fact that a prince does not help a princess escape from himself, I was pretty confident that I would have to handle my rescue on my own.

Chapter 8

Peering out the window, I observed how hard the ground looked from this distance. It was hard to imagine scaling down the wall, especially using sheets as my makeshift rope. As I considered my options, I knew that even if there were thousands of pillows lying underneath my window to cushion my fall there was no way that I would try it. I settled down on the window seat to plan my next move.

The next thing I knew, Mother was standing over me shaking my shoulder. "Wake up, Maxine. It's time to get ready."

I pushed myself up, feeling stiff. It was then that I noticed the small army of scary-looking ladies-in-waiting standing by the door. Oh crud-in-the-butter. Did this mean another beautifying process? Twice in one day? It was every kind of wrong.

Fortunately the beautifying process went more quickly this time, due in part to the fact that there were several women mauling me as opposed to just Mother. When they finished, I surveyed their work in the mirror with Mother beaming behind me. This time I was wearing a cream-colored gown of crushed velvet. A delicate tiara set with small topaz stones was nestled in my unusually tame copper curls. The color of the stones reminded me of the flecks in Connor's eyes and I sighed, a feeling of deep sadness washing over me.

Mother looked at me searchingly. "Maxine, you should know that your father and I really believe that Prince Torstein is an excellent match for you. We think that he's just the man to help you settle down and become the kind of queen that you have it in you to be. But we will never force you to marry someone whom you don't want to marry."

"Oh yes, we will." My father stood in the open doorway with his arms folded over his chest. Ron was standing beside him, looking like he would rather be out slaying dragons than be involved in this conversation. "Alanna, you and I both know that we have put too much into this match to give it up over the whims of a strong-willed girl. Can you imagine what sort of trouble this would cause between the kingdoms if we jilted the prince a week before the wedding? Treagal would declare a war! I cannot allow it."

"How would my jilting Prince Torstein be any different from Ron jilting all of these princesses that he's been rescuing?" I asked.

"Leave me out of this, Max," Ron said warningly.

"Why should I?" I demanded. "You're the one who's going to cause a bunch of wars, not me. How many girls have you ditched now? Fifteen? Twenty? I've lost count. Does anyone else realize that the parents of these girls are *kings* and *queens* of powerful countries and that they are all furious? If any wars begin, it will be because of Ron here and *not me*."

After a short silence, Mother cleared her throat. "We'd better get downstairs. There is a ball in our honor that we should be attending."

Father scowled. "I would rather stay in my room. Confrontations like these give me indigestion."

"That's not an option, dear." Mother took his arm and they walked down the hall. I watched them go, torn between incredulity and anger. Hadn't they listened to a word I'd said?

"Have you ever noticed how oblivious Mother and Dad are?" Ron asked, running his hands through his hair, which was currently its natural golden color. I assumed that this was in deference to his next quest to rescue the Princess *Golden*.

"Yes, I have," I said. "Just now, in fact."

"Your point about the wars was pretty valid, but what did they do? They just wandered away as though you hadn't said anything. And do you know why that is?"

"No. Do you?"

"Sure. It's because they're so used to living in peace, surrounded on all sides by trustworthy relatives, that they don't want to admit that their perfect son is going to bring it all down around their ears. That's why."

It had been awhile, ever since the Cinderella Incident, in fact, that Ron and I had really talked. "Why are you doing it, then?" I asked. "Why don't you just stop?"

He turned and looked at me. His eyes were an odd shade of gold and his expression was sad. "I don't know how to stop anything," he said. "I keep trying to stop being perfect but it's as though everyone is determined to love and admire me no matter what I do."

"So you're going out of your way to cause trouble?"

"I don't know. Maybe. I'm just tired of being something that I'm not."

I hesitated. "Like a perfect prince."

"Exactly."

"But there's got to be a better way than what you've been doing—breaking so many hearts—"

Ron made an impatient noise. "Don't be dramatic. You know as well as I do that none of those silly girls were ever really in love with me to begin with. They had no idea who I am to *be* in love with me. They were just enamored with my good looks, my fantastic strength, my superior intelligence, my unlimited wealth—"

"Yeah, thanks, I get the idea." I had a feeling that if I had not interrupted he would have gone on for quite awhile. "Anyway, I think one of those girls *was* in love with the real you. What about Cinderella?"

He looked away. "I don't know what you're talking about."

"Why did you break your engagement with her, Ron? I could tell that she really cared about you."

"I don't wish to discuss this any further." His expression was cold.

"Fine. But will you at least give up on the quests? Please, Ron. We can figure out another way to deal with everybody."

"I don't think so."

"Why not?"

"Why not?" The anger vanished from his face and he grinned at me. "Because it's fun, that's why not."

Aunt Marge came out of one of the rooms further down the hall. When she saw us she raised an eyebrow. "Didn't the ball start an hour ago?"

I shrugged.

"Maybe the guest of honor should get downstairs." She prodded my shoulder with her finger.

"I thought that this was Weldon's big night," I protested.

"Weldon's engagement ball is tomorrow. Tonight was planned for you and Prince Torstein."

Ron and I looked at each other.

"Guess we'd better get down there," said Ron. He turned and followed Aunt Marge down the hall. With a sigh I followed them, wondering when Ron was planning on leaving to rescue Princess Golden. I wasn't looking forward to facing my betrothed. It was bound to be awkward.

Chapter 9

The sound of music and laughter came to my ears as we rounded the last flight of stairs to the main floor. Aunt Marge and Ron went ahead of me, descending the stairs with grace and confidence. Royalty came so naturally to them.

I took a deep breath. 'Here goes nothing,' I thought, and walked as steadily as I could manage (they had put me into another pair of those terrible high-heeled shoes) up to the Royal Announcer.

"Her Royal Highness Princess Maxine Charming of Veiland!" he bellowed--*right* in my ear. Wincing, I stepped away from him and began my descent down the stairs. Aunt Marge and Ron were in front of me so I watched their backs for something to focus on. About halfway down, I noticed that things had gone unusually silent. I looked away from the ornate stitching on the back of Ron's dress coat to see what was going on and realized with horror that every single person in that enormous room was staring straight at me. Swallowing hard, I continued my decent even while I frantically tried to figure out the cause for this unexpected and unusual attention.

Then I realized: this was my first public appearance dressed like an actual princess. I usually attended these elegant events dressed almost as casually as I dress during the day, which, I admit, is pretty casual. To the disdain of the other princesses and their mothers, I usually favor comfortable dresses that are worn out just right. It had never bothered me to be wearing my plain gowns while everyone else was dressed in velvet and satin.

Now that I was dressed as beautifully as the rest of them, I realized that it just wasn't worth it. Not only was I being scrutinized critically by every female in the room and stared at with unflattering amazement by most of the males, but the corset I was wearing under the gown was about as comfortable as wearing a camel hair shirt stitched with wire. Not that I've ever worn a camel hair shirt with or without wire, but I can imagine.

I forced myself to continue the descent into the ballroom, trying to ignore the weight of hundreds of eyes watching my every move. I knew that they were waiting for me to trip or do something embarrassing.

I guess I shouldn't hold it against them since I usually *do* trip or do something embarrassing.

I made it down the last few steps without incident and Prince Torstein stepped out from the crowd. "Princess Maxine. You look absolutely breathtaking."

I forced a smile and then gave a shot at fluttering my eyelashes like I'd seen other princesses do with their beaus. "Thanks. So do you."

He looked startled, which I took as a cue that I had overdone the lash-fluttering thing. It's hard to understand why girls flutter their eyelashes to begin with. I mean, how could looking like you have something in your eye be considered attractive? I changed tactics.

"Prince Torstein, I am absolutely famished. Would you be willing to get me something to eat?"

"It would be an honor." He bowed and left, wending his way through the crowd to the tables laden with food.

"Brilliant," said a voice in my ear.

I whirled around. It was Connor, looking disturbingly handsome in a black tunic with a simple silver design stitched along the collar and sleeves.

"What'd I do now?" I demanded.

"You find out that you're engaged to the poor guy and already you have him running around like a chicken with no head? The least you could have done was give it a day or two before you have him at your beck and call. You'll have a whole lifetime together for that." He folded his arms and scowled at the people milling around us.

"What are you talking about? All I did was ask him to get me something to eat."

"Sure. It starts small, but then where does it go?"

"Um. I could eat too much?"

He glared at me. "You know what I mean."

"Actually, I don't."

Connor leaned in uncomfortably close. "What do you even know about this guy, Max? He could be anybody! He could be the kind of guy who is cruel to animals or disrespects the elderly--" His voice was rising and people around us were starting to stare.

I grabbed his arm and pulled him over to a small stand of decorative plants in the corner. "Connor, what is going on with you?" I hissed. "This morning you said some things to me that really hurt my feelings--" He tried to say something but I held up my hand. "But it isn't just this morning that concerns me. For the last few months, maybe longer, things have been strange between us and I'm not sure why. I've always thought of you as my best friend, but I feel like I don't even know you anymore."

He looked down, a muscle in his jaw twitching visibly. Then he shifted and rubbed his hands over his face. "I'm sorry. There's a lot going on right now that you don't know about. Someday soon I hope to be able to explain it to you, and when I do...well, hopefully it won't be too late by then." He looked down at me and his expression softened. "Max, do you ever wonder—"

"There you are, my dear!" Prince Torstein paused when he saw Connor, his friendly blue eyes narrowing slightly. "I beg your pardon, Maxine, but is this fellow bothering you?"

"I was just leaving." Connor seemed to deliberately shove against Prince Torstein as he passed him. Prince Torstein's eyes were no longer friendly as his free hand went to his side as though in search of a sword. It's a good thing people come to these balls unarmed.

He turned to me. "Who was that ill-bred man?"

"His name is Connor Landon. He's my Aunt Marge's ward."

"I see." His speculative gaze brought a rush of color to my cheeks.

"We practically grew up together," I added.

"Really. So he's like a brother to you, is he?"

"Uh, yes. Exactly like a brother." Why did I feel so guilty? I turned away from Prince Torstein's penetrating stare and sat down at a nearby table.

"Here are the refreshments that you requested, my dear."

"Thank you." I picked up the silver fork and took a small bite as Prince Torstein sat opposite to me. I was so hungry that I had to really concentrate on eating delicately as a princess is supposed to.

I wasn't even aware of the long silence until he asked, "Do you remember me at all?" Fortunately he continued without waiting for an answer. "I suppose you *were* only six when we met. But I feel as though I know you quite well. I have kept in contact with your Aunt Regina over the years and she wrote regularly, telling me all about you."

I stopped eating and stared at him. This was news. This was *weird* news. Why were my evil Aunt Regina and my betrothed corresponding at all? "I hope that she was kind in her letters," I managed finally.

"I don't imagine that anyone could write an unfavorable thing about you."

Only with the greatest of efforts did I restrain myself from snorting. I could think of a lot of people who would write unfavorable things about me, and Regina was at the top of the list. The fact that Prince Torstein was writing to her was troubling. He could act as friendly and thoughtful as he wanted, but any guy who got along with Regina needed his head looked at.

He reached across the table and grabbed one of my hands. This put a definite damper on finishing my meal; somehow it felt wrong to keep eating with him trying to be romantic. I sighed and put down my fork.

"I know I should have written to you personally," Prince Torstein said, gazing down at my hand, "but I never knew what to say. I started so many letters to you, but I'm not good at expressing myself on paper. I decided that I would come to you when all was ready and let you get to know me properly." His hand gripped mine even more tightly and I had to resist the urge to pull it away. He continued. "I have put several additions on the castle we will share, and have tried to leave many of the rooms open so that you may decorate them as you wish. I want you to be comfortable and feel at home in every way. May I call you Maxine?"

I nodded. He was going so fast my head was spinning.

"And you must call me Tor. It is what all of my close friends call me. Although, I hope that we will be *much* more than friends." He looked at me with such intensity that I felt my cheeks burn. I had never felt so uncomfortable in my life, and given that I am prone to embarrassing and awkward moments, that's really saying something.

I took a deep breath. "Prince Torstein—I mean, Tor. I'm going to be completely honest with you. Until today, I knew nothing about this betrothal. Not only that, but I don't remember you at all. You seem like a nice guy, so I hope you won't be offended when I say that I'm hoping that we can have a little more time to get to know each other before we, um, get married." Provided I was still around by then.

"I agree," he said.

"You do?"

"Certainly. I will be sure to cancel all of my appointments in the upcoming week so that we may spend every possible moment together before our wedding next Saturday." He smiled at me. "I am so glad that you suggested this. It proves to me that our minds are already connected."

I lifted my lips in a parody of a smile while my insides churned. How was I going to get out of this terrible, horrible mess?

Chapter 10

Suddenly an explosion shattered the air, accompanied by red sparks and thick black smoke. People screamed, rushing to get out of the way of the man who was striding through the billowing smoke towards the table where I sat. He pointed his finger straight at me.

"*You*," Wizard Marvelonius growled.

"He's early," I gasped.

Prince Torstein looked at me, his eyebrows drawn together. "Who is this man, Maxine? And what do you mean he's early?"

I looked at my fiancé. "Um...It's kind of a long story."

Marvelonius was wearing his wizard's robes of red and black, with a tall wizard's cap pushed back on his head. It made him much more intimidating-looking. I swallowed audibly as he took the last few steps to our table.

"*You*." Either he couldn't think of anything else to say or 'you' was the worst thing he could think of to call me. His lack of creativity was a little disappointing.

Just then Prince Torstein pushed back his chair, grabbing the first weapon he could lay his hands on. This turned out to be my fork.

In the wide world of weaponry, a common fork does not rate high in the intimidation department, yet Torstein wielded it like it was a blade of the finest steel. "If you value your life, you will stand away from the Princess," he declared, waving the fork with a deadly gleam in his eyes.

I figured I'd better intervene before wizardly sparks and forks started flying. I stood up. "Marv, I'm really sorry about the whole freezing-spell-thing, I just couldn't let you—" I stopped, noticing his forehead for the first time.

Holy unicorns. No wonder he was so angry.

"'*Freezing thing*?'" Marvelonius's eyes were wild and his spiky hair was going in even more directions than usual. "Who cares about the 'freezing thing'?" I got out of that little *fairy spell* hours ago. It's this other matter that concerns me!" He pointed jerkily at his forehead, where, I am chagrined to report, a small portion of my note was still firmly affixed. The rest of the note had been torn away, but where I had dabbed the glue onto his head, in a rough circle, were the distinct words "windswept peaks."

"Huh," I said, and without really meaning to I took a step closer to get a better look. "That's some strong glue."

"*Glue?*" he snarled. "That wasn't just *glue*, you little idiot! It's the strongest bonding substance known to the civilized world! And you swabbed it onto my forehead! Do you realize that I haven't invented a solvent for it yet? And even worse than that, you stole my—"

It had to be done. I reached up and gave a sharp tug on the jagged edge of the paper on his forehead. Just as I'd hoped, he gave a squeak of pain and didn't end his sentence. But before I could step back he grabbed my arms and pulled me up against him.

"Stay back," he growled at Torstein. "This little pest has caused a lot of trouble! Just because she's a princess doesn't mean that she can do whatever she wants. It's time she learned that."

At last I found a use for the shoes that had been vexing me all day. I lifted my foot and brought my heel down on the wizard's toes. The poor guy didn't stand a chance. He yelped and let me go so abruptly that I would have fallen if the prince hadn't caught me.

Aunt Marge made her way through the crowd of scandalized onlookers. "What is going on over here?" she asked. When she saw me, she sighed. "Max. I should have known that you would be in the middle of this."

"Not so!" Prince Torstein spoke up in my defense. "Princess Maxine and I were enjoying a pleasant chat when this scoundrel came and attacked her. It is fortunate that she is wearing those deadly ladies' shoes or she would still be in his grasp."

Marvelonius threw a look of contempt at the prince. "I hardly think—" he began.

"I say! I say! What is the commotion!" Uncle Phillip yelled, emerging into the center of our little drama. He yells a lot, the natural result of living with a wife who pretends she can't hear him.

At the sight of Uncle Phil's round face, a wonderful, brilliant idea came to me, a plan that would distract everyone, hopefully even the wizard, from remembering why he came. I flung my arm out in Marvelonius' direction and proclaimed, "Allow me to introduce the Magnificent Wizard Marvelonius, Producer of the Greatest Spells and Magic Tricks in all of the Kingdom of Veiland!" I smiled at the wizard and began to clap my hands as though he were there to perform.

Uncle Philip, who loves magic shows, smiled and began to clap along with me. Soon everyone was cheering and clapping for a performance.

The wizard drew himself up to his full height. "I regret to say," he began, but was interrupted by, well…me. I snatched his cone-shaped hat from his head.

"The first trick," I declared, "shall be pulling a rabbit from this hat!"

Everyone loved this one so the applause grew louder. Cousin Weldon and his bride-to-be, Helga, came to the front of the crowd, more than ready to enjoy the show. I hadn't seen much of Weldon since he'd been transformed back to his usual form a few months ago. The terrible beast has been greatly exaggerated in the stories, might I add. All Weldon turned into was an enormous bloodhound, but the horror of his transformation came from the huge quantities of slobber that he produced.

I held the hat out to the wizard but he just glowered at me. It was hard to take him seriously with that spot of paper on his forehead.

"The Magnificent Wizard Marvelonius has directed *me* to pull the rabbit from his hat!" I announced. I raised my hand and wiggled my fingers energetically.

Marvelonius' eyes grew wide with alarm. "Wait, don't-"

I had already reached into the hat. My plan was to toss the hat through the air to the wizard in the hope that he would catch it and finish the trick, but I was startled when my fingers ran into something warm, furry and very, very alive.

"What in the name of goblins…" I pulled the furry thing out and held it up. Screams rent the air as the women in the crowd, and a surprising number of men, began to scramble backward.

The wizard looked surprised. "A possum?" he muttered, more to himself than to me. So that's what this odd little creature was. Now what I want to know is who carries possums in their hat? I looked at the wizard like he was crazy, which he obviously was, while the possum snuggled itself into my arms, its long, bare tail curling and uncurling. The naked pink movement did not help matters and some of the guests began to faint.

Cries of, "It's a dragon rat!" filled the air.

"Kill the beast," someone else yelled, causing Weldon to flinch and look around nervously.

"Give me a break," I said. "I'll put it back, alright?"

"Princess Maxine, I think it would be better if you not—" Marvelonius reached out to take the hat just as I went to put the possum back into it. Unexpectedly the hat felt weighted down and there was no room for the possum.

"Hmm," I mused. Without thinking I handed the possum to the wizard and reached into his hat to see what else was in it. The new animal gave a loud chattering sound and scampered up my arm to perch on my shoulder. More screams filled the air.

I looked at the wizard questioningly; it was his hat, after all.

"Whatever you do," he growled, "Do *not* reach your hand into my hat again." The animal on my shoulder screeched and grabbed my ear for balance.

I raised my eyebrows. "Look, Marv, what you keep in your hat is your business. Most wizards usually just conjure a few rabbits out of thin air, but I won't judge you if you have to keep animals in here to make it look like you can do magic."

"I do *not* keep these animals in my hat!" he said through his teeth.

All around us was pandemonium. Women were dragging their husbands to the door, while some of the men were gathered together in a small group, eying the possum and arguing with each other, presumably about who should be the one to kill the dragon rat. Uncle Phillip was leaning over the wizard's shoulder, waiting happily for the next trick while Weldon and Helga were clearly wondering what was going on. Aunt Marge stood watching with her arms folded, an amused look on her face. I looked around, wondering where Prince Torstein had gone.

Marvelonius brought my attention back to him by means of a low growl.

"*Give. Me. My. Hat.*" He had his hand out, his face red beneath the white splotch of paper.

"Gladly." I handed it towards him but was unprepared when the little animal on my shoulder began hopping up and down. My thumb slipped into the interior of the wizard's hat and immediately it sagged under a new weight. I met the wizard's eyes and dropped the hat to the ground.

Chapter 11

The remaining spectators scrambled back with fresh screams as the new arrival crawled out, its stench already pervading the room. Marvelonius snatched up the hat and threw it over the skunk just as it raised its striped tail. The hat moved a few inches and then sagged limply.

"Whoa. What just happened?" I asked, pulling the other animal off of my shoulder as it began to tug on my hair.

The wizard cautiously picked up his hat. It was empty. He sniffed it and wrinkled his nose before placing it back on his head. "It would appear that you have some small talent for magic," he said.

The creature in my arms chattered and I held it out. "What kind of animal is this?"

"It's a monkey," Prince Torstein walked up. Where he'd gone to in all of the commotion was anybody's guess.

"A monkey?" I had never heard of monkeys before. The little guy was kind of cute. "How do you know that?"

"I've seen them before. On my travels."

The monkey chattered again and hopped out of my arms onto Prince Torstein's shoulder. He reached up, grasped it by the skin on its neck and handed it, squealing, to the wizard.

"Hey, wait—" I began, but it was too late. The wizard tossed it into his hat and it disappeared. "Toadstools. I wanted to keep it."

Prince Torstein raised an eyebrow at me. "My dear girl, there is no place in my castle for the antics of a monkey."

"Oh, *really?*" I put my hands on my hips. "Well what about the antics of a—"

"Max, what's going on?" Connor pushed his way through the crowd. He was followed by my parents but I didn't see Ron anywhere. Had he already left, the little sneak?

"Oh, nothing. Marv and I just put on a magic show for everyone." I smiled guiltily at Marvelonius.

The wizard rubbed his neck. "Listen, Maxine, where'd you put it? If you give it back now, we'll put all of the other disagreements behind us." He tapped the jagged bit of paper on his forehead significantly.

"What did she take?" Connor asked.

"Nothing." To my surprise the wizard's voice chorused with my own.

"I say, is that the end of the magic show?" asked King Philip. He was sitting on the floor feeding the possum bits of a cracker.

Just then an icy shadow fell over us, causing Weldon to whimper fearfully. It was Aunt Regina, coming to investigate the rapid departure of her guests. "What is happening?" she inquired in her crystal-cold voice.

Uncle Philip leapt to his feet. "Ah, my dear! You have come just in time to see this wonderful creature that came from the wizard's hat!" He held up the possum.

Aunt Regina gasped at the sight of the rat-like creature, her hand going to her creamy white throat. Then she turned and looked at the wizard.

"Is that animal your doing?" she demanded.

"Madam, your husband is hardly an animal, and I claim no responsibility for him." The wizard smiled at her with an inordinate amount of teeth showing.

They looked intently at each other and a strange buzzing sound filled the air. Aunt Regina made a small, considering sound, and smiled at the wizard with zero warmth. Then she turned to Uncle Philip. "Let us join the remaining guests, my dear," she said. He set the possum down with a resigned sigh and followed her from the room.

"Am I glad she's gone!" Weldon exclaimed, the first words that I'd heard out of him all night. "Well, I am," he said as we all stared at him. "She's one scary woman, even if she is my mother."

I exchanged a glance with Connor, my eyebrows raised. Weldon's time spent as a dog had been good for him. He hadn't been nearly so personable or discerning before. But then again, you know what they say about dogs, how they can sense things that other people can't...

Marvelonius turned towards me. "Listen, Maxine, maybe we should go somewhere where we can talk privately."

"I hardly think so," said Prince Torstein, folding his arms. "Anything you have to say to my betrothed you can say to me."

The wizard glanced at Aunt Marge. It seemed that she shook her head at him slightly, but I wasn't sure if I was imagining things. Marvelonius turned back to me and said in a low voice, "About that little spell that you used on me." He raised his eyebrows.

"Spell?" Realization dawned. "Oh, right! Again?"

"No better time, I would think." He muttered something under his breath just as I pursed my lips and whistled. Everyone except for Marvelonius and I froze into place.

"How come it didn't work on you this time?" I asked.

He smirked. "I was ready for you. You should get going. Your brother left a few minutes ago." He handed me my traveling bag.

"How did you--?"

"Don't worry about it."

"But why are you--?"

"Let's just say that I have rethought matters and concluded that you following your brother might actually be a good idea."

"Oh. Well, thanks. I think."

Marv glanced around at the frozen crowd. "How long are you going to leave them like this?"

"Well, first I have to get the motorcycle, which will take a little time since it's back at home--"

"I've got one right outside."

"Then why were you going on about it?"

"I want *my* motorcycle back. You can take the one outside. You just don't steal a man's bike and expect him to be okay with it."

"What on earth is going on around here?" It was Aunt Regina's voice. I knew from past experience that my freezing spell didn't work on her, which in my opinion was further evidence that she was some kind of wicked witch in disguise.

"You'd better get moving," Marv said. "I'll stall your terrifying aunt."

"Thanks. Four hours on the spell, by the way. Do you think that will be enough time?"

"It should be. Tell me where my bike is!"

I explained where I'd left it and added, "I'm sorry for taking it but I was desperate."

"Desperation doesn't excuse dishonesty," he growled.

Aunt Regina's voice came to us as she tried to revive one of her guests. "Lady Markena! Lady Markena, speak to me!"

"Never mind," said Marv. "I'll lecture you later. Now get going!"

I didn't have to be told twice.

Chapter 12

Hours later I sat on my bike, drenched from the rain, shivering cold, and scratched from numerous encounters with thorny bushes. It had taken me awhile to figure out that the motorcycle had a round lantern built into the front which glowed like a small sun when you pressed a certain switch. While this helped my travels in the dark enormously, the discovery came a little late: not only had the run-ins with the thorny bushes already occurred, but another, entirely unexpected problem had developed: *I was completely, one hundred percent lost.*

I had never been lost before. Even as a child, I'd always had an innate ability to find my way, whether I was navigating the long, confusing muddle of passageways in my family's castle or exploring the lands surrounding my home.

I tried to ignore the feeling of panic fluttering restlessly in my stomach as I stopped and looked for some kind of landmark. I was supposed to be in the Tasia Woods, headed towards a small kingdom called Denitri just below the eastern peaks, but a dark fear had been growing inside that I had somehow strayed from the safety of the Tasia Woods into the dangerous Miraysian Forest.

The Miraysian Forest, which lay in the outer boundaries of Uncle Philip's kingdom, was a place that even I had not explored yet, due to my disinclination to encounter extreme danger. Many a knight known for his strength and bravery had gone in and never returned. Uncle Philip was often criticized for his failure to do anything about the terrible and mysterious creatures reputed to live in the forest, who were said to have an indiscriminate taste for flesh, human or otherwise.

To my relief, the spattering of rain eased and then stopped. I wiped my wet face with my sleeve and began to move forward again. I hoped that by traveling along on the same path I would emerge from the trees eventually. Then I would figure out exactly how off-course I had gone.

The forest growth seemed to be getting thicker, hemming me in on both sides. Fighting a growing sense of panic, I saw with dismay that the path ahead split into two narrow trails. I slowed and then came to a stop. I was debating which trail to take when something moved in the bushes on my right. I froze, my entire body tense as I stared into the shadows, trying to subdue the awful sense that something was watching me. The last thing I wanted was to have an encounter with a wild animal, particularly since if this really were the Miraysian Forest, the chances of said animal being cute and cuddly were slim to none.

Suddenly a creature about the size of a cat burst from the bushes and turned to face me in the light from the motorcycle. It was an ugly little thing, with a flat, narrow face, no ears, and disproportionately long limbs. This was no ordinary forest animal: the beast's almond-shaped eyes seemed to be assessing me with an unnerving cunning that made my flesh crawl. It hissed, revealing sharp, pointed teeth, and I yelped, reaching for my sword. Before I could pull it even halfway from the scabbard, the monster turned and darted back into the deep growth.

Heart pounding, I turned my bike down the trail furthest from where I'd seen the animal. Even though the creature hadn't been very big, something about it terrified me and I revved my bike, taking off at a greater speed than I had previously dared.

What I hadn't taken into account was the recent rain. Following a sharp curve in the trail, the bike tires slid in the mud. Trying to keep it upright brought the opposite effect and the bike tipped, spilling me into a puddle.

I pushed myself up, feeling like an absolute idiot, and wiped muddy water from my eyes. In my attempt to escape the creature I had nearly killed myself. I should have known better than to try to ride the bike in a way that would have challenged an experienced rider.

Picking my bike up, I shut it off and put down the kickstand. It was useless to try to travel further in the darkness. I would camp here and wait until morning, where hopefully in the light of day I would be able to figure out where I was.

My first order of business was to build a fire. Hoping that the light would scare away any animals similar to the one I had just seen, I retrieved my flint from my traveling bag. Kicking around in the undergrowth revealed some kindling that hadn't gotten too wet from the rain. After a few tries my fumbling fingers managed to light a spark and I blew on it to get it going.

"I wouldn't do that if I were you." The words were spoken so near my ear that I felt a puff of warm breath on my neck. I screamed and jumped to my feet only to trip over the pile of wood I had gathered. A looming shadow stood over me, and I thought for a minute that my quest was about to end before it had even really begun. Instead, the newcomer turned and kicked earth over my tiny fire.

"Hey!" I exclaimed, suddenly more angry than afraid. "What do you think you're doing?"

"Trying to prevent you from getting yourself killed."

"By smothering my fire?" I stood up, brushing at the accumulated mud on my rear. "I'm cold. And a fire will scare away animals and…" I hesitated. "Any other things that might be out there."

"Fire may bother natural wildlife, but if you're trying to scare away the Maligios, I've got bad news for you: light attracts them. You'd be surrounded in seconds."

I squinted, trying to see his face, but it was too dark. "The Maligios?"

"The creatures that live in this forest. Isn't that what you were running from?"

I didn't answer. So that horrible little beast had friends.

"Of course," he continued, "they'll come no matter what you do. They can smell you. But light brings them faster."

"And how exactly do you know all of this?"

"I've been through here before."

It occurred to me that this stranger might be as much of a danger as these so-called Maligios. I began to edge towards my bike. "No one travels in the Miraysian Forest," I said. "Or at least, no one does and survives."

He laughed. "That doesn't bode well for you then, does it?"

The sound of his laughter made me pause. He had been speaking in a gravelly voice that identified him as a stranger, but the laugh... the laugh was familiar. I hesitated and then asked, "Do I know you?"

There was a short silence. "You have never known me."

I took a moment to try to figure out this cryptic response. "I guess you're right," I said. "I definitely would've remembered meeting someone as strange as you."

He made an irritated noise. "I didn't say that we'd never met."

"Um. You kind of did, actually," I said.

"No, I did not. I only said that you have never known me."

I decided to play along so we could focus on other, more pressing concerns. Like, say, evil creatures in the forest coming to eat us. "Right. Sorry. So we *have* met, but somehow, in spite of this, I don't know you."

"Yes."

"So where did we meet where I then continued to not know you?" Maybe he was an obsessed peasant. That happened sometimes with royalty, some crazy person following you around, sending you letters, that kind of thing.

"Everywhere. Nowhere. It doesn't matter." He sounded impatient.

"Then why did you bring it up if it doesn't matter, Mister You-Have-Never-Known-Me?" I demanded. "Why aren't we talking about something a little more critical to the moment, like how to get out of these woods without getting eaten?"

"If we try to leave before they have fully gathered, we won't stand a chance," he said. "So forgive me for being so chatty, but I'm waiting for the right moment."

"Why--" I broke off what would have been the beginning of an in-depth interrogation and peered into the darkness. I had heard something. In the resultant silence, the sound of countless creatures moving swiftly through the brush could be heard.

The stranger took a step forward.

"Stay where you are!" I ordered.

"If you insist. They're getting closer and soon it will be time to move."

"How can you tell?"

"Just trust me."

Hah. I challenge anyone to feel trusting when they're in a dark, evil forest surrounded by monsters and an enigmatic stranger who won't even tell you who he is. I leaned over and found the switch on my motorcycle, flooding the woods with the brilliant white light from the circular lantern. Illuminated in the light were hundreds of the Maligios, their eyes reflecting with flashes of red.

"I told you that they're attracted to light!" The stranger sounded angry as he ran towards me.

"I wanted to see how many there were!" I tried to back away, but he grabbed me before I could get anywhere. "Besides, if they're gathered around already it's not like the light would cause anymore damage."

"We don't have time to discuss your mistakes. Get on!" He straddled the motorcycle and pulled my arm until I got on behind him. I opened my mouth to ask him if he knew what he was doing when he revved the bike and shot forward.

The Maligios gathered together, blocking our route. I flinched, certain we were going to run into them, but at the last minute they scattered out of the way. One of the monsters latched onto my wrist as we went by, its claws digging into my skin. The weight of the creature almost overbalanced the bike, but the stranger righted it and then executed a sharp turn, causing the bike to lean sideways so far that we were sliding through the mud. The claws holding my wrist fell away and in the next instant we were off on a narrow trail, flying along at such breathtaking speed that I gulped and buried my face into the stranger's back.

The sounds of pursuit faded but we continued on at the same harrowing pace from one narrow trail to another. He seemed to know exactly where he was going.

We rode for what seemed like a long time. The trees began to thin and the first rays of the morning sun stretched like long fingers into the sky. The stranger brought the bike over to the side of the road and stopped. The silence following the growl of the motorcycle weighed on my ears as though someone had stuffed them full of cotton.

I stepped off the bike as my rescuer turned to face me, his features shadowed by the rising sun behind him.

"We should get some rest," he said. "It's going to be a long day."

I nodded and then just stood there. I was so tired I could hardly stand upright.

"Come on, then," he said, sounding amused. Too tired to care I followed him, watching as he spread out my cloak on a patch of thick grass. "Lay down," he ordered. Without thought I obeyed and that was the last thing I was aware of for several hours.

Chapter 13

I woke slowly, unsure of who I was or where I was or if it even mattered. I was contemplating going back to sleep when I noticed the stranger watching me from across a small fire. The sun was bright overhead and the trees on the outskirts of the forest actually looked pleasant and cheery with the sky visible through the brilliant green leaves. I would have concluded that last night was merely a nightmare if it weren't for the solid evidence of my rescuer sitting across from me.

I sat up, pushing my hair away from my face. "Hi," I said awkwardly. "I guess I should thank you…" My voice trailed off as I got my first real look at him. I squinted, not sure if I was imagining things.

He was wearing a mask. A very ugly mask, might I add, shaped in the form of a face with an opening for his eyes and mouth. The mask's nose jutted out like a defiant rock formation over a thin, wide mouth. Heavy brows seemed drawn together in a perpetual scowl and a crowded forehead and elongated jaw combined to create a remarkably hideous image.

"Good morning." He smiled, and I gazed in amazement as his mouth moved as though it were real.

"How do you get your mask to move like that?" I asked. As conversational starters go, this wasn't my most tactful. I watched with interest as his mask's eyebrows went up and his eyes widened in surprise.

"How could you tell I'm wearing a mask?" he asked.

"Well, no offense or anything, but it's kind of obvious."

"I have encountered many people and no one has ever seen that I am wearing a mask. They see this as my true face." He sounded almost insulted.

"That's hard to believe. It's pretty clear that it's a mask." I studied him. "Were you wearing it when you and I originally met? You know, the meeting where I didn't know you?"

He hesitated. "I can't say."

"Which means that you weren't."

"How do you figure that?"

"Because if you *were* wearing it you would have just said so. Besides, I doubt I would've forgotten meeting a guy with a moveable mask."

I watched with interest as his mask contorted into all sorts of angry lines. "Don't jump to conclusions, Princess. It's not a healthy form of exercise."

"Anyway," I continued, "if I were going to go to the trouble of wearing a mask, I'd at least make sure it was an attractive one."

He glanced up at me from under that forbiddingly heavy brow. "Are you saying that you think I'm ugly?"

"No, I'm saying that I think your *mask* is ugly. It's probably the ugliest mask that I've ever seen. If I were you I would take it off and burn it."

"Oh would you?"

"Definitely."

He smiled unexpectedly. "Well, you're not me. So I guess I'll just leave it on."

"Is your mask an improvement over how you really look?"

The smile vanished. "Is that all you care about? Appearances?"

I rolled my eyes. "I can tell that you aren't a morning person. Look, I need to…um… I'll be right back." He chuckled as I got up and hurried off into the woods, feeling the familiar burning sensation in my face that told me I was blushing bright red.

Memories of last night's events crowded into my mind and I wondered what the Maligios would have done if the stranger hadn't come along when he did. It made me realize how vulnerable I was traveling alone. In all of my map-making travels, I had always had a full retinue of trusted guards to protect me. While I was only a few hours from Denitri, the idea of continuing to travel alone made me nervous. And even though I hadn't had more than a few moments of conversation with this odd, mask-wearing stranger, I felt an inner conviction that he was someone I could completely trust.

I re-braided my hair and washed my face and hands at a small stream. My stomach rumbled as I caught the mouthwatering scent of bacon cooking. That settled it. If this guy was willing to cook, I would definitely keep him around for a while. *Then* we would go our separate ways.

I walked back and settled down in my spot opposite the stranger. "I've decided to allow you to travel with me for a few days," I announced. His heavy eyebrows lifted in surprise and he opened his mouth to respond but I held up my hand. "I know, I know. It's not really proper for us to travel together without chaperones. But there are extenuating circumstances and as long as my parents don't find out it will be fine."

"Your kindness is overwhelming."

I ignored his sarcasm. "I guess it's time we introduced ourselves."

"I already know who you are."

"Yeah, that's what gets under my skin. You say that we've met before, but you won't take off your mask so I can see your face. And what makes you so sure that I 'have never known you'? You might be surprised at how much I know."

"There are different levels to knowing a person."

"You're really into being mysterious, aren't you?"

"It comes with the mask. Something about it just makes me feel full of mystery."

I gritted my teeth. "You are the most annoying person I have ever met. I'm starting to think that it would've been preferable to be eaten by the Maligios than try to hold a conversation with you."

He shook his head irritably. "Marvelonius sent me."

"What?"

"The Magnificent Wizard Marvelonius."

"I know who Marv is. My confusion stems from why he sent some guy with bad taste in masks to follow me."

"You really ought to work on getting used to the fact that I am wearing a mask and am not going to be taking it off so that our conversations will be more productive."

"*Fine.*" I glared at him. "How do you know Marv?"

"It's a long story."

"I'm listening."

"It's a long story *and* I'm not going to tell it to you."

We stared at each other over the fire in a sort of battle of wills. I could tell by the look in his eyes that he wasn't going to back down. "At least tell me your name," I said. "We'll start with the easy stuff and work our way up, shall we?"

"I don't have a name," he said.

"Look, are you always this weird or am I getting special treatment?"

He laughed. "I don't think I'll answer that."

"Do you really expect me to believe that you've lived your whole life without a name?"

"I have been called many things," he said. "But I have not been given a true name. There is a difference." He lifted the bacon out of the pan and placed the strips onto two plates alongside thick slabs of bread. As he moved, setting the pan aside and gathering mugs, I felt a strong sensation of recognition, but it was so fleeting that I couldn't pinpoint it.

He shifted uncomfortably under my gaze. "If you're not hungry I'll eat your share."

I grabbed a plate. "So how about *I* give you a true name?" I asked.

"You can't. It has to come at a certain time in a certain place from a certain person."

I looked around the sunlit woods. "How do you know that this isn't it?"

He just looked at me.

I sighed. "Fine. One can only assume that you're under some kind of evil spell that impels you to wear an ugly mask and go without a 'true name.' So until this exciting *certain time* comes, I will take it upon myself to give you a temporary name." I thought about it. "I once had a dog named Jack. Poor Jack, he was so ugly, people cringed at the sight of him." I slanted a look at the masked stranger and asked, "How about I call you Jack?"

Instead of looking insulted, he grinned. "Jack is fine."

"So let's talk, *Jack.*"

"Do we have to?"

I ignored his comment. "You say that Marv sent you to help me. Even if you are friends with the wizard, why should you devote a significant amount of time to helping someone you hardly know? And why should I trust you?"

"You trust me enough to eat my food."

I paused mid-bite and considered this. "I'm hungry. Besides, you're eating it, too."

He laughed and began to clear up camp without bothering to answer any of my questions. Not that I was surprised by this.

Just so long as he understood that his driving the motorcycle last night was a one-time deal. I was the temporary owner of that lovely piece of machinery and I would insist on his riding behind. There was no way that I was going anywhere as a passenger.

Chapter 14

"If you don't slow down we're going to wreck, and you'll be the one who has to explain to Marv that you destroyed his motorcycle!"

"What makes you think that he cares about this bike so much?" Jack asked, plunging recklessly down another hill just to annoy me.

"It doesn't matter if he cares about it or not. He loaned it to me, and I would like to return it to him in one piece." The plan to have Jack ride behind on the bike lasted about as long as Ron's engagements to his rescued princesses— meaning it was basically over before it began. This was why I was now holding on around his waist as though my life depended on it.

Which it did.

It seemed to me that every time I relaxed enough to loosen my hold, he'd do something crazy and next thing I knew I was about to crack a few of his ribs in my efforts to not fall off. It hadn't taken me long to realize that he was doing it on purpose. My arms were getting tired, my eyes were streaming and I had enough dust in my mouth to grow a garden.

"I thought you wanted to get out of the forest before it got dark," Jack flew up the next hill and down the other side so fast my stomach somersaulted.

"We've been out of those woods for hours now. And I would appreciate it if you would slow down so I can catch some of this air and put it in my lungs."

"Just put your face on my back. You'll breathe easier with me shielding you."

"No, thank you. I prefer to watch so I'll be aware of the precise moment we go careening off the road to our deaths."

He didn't answer.

Sitting so close behind him had given me a perfect opportunity to look for the defining line where his mask left off and his real skin began. Although I'd studied his neck with all the diligence of a scholar, so far I had failed to find anything out of the ordinary; his skin seemed to smoothly meld into the mask covering his face.

"There's Denitri," Jack said. Ahead a cluster of stone buildings crouched in the shadow of the eastern peaks, while on a rise above the village was a castle. The place looked beyond neglected, with the cottages leaning haphazardly and a pall of grey smoke overhanging everything.

Appearances did not improve upon closer inspection. Garbage was piled in front of every cottage, spilling out into the street. Combined with the trash was an almost unbearable stench: an unholy combination of unwashed bodies, sewage, wet dogs, and a hint of stale garlic. It was the kind of smell that you can almost taste.

"Try not to breathe," Jack advised when he heard me gagging. Given the circumstances it was good advice. I eyed the people of this wretched place, wondering how they could stand it.

The road was full of ruts and deep holes, forcing Jack to wend his way cautiously through. Before we were even aware of it, the people in the village crowded forward, forming a circle around us that slowly tightened into a wall of sullen humanity.

Jack came to a stop in front of those directly in our path. "Excuse me," he said. "Would you mind moving out of the way?"

No one spoke. Even more people gathered around, effectively blocking any escape route. While the villager's faces were expressionless, there was a hostile gleam in their eyes.

"I don't like this," Jack muttered.

I tried for optimism. "They're probably just curious about the motorcycle."

"Maybe, but I've got a bad feeling."

Just then the crowd parted enough for a man to come through. He strolled forward with an arrogance I recognized from years of associating with royalty. "Welcome to Denitri," the man said. "We don't often have visitors. Three in as many days is really quite an event, wouldn't you say, Parker?"

"Indeed so, Prince Jaspien." Parker, a well-muscled chap, stood with another fellow behind Prince Jaspien. I guessed that they were his bodyguards.

"I can only assume that you are lost like our last visitor claimed to be?" Prince Jaspien inquired with a sneer.

"Not really," Jack said.

"That's a shame," said Jaspien. "It would be better for you if you were. This kingdom is closed to all travelers. Did you not see the many signs that were posted?"

He was lying—there hadn't been any signs posted. Given the circumstances, however, it didn't seem like it would be the most brilliant move to call him on it. "We weren't aware that Denitri was closed," I said.

"Parker, inform these travelers of the consequences of their ignorance," Jaspien commanded.

Parker unrolled a parchment and cleared his throat. "It is hereby decreed that all miscreants who dare to trespass into the Kingdom of Denitri shall suffer a penalty of death by torture and beheading. Know ye that death shall come only after extreme suffering and pain. Decreed by His Lordship Prince Jaspien."

"Out of a sort of futile curiosity," Jack said, "dare I inquire into your failure to observe the Traveler Protection Act that was established between the kingdoms years ago? Isn't there something in there about the freedom for all to pass through every land without fear of persecution or harm?"

Prince Jaspien's eyes narrowed. "How delightful to hear that someone in this world still studies those old international laws. However, based on the fact that you are both obviously thieves, the Protection Act doesn't really apply, now does it? Parker, Franklin, escort these criminals to the prison."

"What do you mean?" I demanded. "We aren't thieves!"

"Really?" Jaspien's eyebrows rose in mock surprise. "Then you would have me believe that humble travelers like yourselves have somehow been able to purchase a riding contraption like the one you're on? Unless you *aren't* poor? Perhaps your families would be anxious to pay for your freedom?"

I hesitated for a second, trying to figure out the best way to respond.

"While you fabricate additional lies to entertain me with," Jaspien said, "I will take it upon myself to confiscate the riding contraption. Right now, if you please. You will have no use for it without heads, after all." He smiled.

This is the problem with bad guys: not only do they take your freedom and make unpleasant decisions to detach your head from your body, but as the final insult they steal your belongings and then say that *you* are the thief.

"Saw that coming a mile away," muttered Jack as the guards more or less pulled us off the bike. Parker patted Jack down, finding several wicked-looking daggers.

I was wearing my grandfather's sword at my waist and even though I knew from experience that no one could see it I still felt nervous when the other guard approached me. To my relief, he merely grabbed my arm and pulled me along behind Jack and Parker towards a small stone building.

"Get in," Parker ordered, pushing open the heavy wooden door. We obeyed and the door slammed shut behind us, plunging us into a pungent darkness. I waited for my eyes to adjust, sensing Jack at my side doing the same. The guards outside muttered amongst themselves and then tromped away.

"You all right?" asked Jack.

"Oh, I'm great. You?"

"Never better. I can't wait to have my head chopped off."

"Don't forget that we get to be tortured first."

We were interrupted by a sleepy-sounding voice. "I hate to be rude, but I am trying to sleep."

Jaspien had mentioned that there had been three travelers in as many days. I should have guessed that the third person was Ron. "Ron, it's late afternoon," I said. "If you sleep now, you won't get a good night's rest."

There was a rustling sound as Ron got to his feet. I could barely make out his outline as my eyes became used to the gloom. "Max? What in the name of gnomes are *you* doing here?" His tone was not exactly welcoming.

"Well, Prince Jaspien said that we're thieves, so he--"

"That is not what I meant," he growled. "I can't even begin to tell you how complicated this makes things! Of all the stupid, idiotic..." I heard him breathe deeply as though he were trying to master his temper. When he spoke again, he was the usual courteous Prince Charming. "I apologize. I shouldn't have snapped at you; I've just been feeling a bit tense lately. How are you, Max?"

"Um. Good?"

"And I can only assume that I have not met your companion, although I do wonder that you are traveling alone with a man. Unless...don't tell me that they've already married you off to Torstein?"

I heard Jack shift beside me and I wondered again how much he really knew about me. "I don't think Tor and I will be getting married anytime soon if I can help it," I said. "Ron, I'd like you to meet my friend here. I call him Jack."

"How do you do, Jack? I hope that your travels have been pleasant?"

"Yes. Thank you. Do you have an escape plan?" Jack sounded impatient with Ron's attempts at royal courtesy.

"I do. Of course, your arrival does complicate things."

"Perhaps I may be permitted to inquire into the details?"

Before Ron could respond we heard the guards return to their post, signaling an end to our conversation. I sighed and sat down. As I did so, I felt my sword brush against my hip. I'd forgotten about it for a minute. "Hey, you guys," I whispered.

"Not now, Maxine," they both hissed in unison.

"But—"

"Shhh!"

I *hate* being shushed. I folded my arms and glowered into the darkness. If they didn't want to know that I was the possessor of a magical sword that was invisible to the eyes of the enemy, then that was their loss. Besides, if I told them about it they'd no doubt make me give it to them.

In the meantime, I had nothing better to do than plot my own escape. If Ron and Jack were lucky, I'd consider letting them come along once I busted out of this moldering little prison.

Chapter 15

Hours later, I finally heard the sound I'd been waiting for: the deep, peaceful snoring of the guards. I stood up and stretched. "Well, boys, it's been fun, but I've got to get going." I slid my sword from its sheath and stabbed it into the thatched roof above my head. The moldy straw crumbled easily away, allowing the brilliant light of the moon to pour into our little prison.

"I hate to remind you of this, Max," said Ron, "but there are guards right outside who will be awakened by the sound of you knocking a hole in the roof." His tone was condescending. I was tempted to leave him behind for it.

There was a rustling sound beside me as Jack stood up. "Max, you're brilliant," he said.

"How do you know what I'm going to do?"

"Remember, we've met before."

"If one of you would be so kind as to let me know what you're talking about?" Now Ron sounded petulant.

We ignored him. "You do realize that this will only work on people within hearing distance," said Jack.

"I think that I understand the scope of my power a little better than you," I said.

"Oh! I get it—" began Ron.

"Plug your ears, gentlemen." I commanded. I waited until they'd had time to obey before whistling. The snoring outside stopped as though it had been shut off like the switch on the motorcycle. Satisfied that the guards were in a state of unmoving stupor, I nudged Jack and Ron so they would know they could unplug their ears.

"What I want to know is how come you got to keep your sword when they took all of my weapons," Jack muttered.

"Yeah! They took my sword, my arrows *and* my favorite dagger," said Ron.

I began to enlarge the hole in the roof without answering.

"Would you like me to finish that for you?" offered Jack.

I blinked as dust and bits of straw showered down on my face. "I would," I said, wiping at my streaming eyes with my free hand.

Jack took the sword from me and went to work cutting a larger hole in the roof. "I didn't even see that you *had* a sword," he continued after a moment. It was obviously really bothering him. "You'd think that I would have noticed something like that since you had to have been wearing it."

"Apparently you're not very observant," I said. "I've had it on this whole time."

He grunted. "I don't know. It just seems like something I would have noticed." He worked for awhile in silence and then stepped back to survey his work. "Alright, that should do it." He returned the sword to me. "So what are our plans once we're out of this box?"

"I was thinking of galloping away on my noble steed," said Ron.

"*Great* plan. Princess Maxine? You have anything with a little more detail?"

"Well, I'd like to get my motorcycle back."

"It must run in the family." Jack sounded annoyed. "Have either of you bothered to study the peaks we're planning on scaling in the very near future?"

"We found Ron," I said. "I figured that we would just head home." Jack boosted me through the hole in the roof and then he and Ron followed behind.

"Is that why you're here?" demanded Ron, straddling the wall beside me.

"Obviously," I answered, peering down. Fortunately for my fear of heights, the prison wall wasn't very high.

"Then you've just wasted your time," said Ron. "And for your information, I already had an escape plan."

"Which was?"

"Her." Ron pointed. A young lady stood a little ways back from the prison, unmoving courtesy of my spell, with a shovel clutched in her hands.

"You were going to dig your way out?"

The moonlight gleamed on his sheepish look. "Actually, *she* was going to dig my way out."

I rolled my eyes. "I hate to remind you of this, Ron, but there are guards right outside who would've been awakened by the sound of her digging. Though I know as a prince you've never tried it, shoveling does make some noise as the blade of the shovel is pushed into the earth--"

"Sorry to interrupt," Jack's voice on my other side was calm. "But someone's coming."

We looked towards the village. Judging from the quantity of torches headed our way, the whole kingdom of Denitri was coming. "Dragon snot," I said.

As the crowd approached, the light of their torches fell on Ron's would-be rescuer. "There she is!" shouted a voice I recognized. "Sister, what are you doing out here?"

I raised my eyebrows at Ron.

"I didn't know she was Prince Jaspien's sister," he hissed.

"Quick, plug your ears again," I whispered.

Ron and Jack obeyed as Jaspien seized his sister's arm. Her stiff form nearly toppled over and he had to grab her with both hands to keep her upright. As soon as she was steady, Jaspien snatched his hands away as though her stiffness was contagious. "What has happened to her?" he roared.

Everyone fell silent, which I thought was quite obliging. I whistled as piercingly as I could and then poked Ron and Jack. "Alright guys, let's get going."

They didn't move.

"Guys?" I tugged on one of Ron's arms, trying to pull his finger from his ear, but it didn't budge an inch. Jack was equally unmoving on my other side. I stared at their stiff forms in horror. I must have whistled so loudly that the ear-plugging wasn't enough protection.

This just had to happen as we were sitting on top of a prison wall in a hostile kingdom with who knew how many more people waiting to attack us. I tried to remember if my fairy godmother had left any instructions on a freezing spell gone wrong. Nothing came to mind, but that was hardly surprising since she hadn't left me any instructions, period.

I could say the word to release everyone from the freezing spell right away, but how would I re-freeze the mob without freezing Ron and Jack again as well? And I couldn't whisper to release them alone since their fingers were plugging their ears. The trick was to somehow get them free from my spell while leaving Jaspien and his men as they were.

Things were getting way too complicated.

Then I remembered my silver jug with the never-ending supply of water. As far as I knew, the jug's only power was that the water supply never ran out, but maybe there was a little magic mixed in that would help revive them. I jumped down from the wall and hurried to the stables where my bike was parked.

I was opening my pack when a voice said, "No, you don't, little missy." A large hand clamped over my mouth while an equally enormous arm encircled my waist, lifting me from the ground. "Hey, Charlie," my captor said, turning towards the stable doors. "Look what I found."

An older man stepped into the stables. "Where on earth did you come from?" he asked. Given that my mouth was currently covered with a hand the size of a small country, I wasn't able to respond. Charlie turned. "Monty?"

Another man appeared in the doorway. "Sir?"

"Go check on our lookout. Something's not right."

We didn't have to wait long for Monty's return. He came rushing back with a wild look on his face. He and Charlie spoke in urgent undertones for a moment before coming over to where I still hung in the arms of my giant captor.

"Monty tells me there's a crowd of curiously stiff people in front of that prison over there," Charlie said, watching me closely. "It occurs to me that you might have had something to do with it. After all, why is it that you are not with your friends on top of the jail wall, sitting like a guilty statue?" He didn't seem to notice that the giant's hand was preventing me from responding.

"I have a deal for you," he continued. "I believe that we are on the same side, given that your crowd was imprisoned by Jaspien and I have my own grudge against him. What do you say to joining forces? You can help us by not turning us into statues, and we will help you by getting your friends down and away to safety. Sound agreeable?"

I nodded, which wasn't easy given that my head didn't have a lot of mobility at the moment.

"I don't know why I should trust you," mused Charlie. "I usually make it a point to not trust anyone. Yet instinct tells me that by working with you, I will succeed in my ultimate quest." He pointed at me threateningly. "But I warn you that if you betray me I will not rest until you are punished. Do you understand?"

I nodded as energetically as I could and Charlie signaled to the giant to let me go.

"Thanks," I said, trying to catch my breath.

"Don't mention it. I'm Charles Derby."

"Maxine Charming."

"A Charming, eh? I've heard of your family." He laughed at the look I gave him. "That's not necessarily a bad thing. Now let's go get your friends before Jaspien and his crowd stop playing statues."

Chapter 16

Getting Jack and Ron down from the prison wall was a tricky procedure given that they were about as pliable as blocks of granite. We laid them out on the ground with their fingers still plugging their ears, their bodies stiff and awkward-looking.

I had chosen Jack as the first victim in my experiment since his mouth was open slightly wider than Ron's. Kneeling beside him, I poured water from the silver jug down his throat, hoping that he wouldn't drown. The water overflowed from his mouth and ran down the sides of his face. I set the jug aside and bent over my subject, watching anxiously for any sign of movement.

"What did you say you were doing again?" Charlie asked after it became apparent that the water wasn't having any visible effects.

"This is a magical jug that never runs out of water," I said, "So I thought that maybe, since it has magic in it..." My voice trailed off as I realized how pathetic my idea really was.

"Looks like ordinary water to me," Charlie observed helpfully. "How did you get these people like this in the first place?"

"I'm not sure..." I hesitated. I didn't really want to tell him about my fairy godmother gift. It's not the kind of thing you want to spread around.

"That you want to admit what happened? That's all right, I can guess. Let me see..." He tapped his chin as though he were deep in thought. "I know: you sang to them! Am I right?"

"Not exactly."

"For some reason princesses all seem to think that they should be able to trill like little birds." He shuddered. "Petrification is actually a better fate than being forced to listen to some of these daughters of kings. This one fellow I know—and I swear this is true—his *ears* fell off. Right off! It was terrible. We had the dickens of a time getting them back on again."

I glared at him. "I didn't sing, alright?"

Charlie shrugged. "Sure. I believe you. But whatever it was that you did, you might want to try *un*doing it or you're not going to get very far."

I returned my attention to Jack. "C'mon, c'mon, wake up," I hissed, patting his cheek. His skin felt clammy but I wasn't sure if that was because he was in the throes of my spell or if it was due to the mask he was wearing.

I paused. I had forgotten about the mask! When would I ever get a better opportunity to sneak a look behind it than now? The temptation was too much to resist. I scooted closer to Jack and felt along his jaw line, trying to find the edge of the mask to peel back.

I was so intent in my efforts that I forgot about Charlie until he said, "So in lieu of waking that poor boy up, you've decided to just rip his face off?"

I looked up at him guiltily. "No, see, he's wearing a mask. I want to take it off so I can see what he really looks like."

"A mask."

"Sure. Can't you tell?"

Charlie studied Jack for a moment and then shook his head. "Not seeing it."

"Are you kidding me? He's got this hideously ugly mask on and you can't see it?"

"Hideous? I'm not really a connoisseur of the male appearance, but I'd say that he's a nice-looking young man. Trust me, I've seen hideous, and this boy isn't it."

I looked back down at Jack to try to see what Charlie was seeing. The light of the mob's torches glowed on his still face, elongating the shadow from his hooked nose and impossibly bushy eyebrows. *Nice-looking*? Were we talking about the same guy?

I leaned in closer to Jack's face. His eyes had been open when I'd performed the last freezing spell and it was a little eerie seeing them staring back at me so blankly. Suddenly the eye I was looking into moved and I fell back with a yelp, landing near Charlie's feet.

"Looks like he's coming around. You give the other fellow some of that fancy water while I go get you some horses." Charlie strode off in the direction of the stable.

Jack took a shuddering breath, which unfortunately caused him to inhale some of the water that had pooled in his mouth. He started coughing while I sat back and tried to look innocent. Eventually he recovered enough to sit up and swipe his wet face with his sleeve. "What did you do?" he rasped.

I cleared my throat. "What do you mean?"

"Well, first of all, why am I all wet? And secondly, if that was your whistling spell, don't ever let it happen to me again. It's absolutely the worst feeling ever."

"It's not like I meant for you to freeze up. And you're lucky I had this magic water with me." I shook the jug at him.

"Magic water, my foot. I don't think I was all the way out since I had my ears plugged."

Just then Ron groaned and his body relaxed from the frozen position he'd been lying in. Feeling sheepish, I corked the silver jug and stuffed it back into my bag. I watched Jack massage his shoulder with one hand. "So, uh, do you remember anything?" I asked.

He looked up sharply. "What do you mean?"

"You know. While you were…out?"

"Why?" His eyes narrowed. "Alright, tell me what you did."

"Nothing! I just…nothing."

"You tried to take my mask off, didn't you?"

I looked away. "Why would you think that?"

"You're a woman. Women are always opening boxes and going into forbidden rooms and doing all sorts of things that they've been warned not to do. It only serves to reason that you tried to have a look at my face."

"Oh yeah?" I glared at him. "Well, men are always going off exploring and having adventures, yet when a girl tries to do the same thing, she gets into trouble for it."

"Max, you tried to peel my face off. I don't care if you explore and have adventures, but the least you could do is refrain from attacking me while I'm unconscious."

Ron groaned again, giving me the perfect excuse to get out of making promises I wouldn't be able to keep.

"Are you all right, Ron?" I asked, kneeling beside him.

He shook his head. "I feel awful. I don't know if I could fight off a *puppy* in this state."

"Can you ride?" Charlie asked, emerging from the darkness. He was leading three horses.

"Of course."

"Excellent. Let's say you leave the puppy fighting for another night and get out of here before Jaspien and his men wake up."

After I introduced Ron and Jack to Charlie, I pulled him aside and whispered, "What about my motorcycle?"

"That machine would never make it up those mountains," Charlie answered. "You're better off leaving it with me."

"You don't even know how to ride it!"

"I'm quite sure I will be able to figure it out." He grinned and lifted me into the saddle of a little brown mare. "Off you go," he said, hitting the horse's rump. The mare trotted over to where Ron and Jack were mounting their horses.

"Let's go," said Jack.

"But what about my bike?" I asked, peering back at Charlie.

"Good luck," Charlie called, waving.

"*Toadstools.*" I faced forward. "That guy is really annoying."

"I found him quite helpful," said Ron. "He even gave Chester back to me." He patted his white stallion fondly on the neck.

"Yeah. Great. You can probably tell I'm ecstatic."

We spurred our mounts forward, following a narrow trail through the trees. The eastern peaks loomed ahead, imposing walls of grey rock that didn't appear very traveler-friendly. The closer we got, the higher they grew, and I began to worry about actually attempting to climb them. All along I had assumed that as soon as I caught up to Ron, he would somehow realize the error of his ways and meekly follow me home.

Evidently my quest to force him to come home had not been well thought out. One would think that after fifteen years of acquaintance, I would have realized that the mild surprise of having me show up in the midst of my brother's latest rescue attempt would not be nearly enough incentive to inspire him to change his ways. Princes tend to be incredibly stubborn people.

We fell into a silence that lasted into the coming of dawn, stopping only once to eat and stretch. It seemed like it had been forever since I'd had a good night's sleep and I thought longingly of my comfortable bed back home.

"We're almost at the peaks," said Jack, snapping me out of my half-asleep daze.

"I'll take it from here," announced Ron. "Thank you both for your help. I hope your trip back to Veiland goes well." He made a shooing motion with his hand.

I glared at him. "Nice try, Ron, but you're not getting rid of me so easily. Why don't we *all* go home and let someone else rescue the little ninny?"

"I would appreciate it if you would start treating me with some respect, Maxine," said Ron, glaring back. "Has it occurred to you that one day I will be *your king*? You might want to think about that for a minute."

"Here we go," Jack muttered, spurring his horse to ride ahead.

"And maybe," I growled. "you should think about the fact that if I marry Prince Torstein, I won't be your subject—I'll be a queen over my own country! If you don't treat *me* with respect, I'll come and conquer your kingdom."

"Hah! I'd love to see you try." Ron reined his horse around so he could sneer at me more conveniently. "The armies of Veiland are infinitely superior to the armies of Treagal. Besides, what would Mother and Dad think of you trying to invade their lands? Their own daughter? Really, Max."

"You are so aggravating! *Prince Charming*, indeed. Prince Obnoxious fits you much better."

"And you are the least like any princess that I have ever met. You're a disgrace to your title."

I flinched. That hit home more than he knew. I drew my sword. "I say we are going home."

"And I say that you may go wherever you like. *I* am going to rescue Princess Golden." His eyes dared me to go ahead and try something with the sword.

One reason brothers are so annoying is that they know you can't really behead them for multiple reasons, the most compelling of which being what your parents would say if you did.

I growled and lowered my sword. "*Fine.* But I'm coming with you."

Ron looked at me with exasperation. "Max! Just go home!" He ran a hand through his hair. "What will people say if they hear that Prince Charming rescued another princess...*with the help of his little sister?*"

I pursed my lips to whistle and Ron's hands flew to cover his ears. "Don't whistle! Look, you can cross the eastern peaks with me, alright? Then you'll go home."

That's what he thought.

Chapter 17

"Done arguing?" Jack's voice floated back to us.

"I guess so," I said. "Why?"

"Because, and correct me if I'm wrong, there appear to be trolls guarding the peaks. We need to figure out what we're going to do about that."

We rode up beside Jack and looked. Now that we were closer, I could see winding switchbacks carved into what otherwise looked like a sheer wall of rock. All along the lower end of the switchbacks a line of menacing figures stood waiting for us.

"I could whistle," I offered.

Jack shook his head.

"Why not?"

"Trolls don't have ordinary hearing. They can hear the sound of a stream hundreds of feet underground. They can hear a sigh or a song from miles away. And they can hear what I'm saying right now. This is just a hunch, but I don't think that your whistle will affect them in the slightest."

"How do you know all of this stuff?" I demanded.

"Like I said before, I travel. And I read a lot."

"I'd like to borrow whatever books you've been reading," I muttered.

Ron looked worried. "I forgot to get my weapons back."

"And here I thought that you had experience with this quest thing," I said. "You'd think that keeping a weapon on hand would be one of the first things you would worry about."

"My quests usually go more smoothly than this. Besides, when you froze me it took awhile to recover. I'd like to see how you would feel under the effects of your awful fairy godmother gift."

"Arguing isn't going to solve anything," Jack interrupted. "We need a plan."

"What's the point of planning if they can hear everything we're saying anyway?" I asked. "I say we go talk to them and see if they'll just let us pass by."

"But what if they're dangerous?" Ron asked. "Who knows what these trolls might do to us?"

"I could tell you." We jumped at the unfamiliar voice and looked around. No one was in sight.

"First," the voice continued, "they will relieve you of your valuables. I notice, for example, that the golden-haired fellow wears a fine ruby ring, and the lady has a sword which gleams of magic. The man with the enchanted face, though...I wonder of what value his true heart is in circumstances like these?"

Jack reached into his boot and withdrew a wicked-looking dagger that Jaspien's men had obviously missed. "Show yourself!" he ordered.

The unseen speaker chuckled. "There is no need to be violent. I am only telling you what to expect from the trolls."

"And how do you know what the trolls will do?" Ron asked.

"I have a lot of experience with them. After all, I am their king." A misshapen, extraordinarily ugly creature appeared on the path in front of us. "How do you do?" he inquired.

Our horses didn't like having a gigantic troll abruptly appear under their noses. They showed their displeasure with a series of dramatic snorts, squeals, and fancy footwork. After bringing my mount under control, I extended my hand to the newcomer. "It's a pleasure to meet you, Your Majesty," I said. "I'm Maxine Charming and this is my brother Ron and my friend Jack." The Troll King stepped up to my mare and grasped my hand in his warty fingers. A glint of amusement shone in his orange eyes. His face was fierce, with flaring nostrils and a wide, stern mouth, but I noticed that there were smile lines around his eyes and his grip was warm and firm.

"And why is it that you are so determined to climb the peak to rescue the Princess Golden?" the Troll King asked. He looked at Ron as he said this so I figured I was off the hook for providing an answer.

Ron rubbed the back of his neck. "Because she needs to be rescued, I suppose. If someone needs it, I rescue them."

"I see. That is an important line of work." The Troll King's gravelly voice didn't reveal what he thought of Ron's explanation.

"Sire, perhaps you could give us some advice on our quest," said Jack. "We've heard that Princess Golden is being held captive by three vicious beasts, but that's about all we know."

"Certainly I can give you advice regarding the princess and her dreadful captors," the Troll King said. "For a price."

"Naturally," said Ron, pulling a coin purse from his saddlebag.

"The price being that after you have attained the top of the peak, you surrender all of your weapons to me," the Troll King continued, ignoring the coin purse Ron was holding out.

Ron gaped at him. "But Sire—with all due respect—we will need weapons to rescue the princess!" He looked at Jack and me for support.

"This quest might prove to be different from the others," said the Troll King. "You will find that your most useful weapons will be found within."

Ron looked confused. "Within? Within what?"

The Troll King smiled. "Within your heart, of course. Sometimes the enemy is cleverly disguised. You should not be too hasty in condemning those whom you perceive to be your enemies."

"Perhaps," I interjected, "you could tell us whatever it is that you're trying to tell us a little more plainly. We're not all that good at interpreting deep, meaningful statements, so feel free to give us the names of those who aren't our enemies so we don't accidentally condemn them."

The Troll King continued as though I hadn't spoken. "Often those who profess to be the most wicked have the greatest potential for good. Know also: the lady whom you go to rescue may not need your help. But others do."

"Are you saying Princess Golden doesn't need rescued?" demanded Ron, sounding frustrated.

"The fair damsel harbors secrets of her own."

I took a deep breath. "Not to harp on the details too much, Your Majesty, but could you at least tell us what her secrets are?"

The Troll King's voice grew stern. "Beware enemies of the heart." With that he was gone, leaving a small puff of dust as the only proof he had been there.

"Why are people always going around saying things without really saying anything?" I demanded. "You ask a simple, straightforward question, and everyone goes out of their way to *not* answer you. I can tell you one thing: I'm going to make sure I say what needs to be said without any vague beating around the bush."

"And how is this going to be any different than how you already are?" asked Jack with a suspicious twinkle in his eyes.

"I am sure that I do not know what you mean, Maxine," Ron interjected before I could answer Jack. "I found the information the Troll King gave us quite enlightening."

I paused, staring at him incredulously. "Wait a minute. You were just as confused as I was a second ago. How is it you suddenly find his help enlightening?"

"Well, now we know that Princess Golden may not need rescuing. And, uh…" He became absorbed with a loose string on his sleeve. "Well, you know."

"Exactly. You don't have any more of an idea of what he was talking about than I do." I folded my arms.

"I don't see why you're being so belligerent," said Ron. "You're acting as though there are people keeping secrets from you at every turn."

"That's because there *are*," I growled. "Did you know that we have a prime example of someone keeping secrets right here?" I pointed at Jack, who shifted uncomfortably and looked away. "*Jack* isn't even his real name! He says that he hasn't received his true name yet."

Ron shrugged. "So? If he hasn't received his true name, then he hasn't received his true name. I don't see what the big deal is."

I hadn't expected this matter-of-fact reaction. "Well, what about the fact that he's wearing a mask? What about that?"

Ron looked at Jack. "So that's what the Troll King meant about the fellow with the enchanted face. I thought that he was talking about me, because, you know, my eyes are really blue, not gold. Of course, my hair is naturally this shade of blond."

I ground my teeth and tried again. "Ron. Focus. Can you tell that Jack is wearing a mask?"

Ron studied Jack. "I suppose not. Although, you do remind me of someone."

Jack looked down at his hands. I could tell that he was afraid that he was about to be unmasked, if you'll pardon the expression.

"Yes, you do remind me of someone. Are you by any chance related to Pierre Aulier? He's a good friend of mine from the university."

Jack glanced up, obviously surprised. "I, uh, I don't think so."

My eyes narrowed. I was beginning to suspect something about Jack's mask. "Ron, will you describe Jack's facial features for me, please?"

Ron looked at me like I was crazy. "Why would you need me to do that? He's right in front of you."

"Just humor me."

Ron rolled his eyes. "If I don't do as she asks she'll just keep pestering me," he explained to Jack. "Now, let me see...Well, he's got kind of skinny eyebrows, a rather small nose, puffy lips..."

I looked at Jack. To me, his eyebrows were thick and bushy, his nose enormous and jutting, and his lips were a thin strip across his face.

Ron and I were seeing two different images.

Jack watched me, waiting for my thoughts to process. Unfortunately, other than having proved that what I saw wasn't what others saw, I didn't have much to conclude.

"The day isn't getting any younger," said Ron. "Now that we've established what Jack looks like, I suggest that we get moving." He spurred his horse towards the peaks.

Jack and I sat looking at each other. "Why are you so familiar to me?" I asked. "I wish that you would trust me enough to tell me who you are."

"I do trust you."

"Then tell me how I know you."

"I can't."

I thought about it. "All I can say is, you'd better not turn out to be that bully Prince Norbert or I will kick you. He was this kid who used to torment me all the time."

Jack laughed. "I'm not Norbert."

"Thanks. That narrows the field down considerably."

Chapter 18

The ride to the base of the eastern peaks went quickly and before I knew it we were starting up the switchbacks. The trolls had all disappeared with no sign that they had ever been there.

At the start of the switchbacks the trail was wide and fairly level, but the higher we got, the narrower and steeper it became. Worse than that, there were loose rocks and gravel coating the path and my horse's hooves kept slipping. I gripped the pommel of the saddle and tried to keep my breathing even. My entire body was tensed to the point where my muscles were starting to ache. I wanted to get off the horse and walk but didn't dare try dismounting on such a narrow trail.

My mare slipped again, this time seeming like she was going to fall right over the edge. She snorted and stumbled a bit before righting herself. I distantly heard the pounding of blood in my ears as the edges of my vision began to darken.

"Maxine." A strong hand gripped my arm. Jack had dismounted and was standing against the side of the cliff, one hand holding my reins. I sobbed a little and slid off the horse into his arms. He held me close and stroked my hair until my breathing calmed a little. Then he took my hand and began to lead me along the trail with the horses following behind.

"I'm scared of heights," I managed to say after a minute.

"I wasn't sure that you were scared of anything."

"You two all right?" Ron called from ahead where he was riding jauntily along the treacherous path in the most irritating manner.

"We're fine," Jack called back.

"Speak for yourself," I said, watching the ground and choosing my steps anxiously.

He laughed. For a few minutes neither of us said anything. "How are you feeling?" Jack asked.

"Still pretty nervous," I admitted.

"I'm not much of a story teller, but would a story help distract you?"

"At this point anything would help."

"Let me see what I can do," he said. "Here goes. Once upon a time—"

I interrupted. "Why does everyone start their stories that way?"

Jack tugged at my hand. "Don't argue with me," he ordered. "It's a great opening line."

"If you say so."

"It is. It happened once and it happened upon a certain time." He paused to see if I were going to argue with him further but I kept quiet. After a moment he cleared his throat and began again. "Once upon a time, there was a young prince who lived in a beautiful castle by the sea. The boy was happy with his parents who loved him, but tragedy struck early when the boy's parents were secretly murdered by the king's own chancellor."

"Did I mention I like happy stories?" I interjected.

He raised an eyebrow. "Happy stories are boring. Now be quiet." He continued. "A trusted friend of the deceased king and queen found out about the chancellor's plans to murder the prince next, so he took the boy to a remote land where he could grow to manhood and one day reclaim his kingdom.

"As the young prince grew, stories of the chancellor's cruelty and tyranny came to him and he felt increasing frustration in his inability to do anything. Yet when the time came where he was of age to return and be crowned king, it was discovered that the chancellor had acquired an army of loyal followers. Furthermore, the chancellor had substituted his own son in the prince's place. Since the two boys were the same age, few knew that a switch had been made, particularly since the chancellor claimed that his own son had died.

"Those who suspected the truth didn't dare say anything for fear of their lives. His kingdom was lost to him, and the prince despaired of ending the chancellor's tyrannical rule."

Jack stopped. I waited for a minute and then asked, "And then what?"

He blinked, looking as though he had been miles away. "What? Oh, that's the end."

I looked at him in disbelief. "But that was a terrible ending! It was more like the middle of the story, not the end."

He shrugged. "Not all stories end in happily ever after," he said.

"But stories ought to at least *end*. I'm telling you, that was a middle-of-the-story break. I need some closure here."

"Yet my story was successful."

"How?" I demanded.

"We made it to the top of the peaks," said Jack.

"We did?" I looked around. Without my realizing it, we had climbed up the last of the switchbacks and were now standing at the top. Ahead a pretty meadow stretched out in shades of brilliant green. The roofs of a village stood in the distance, and overshadowing the village was an enormous white castle.

"Holy unicorns," I said in amazement. "We made it. I thought for sure I was going to faint."

"I'm glad that you didn't."

"Me too."

"Because if you had, I would've had to carry you."

"Thanks a lot."

Jack grinned at me, and in spite of his unattractive face, something about the look in his eyes made my heart beat a little faster.

"And now I finally know something about you," I said.

"What do you mean?" He looked uneasy.

"You can't pretend that the story you just told me wasn't about yourself. You're the orphaned prince, aren't you?"

Jack rubbed his chin. "I guess I shouldn't have told you that particular story."

"Why not? After we finish up with Princess Golden we can go on a quest to your kingdom. Is that why you don't have a name? You have to be acknowledged in your identity as the prince to assume your true name, don't you?"

Jack didn't answer.

"Sometimes I awe myself with my brilliance," I said smugly. "So which kingdom is yours? You can tell me, you know. I mean, you'll have to tell me, since we'll be heading there after we're through here. We can sneak in pretending to be peasants like we've been doing, gather together your loyal followers—"

"Princess Maxine, 'we,' as in you and I, are not going anywhere together after this. You will go home and I will go my own way. And that will be that."

"You're just going to leave your people in the hands of that wicked chancellor and his son?"

"I didn't say that."

Ron came riding back. "Is there something going on here that I should know about?"

I looked pointedly at Jack. "No. Nothing is going on. That's the problem."

"If you two want to wait here while I dash in and rescue the princess, that's fine with me," said Ron.

Jack turned to me. "If you want me to leave I will."

"I don't want you to leave. I want you to let me help you."

"People, please. There is a princess waiting to be rescued and I feel that it ought to be done sometime today."

Jack and I stared at each other.

"Obviously I am the only one who understands how to conduct a quest. Farewell, you blithering simpletons, I am off to save the fair Princess—whoa."

The last whoa came out of nowhere. Jack and I looked to see what had inspired the utterance and saw that we were surrounded by trolls. It seemed that appearing out of nowhere in seconds was a particular troll skill. The Troll King stepped forward. "The promise," he said.

I glanced down at my sword only to realize it no longer hung at my waist. Looking up I saw that it was already in the Troll King's hand. He also held Jack's boot dagger and several small, deadly-looking darts.

"Where did those darts come from?" I asked.

"That's what I was wondering," said Ron.

We both looked at Jack and saw him reaching into his vest and pulling out one last dagger. "You missed this one," he said, grinning. He tossed it to the Troll King.

The Troll King caught it and then threw it back. "Any man that carries that many weapons has a reason for it. You might need it. But not for rescuing the princess."

"Thanks." Jack tucked the blade back into his vest. He glanced over and caught Ron and I staring at him. "What?"

"Nothing," we said in unison, looking away.

I realized that even though I had found out part of Jack's past, I still didn't know who he was or what made him the kind of person who felt compelled to carry so many weapons. And that bothered me.

Chapter 19

We rode side by side towards the village. "So what's the plan?" I asked Ron. We'd said farewell to the trolls, and they let us by without any further words of advice, helpful or not.

"Plan? We rescue the princess, *somehow* without any weapons." Ron scowled as he contemplated his defenseless state. "Then we ride off into the sunset."

"I have a problem with that plan," I announced.

Ron threw me an exasperated look. "Now what?"

"In case you haven't noticed, the sun is already setting. If we want to ride off into the sunset, we'd better hurry."

"And here I thought her objection was going to be logical," Jack muttered.

I ignored him. "How long do these rescues usually take?"

"It should go pretty quickly," said Ron. "It's never taken me more than an hour or two to save the girl and ride away."

"Yes, but that's because most of those girls *arranged* for you to rescue them. Staged rescues are bound to go quickly."

Jack cleared his throat. I glanced at him and saw that his eyes were shining with suppressed laughter. "Do *you* have a plan then, Princess Maxine?" he asked.

"Me? I'm only here as a sidekick. Ron's the one with all the experience."

"Yes, but you've just suggested that his experience was based on him being set up. So unless Princess Golden has also elaborately staged her imprisonment, this may be his first real rescue."

"I refuse to accept what is being suggested about my work as a rescuer of downtrodden maidens," Ron exclaimed. "Rapunzel was trapped in that tower—"

"Ron, she had a key to the tower all along. She wore it around her neck."

He was quiet for a minute. "Huh. I wondered how she retrieved her favorite hair comb that she'd forgotten in that tower. She told me some story about getting a little bird to fly it down to her, but I wondered at the time... Fine, but I definitely rescued Snow White. I mean, no princess in her right mind would bite into a poisonous apple just so I would come along and save her."

"Whoever said that Snow White was in her right mind?"

"Good point." He slumped dejectedly in his saddle. "So what you're telling me is that all of my quests have been a fraud; a dupe to trick me into getting married."

"Look on the bright side: at least you didn't actually marry any of them. And Cinderella was real. She wasn't trying to fool you."

He didn't look comforted. "Yes, but what did I really do for her? All we did was dance at a ball, and I only found her later because she fell out of her stupid shoe."

"Prince Charming," Jack said, "whether or not these rescues have been staged is secondary to the fact that you were willing to go out and help those who needed you. So maybe all of these princesses haven't been held captive by real witches and ogres. At least you keep trying because you care."

We rode in silence for a few minutes. "So, what's the plan?" I asked. "Did we ever resolve that?"

Jack looked at me with exasperation.

"What?" I asked. "Do we need a plan or don't we?"

He sighed. "Yes, we need a plan. And since you Charmings aren't so great at details, here's what I think: we get a room at the inn—"

"Two rooms," I interrupted. "I'm not sharing with either of you."

"Right. We get *two* rooms at the inn, have a hot meal—"

"And a bath," I said.

"Yes. Please stop interrupting. I know that you think it's amusing, but let me finish."

I snickered.

"And in the morning, after a good night's sleep," Jack glanced at me but I only raised my eyebrows and nodded for him to continue, "Well, based on what we find out from asking around the night before, we go from there. That's the plan."

"That doesn't sound any different from what I had in mind, only with a lot of eating and sleeping mixed in," muttered Ron.

We rode into the village as it was starting to get dark. The various shops were closing up and the villagers were hurrying home.

After a few minutes of watching this, Jack asked, "Notice anything kind of funny?"

"What do you mean?" I asked.

"Well, for one thing, look at these people. They aren't talking or anything, they're just rushing around as though their lives depend on it."

"Yes, you're right," said Ron. "And they all look worried."

I glanced around. Now that they mentioned it, the people did look kind of troubled. I noticed something else. "Look at how clean everything is!"

"And is it just me or are the people dressed kind of funny?" asked Ron.

"What do you mean?" Jack asked.

"Their clothing looks like what people wore hundreds of years ago, only not. It's like they've made up their own styles based on an old-fashioned kind of look."

"Trust you to notice that," I said.

Jack shook his head. "Let's find an inn. We'll find out more there."

We rode along the well-tended streets without talking, moving almost subconsciously at the fast pace set by the villagers. "There's one," said Jack, pointing ahead. We rode up and went inside.

An innkeeper came up to us, drying his hands on a towel. "May I help you?" he asked, so quietly I almost didn't hear him. A woman who I assumed was his wife stood behind him, staring at us suspiciously.

"Yes, thank you," said Jack. "We'd like to rent two rooms for the night and get something to eat."

The people sitting at the tables had stopped eating and were staring at Jack with wide eyes.

"Sir!" exclaimed the innkeeper in a shout-whisper, "Sir, there is no need for you to raise your voice. We can accommodate your request without a display." He showed us to a table and marched away.

"I wasn't—" Jack began in a normal tone of voice. He stopped and looked around. Everyone was still staring at him. "I mean, I wasn't raising my voice," he whispered.

A woman in an apron came over to our table. "What can I get for ye?" she whispered.

"Do you have any roasted beef?" I asked, remembering to speak quietly.

A look of panic crossed her face. "Why d'ye want *beef?*" she asked.

"Um. Because it sounds good?"

A gleam of sweat broke out across her forehead. "I will see if it is possible, milady," she said. "And you, sirs?"

After her reaction to my simple request, Jack and Ron looked a little nervous about ordering.

"What's on the menu?" whispered Jack.

She looked relieved. "Why, sir, we offer porridge. Nice and delicious it is, too."

"Porridge?" asked Ron. "Isn't that a breakfast food?"

The panicked look came back. "Sir, it is an *every meal* food here."

"Right, right. Porridge it is for both of us," interrupted Jack.

Ron looked mutinous. "I don't *like* porridge!" he said. "I never have!" He forgot to speak quietly. Spoons clattered as the other guests let out a collective gasp.

Instantly the innkeeper was back at our side, looking furious. "What seems to be the problem?" he hissed. He was getting louder by the minute. With us in his hair, he'd be shouting for real soon.

"First this lady ordered *roasted beef,*" whispered our server, "and then this gentleman here said that *he didn't like porridge.*"

The innkeeper's face turned an interesting shade of purple. "I hate to be rude in any way," he growled, "but if you are going to be fractious, we will have to ask you to leave."

"I'm terribly sorry, sir," Jack whispered. "We'll all eat porridge and don't worry about the beef—" I opened my mouth to protest and felt his foot fall on mine under the table. "Please bring us three bowls of your delicious porridge."

Mollified, the innkeeper nodded once at the serving girl and left. "There it is, then, three bowls of porridge," she said, and scurried away.

"Why did you have to ruin everything?" I asked. "I was in the mood for some real food."

Jack shook his head. "I think that while we're here we ought to eat what we're expected to eat. There's something strange about this place, and until I figure out what it is, I don't want to do anything that will make us stand out too much."

"I think it's too late for that," observed Ron as the other patrons continued to dart glances our way and whisper to each other.

The serving girl came back with our order in record time. "There ye go. Enjoy your meal."

We gazed down at our supper without much enthusiasm. "We'd better eat," said Jack, picking up his spoon. "We're getting even more attention by just gazing at this sludge." He took a bite. "Not bad," he said.

I took a reluctant bite. It was smooth and creamy, pouring down into my stomach with comforting warmth.

"Hey, it is pretty good," Ron whispered, digging in with enthusiasm.

We ate quickly and went upstairs. After arranging to leave at sunrise the next morning, I said good night to Jack and Ron. Alone in my room, I contemplated what the next few days would bring. Hopefully rescuing Princess Golden would go as quickly and smoothly as Ron expected. Afterwards I had a new goal: to aid Jack in recovering his kingdom from the hands of the murderous chancellor and his imposter son. I imagined Jack's gratitude for my help and all of the elaborate speeches he would make until finally I fell asleep.

Chapter 20

The next morning I awoke to the sound of a maid bustling around in my room. She was humming quietly to herself as she set a tray of food on the table and a pile of clothing at the foot of my bed. I yawned and stretched.

"Good morning, milady," she whispered.

"Good morning," I croaked, rubbing at my eyes. "Do you know what time it is?"

"It's half past eight and counting."

"What?" Instantly I was wide awake. "Are you sure?"

"Yes, ma'am." She left, pulling the door closed behind her.

I leapt from the bed in a panic. Jack and Ron had gone on to the castle without me, I was sure of it. I grabbed the neatly folded pile of clothes that the maid had set down and then stopped. After my bath last night I had sent my trousers and tunic downstairs to be washed. In my hands was a pretty blue dress with a fitted waist and square neckline. They must have sent me someone else's clothing by mistake.

I went to the door and poked my head out. "Miss? Miss!"

The door next to mine opened and Ron poked his head out. His hair was wildly askew and his eyes were heavy with sleep. "Maxine, keep it down, will you? Some people are trying to sleep."

"You're still here!"

"Of course I am. Why wouldn't I be?"

"It's after eight."

Ron's eyes widened. "Ogre's breath! I thought it was the middle of the night."

"I guess we were all a lot more tired than we thought," I said. I peered down the hallway. "Where'd that maid get off to? Miss!"

My loud voice brought her running. "Is everything alright, milady?" she asked.

"I need my clothes, please," I said, holding out the dress. "This must belong to another one of your guests."

She shook her head. "No, milady. That dress was made especially for you last night. One of our seamstresses sat up all night and sewed it for you so you would be dressed properly."

Jack appeared in the open doorway, scratching his head and yawning. "What's going on?"

"They won't give me my clothes back," I said, glaring at the maid.

"So what's that you're holding in your hand?" Jack asked.

"It's her dress," said the maid.

"No, this is *not* my dress," I said. "I would like for you to bring me my trousers *right now*."

The innkeeper's wife came rushing up the corridor. "Nancy, you may go," she said to the maid's obvious relief. The innkeeper's wife folded her arms. "What is the problem?"

I jutted my chin up. "I want my clothes back."

"I'm afraid that's quite impossible," Her tone was smug.

"Why is that?"

"We burned them."

"You *burned* them?" I was incredulous. "How dare you burn my clothes?"

Jack grabbed my arm and pulled me back a step. "Maxine, what are you doing? They were a pair of pants, not your grandmother." He turned to the innkeeper's wife. "Ma'am, I apologize for my friend. She tends to be rather irrational in the mornings. Thank you so much for making her this nice dress."

I growled and went back into my room, slamming the door. I had gotten used to the comfort of wearing trousers. Muttering to myself, I put the dress on. It fit perfectly and I wondered about the strangeness of a kingdom where seamstresses sat up all night sewing so one would be "dressed properly."

There was a tap on my door and Ron poked his head in. "Hey Max, it's time to get going." He paused. "You look nice."

I sighed. "Thanks."

I packed up my things and went out. Jack was engaged in a whispered conversation with the man who had stabled our horses the night before. There was no side saddle on the brown mare and I stood there wondering how on earth I was going to ride a horse astride in a dress.

"Excuse me, ma'am, but that horse is taken."

I turned around. Jack's eyes widened when he saw that it was me and I smiled, amused that he hadn't recognized me.

"Max! I didn't realize--I mean…" He cleared his throat. "You look really pretty."

I felt myself turning red. "Thanks."

Jack turned hurriedly away as though he felt uncomfortable and arranged for a sidesaddle to be put on my mare.

Soon we were on our way, headed in the direction of the castle. "So now what?" asked Ron. "I couldn't find anyone willing to talk to me."

"What?" asked Jack. I glanced at him, surprised at his lack of focus, and saw that he had a grave expression on his face. I wondered what he was thinking about that made him look so somber.

"The plan?" prompted Ron. "Remember? We were supposed to talk to people and see what we could find out."

"Oh. Well, I was thinking that we would just go in and rescue the princess."

"Jack. You're sounding like *me* now," said Ron. "That isn't good. Don't you think that we ought to come up with something a little more detailed?"

Jack shrugged.

Ron looked at me. "Max? Do you have any ideas?"

I tried to think. I'd eaten porridge again for breakfast and it sat thick and heavy in my stomach. "I suppose we could just go up to the castle gates and ask to see her."

"See who? Princess Golden?"

"Sure."

"Max. Why would she be at home with her parents if we need to rescue her? We have to find out where the ferocious beasts, with their claws dripping blood, are keeping her captive. You do remember that she's being held captive? Seems to me that you would remember a detail like that."

"I definitely don't remember the part about the bloody claws."

"Well, they *probably* have blood on their claws. And we don't have any weapons."

I glanced at Jack, hoping for one of his sensible comments, but judging from his expression it was obvious that he wasn't listening to a word of our conversation.

"The Troll King seemed to think that the fair damsel might not need our help so much as others do," I said. "And he said something about our most useful weapons being within ourselves."

"Great. So what am I supposed to do, *spit* on the enemy?"

"I'm pretty sure that's not what he meant, Ron."

"I think that we've been going about this all wrong," Jack interjected.

"What do you mean?" I asked, relieved to finally have his input.

"Well, we've been going into this thinking that we need to rescue a princess, right?"

"No offense, but that is kind of the point," said Ron.

"Yes, but like Maxine just pointed out, the Troll King said that the princess might not need our help. So why are we still so intent on rescuing this girl if we've already been told she doesn't need rescuing?"

We didn't have an answer for that.

"But," continued Jack, "the Troll King did say that others might need our help."

"Not to be difficult or anything, but what are we supposed to do with such vague information?" I asked. We were almost to the castle and I was anxious to get things figured out. "*Who* needs our help? How are we supposed to find this group of troubled individuals?"

"I suppose by finding Princess Golden we'll find the ones who really need rescuing," said Jack. "And then we'll just have to go from there."

We arrived at the gates of the castle and dismounted. Just inside the gates, two castle guards stepped forward and stood glowering out at us. "State your name and purpose," one of them ordered.

This not unreasonable request was met with a stunned silence. "*I said,*" the guard growled, "state your name and purpose."

We stood with open mouths, staring. There was no mistaking the menace in the big guy's voice; it was just hard to take him seriously. See, that's what happens when you dress a guard in pink—in spite of his strength and ferocity, you can't help but think how adorable he looks. And these guys were arrayed in a soft, pretty shade of pink usually reserved for newborn babies, from their helmets down to their large boots.

"Oh, great," muttered Ron, recovering his speech enough to be obnoxious. "We got here before we could finish planning. This is your fault, Maxine."

"What do you mean by blaming this on me?" I demanded.

"It would please me to inform you that Her Majesty does not permit contention in her kingdom," the guard said.

"But we weren't contending, we were discussing—"

"It would please me to inform you that Her Majesty does not permit her subjects to contradict her royal guards."

"Then I guess *we* don't have to worry, now do we, since I'm not one of Her Majesty's subjects," I said, putting my hands on my hips.

"Oh, Max, you and your big mouth," whispered Jack as the guard swung the gate wide open.

"It would please me to inform you that you are under arrest for violating three of Her Majesty's royal laws in a matter of minutes," intoned the guard.

"Three? So far I've only contended and contradicted. That's only two, math boy."

The guard glared at me. "You were impertinent. This is also not permitted. Now you are under arrest."

"All of us?" squeaked Ron.

"You are condemned by associating with the condemned."

"But I didn't do anything wrong," Ron said. "Just because I'm in the company of this ninny doesn't mean that *I* should be put under arrest! I am a prince, by golly! I have rights! I demand--"

The guard stopped Ron's speech by the simple means of prodding him in the stomach with his staff. "You're a prince?" he asked.

Ron clutched his stomach and nodded.

"Oh, good," said the guard. He lowered his staff. "Her Majesty is waiting for you."

"She is?"

"Right this way, please."

The two guards stalked off with Ron, leaving Jack and I to contend, contradict and be impertinent all we liked. We looked at each other, shrugged, and then followed along behind them.

Chapter 21

The guards marched up to the beautiful white castle with Ron between them while Jack and I followed at a discreet distance, trying not to be noticed. As we drew closer to the castle I saw that it was surrounded by a moat filled with murky, green-brown water. We crouched behind some bushes, watching as the drawbridge slowly squeaked down and landed with a thud in front of the guards.

The burly guards suddenly seemed nervous, talking quietly amongst themselves and stretching as if in preparation for some daring feat. Ron stood back a few feet, watching them and looking bewildered by their behavior.

"They look like they're getting ready to run a race," whispered Jack.

"Maybe there's something in the water," I said. "Maybe they're going to have to outrun something."

He shuddered. "Don't."

"Don't what? Talk about moat monsters?"

"I don't like deep water, alright? I don't like not knowing what might be in it."

"You do realize that we're going to have to cross that bridge ourselves if we want to get into the castle."

"Yes, obviously. I just need a minute."

"Ready?" One of the guards shouted, bringing our attention back to the group in front of the drawbridge. Apparently they were through with their stretches. *"Ready? And go!"*

They set off running across the moat bridge, with Ron keeping pace only because they were dragging him along with them.

"Jack, they're going to close the drawbridge. We've got to go."

He took a deep breath and nodded. We scrambled out from behind the bushes, our feet slipping in the gravel. The guards were already across and had disappeared around a corner in the courtyard, presumably to crank the lever that would pull up the bridge. Jack ran ahead of me, his speed as he flew across the bridge lending weight to his claim of being afraid of deep water.

I was halfway over when I heard splashing sounds coming from my left. A shadow fell across my path and a few drops of water dripped onto my face. I increased my speed, hoping like mad that it was raining and that the shadow hovering over me was a cloud.

Jack made it to the courtyard and turned around to see where I was at. His eyes grew wide as he tilted his head way back, as though he were looking at something enormous looming over me.

This was not comforting.

"Run, Max!" he shouted, gesturing with his arms frantically.

What did he think I was doing? Strolling? Too breathless to say so, I hitched up my skirt and ran as I never have before in my life. A damp gust of air blew against my neck, filling my nose with a stench of mud and decay. Jack shouted indistinguishably as something cold brushed against my back.

In desperation I threw myself forward, my arms spread wide. It seemed for a moment as though I were soaring through the air like a bird. A gust of wind swept just behind me, carrying with it the powerful odor of rotten fish. In the next instant I landed on Jack and he stumbled and fell backwards. "Are we safe?" I panted, looking down into his face.

"No idea," he gasped. "Get off."

We scrambled to our feet and faced the water. The surface was rough, with waves splashing against the outer banks of the moat, but nothing was in sight.

"It must have gone back underwater," said Jack.

"It? What was it?"

He ran a hand through his hair and I noticed that he was trembling. "I'm not sure. I think it might have been --" He stopped. "I'm not sure. Let's just say that you're lucky you ran as fast as you did, because I don't think it wanted to be friends."

The drawbridge started to crank back up and Jack and I sighed with relief when it finally slammed into place.

The courtyard was neatly tended with green shrubs and little benches lining a path which led to large white doors. Ron and his guards were no longer in sight. Jack looked at me and shrugged. "Let's see if we can find out where they took him," he said.

We followed the path to the castle doors and Jack opened them wide. "After you," he said, bowing. We stepped into a large, well-lit hall and then stopped.

There are certain occasions in life where the color pink is welcome. In the cheeks of a baby. A fairy godmother's dress. And everyone wants healthy pink gums. But too much pink is just plain wrong, and the interior of this castle was proof of it. Our wide eyes scanned the room, taking in the hot pink couches and vibrant pink wall tapestries. There were pink side tables, pink rugs, pink vases, pink draperies, and a pink suit of armor standing next to a painting of pink sheep in pink pastures.

The viewing sensation was not unlike twisting around and around in a swing when you already have the stomach flu.

"What kind of sick person would do something like this?" Jack asked in a subdued voice. "Pink isn't such a bad color in moderation, but this... it's enough to give a person nightmares for the rest of their life." He looked at me. "This queen must be absolutely nuts. I've never been anywhere where people only eat porridge and where everyone tiptoes around whispering fearfully and where entire castles are pink. I don't know about you, but I'm starting to think that we should have hogtied Ron and brought him back home instead of letting him continue on with this idiotic rescue."

It didn't seem like it would do any good to remind Jack that this was what I'd wanted all along. There isn't much satisfaction in being proven right if everyyhing still ends up wrong.

A movement down the hall caught our attention. Ron, escorted by the guards, was being led through ornately carved pink doors at the far end of the room.

Jack raised an eyebrow and looked at me. "Should we go watch the show, thereby risking a possible visit to the dungeons, or stay out here where it's relatively safe?"

"And miss seeing the Pink Queen in person?" I gestured at the room around us. "It might be worth losing our freedom to get a glimpse of this Majesty of Madness."

Jack grinned and we went down the hall and through the doors. The room we entered had the same color scheme as the hall, only somehow a little more obnoxious to the eyes. Ron stood in the center of the room surrounded by his guards, while more guards, similarly arrayed in pink, stood in morose clusters all along the walls. They were watching Ron with such close attention that our unannounced presence went entirely unnoticed.

Ron stood facing what at first looked like an empty throne. Then I realized that a woman was sitting there, swathed in extravagant layers of silk and lace that matched the room around her. Even her hair, which was swept up in a tower of shimmering ringlets, was a vibrant shade of pink.

"Welcome to my kingdom, Prince Charming," she said. Her voice was high-pitched and almost childish. "I am so delighted that you are here."

Ron bowed, every inch the dashing prince. "Most Royal Queen, it is my greatest honor to visit your lovely kingdom and offer my assistance in the rescue of your daughter."

"It is a lovely kingdom, isn't it? I can't tell you how much work it was to get it this way."

"Your Majesty--" Ron began.

"Call me Amelia," she simpered, fluttering her eyelashes at him. I realized that the fluttering of eyelashes could actually be done in a way that did not make one appear to have something in one's eye. I watched attentively, trying to figure out how she managed it.

"Thank you, Amelia." Ron shifted uncomfortably. "Now, it has come to my attention that your daughter is being held captive by ferocious monsters. I am here to rescue her and restore her to your loving arms."

Jack glanced over at me and caught me trying my hand—or eyes, really—at eyelash fluttering. "What are you doing?" he whispered, sounding alarmed. "Is something in your eye?"

I stopped abruptly and shook my head, trying to will away the flush of red spreading over my face. Jack watched me quizzically for a moment before shrugging. He returned his attention to the scene before us.

Amelia waved her hand impatiently to stop Ron's continuing speech regarding his rescue of her daughter. "Yes, of course. How wonderful of you. But first, are you hungry?"

"Er, I think that the urgency of your daughter's situation-"

"Naturally it is quite urgent, but it never serves to go into battle on an empty stomach, wouldn't you agree?"

"I... Your Majesty--"

"Amelia, remember?" She shook a dainty little finger at him.

"Amelia. I must say that I would prefer to rescue your daughter with all haste."

"My daughter has been held captive for quite some time now, Prince Charming." The Pink Queen's chirpy voice took on an edge of steel. "I am confident that a few more hours in that situation won't make much of a difference. Therefore, I insist that you dine with me prior to her rescue."

"If you insist." Ron sounded troubled.

"I do, actually." Already the queen was directing her attention elsewhere. "Dare I inquire as to why these creatures are marring my decor?" I glanced behind us to see the creatures and then realized that her attention was focused on Jack and me. "Come forward," she commanded.

Jack and I stepped before the Queen and bowed like our lives depended on it.

Which they did.

When we straightened up, I was surprised to see that the Queen was smiling. Specifically, she was smiling at Jack. "Well, well," she said, "Who are *you*?"

Jack swallowed. "My name is, uh, Jack."

"How delightful to meet you, Jack." More eyelash fluttering. How did she do it? The Pink Queen's gaze shifted to me. "And who is this scraggly-looking girl with the nasty-colored hair beside you, Jack?"

I bristled. Scraggly? Nasty-colored hair? Who was she to talk? At least *my* hair was a natural color. I opened my mouth to tell her so when Jack wrapped his arm around me, pushing my face into his shoulder. "This is my little sister Rose. She's always wanted to meet you, Your Highness, so Prince Charming and I let her come along. I hope that's alright."

The Queen laughed. "I can understand that. A homely little thing like her ought to be exposed to beauty once in awhile."

It was getting hard to breathe. I poked Jack's arm until he loosened his hold enough that I could pull my face free. He kept his arm around my shoulders, his fingers digging into my shoulder painfully, warning me to not say a word.

The queen stepped down from her throne. "My servants will show you to your rooms and then we'll see about a nice luncheon," she said, waving her hand in dismissal.

Ron and Jack both bowed, Jack taking me down with him. Then we turned and followed the guards out of the room and up the stairs.

Chapter 22

As soon as the guards left us in our assigned quarters I slipped out of my room and burst in on Jack. "What was that all about?" I demanded. "You almost suffocated me!"

Jack sat down on a pink embroidered couch and surveyed me calmly. "I was trying to keep you from getting yourself killed. I could see her decreeing your death as easily as she would ask for another vase of roses."

He had a point. "Well, next time give me a little more breathing room."

"Hopefully there won't be a next time." He paused. "She was being pretty mean, Max."

I wandered over to the window. "I should be used to comments like that. It happens all the time."

"I don't understand why." He sounded angry. "I've always thought that you are beautiful."

I had been fiddling with a pink tassel on the curtains, but on hearing this I turned around. It was hard to know what I should focus on: the part where he said that I was beautiful or that he had *always* thought that I was beautiful.

Jack's ears turned red and he looked away. "Anyway, we should--"

I cut him off. "Will you please tell me how you know me?"

He sat with his shoulders slightly hunched. "I can't. I've already told you that I can't."

"Why not?"

He didn't answer.

"Jack?" I walked towards him and put my hand on his arm. "If you're ashamed of something in your past, you can trust--"

He stood up abruptly. "I'm not ashamed of anything in my past. I'm not hiding who I am because of some terrible thing that I want to conceal from you. I just..." His voice trailed off. He was standing so close that I could see flecks of gold in his eyes. His eyes looked so warm, so familiar. "Maxine," he murmured.

"Have you ever in all your life met such a creepy lady?" Ron demanded, slamming the door behind him.

Jack and I jumped away from each other. Ron looked first at me and then at Jack. He cleared his throat. "So, anyway, Queen Amelia is really something, isn't she?"

Jack crossed over to the window and stood looking out.

I forced myself to focus on Ron. "Maybe we should try to sneak out of here," I said.

"This may surprise you, but I've already considered that. There are way too many guards. Not only that, but did you two happen to notice the moat when you came in?"

"Unfortunately," said Jack.

"That thing has some kind of creature in it. I'm not sure what it is because the guards rushed me across so fast, but they were scared out of their minds."

"It's a sea serpent, I think," Jack muttered.

"A *sea serpent*? In a *moat*?" Ron looked appalled.

"I know. I almost didn't believe it at first. Anyway, climbing down from the window to swim across is out." Jack turned to face us, his hands in his pockets.

"Sorry to break it to you, but climbing down has never been *in*. I don't do escape by any means which involve heights," I said.

"So what are we going to do?" Ron asked.

"Go eat a nice meal, is my guess," Jack said. "Then we'll rescue the princess, or attempt to."

A knock at the door interrupted us and Jack's eyes grew wide. "Hide!" he hissed.

"Why?" asked Ron.

"I don't know," whispered Jack, herding us across the room. "But I have a feeling that it wouldn't go well for any of us if either of you are found in here."

I didn't question him. If I could get arrested for being contentious, I could get arrested for standing in a room talking. I dove under the enormous bed while Ron climbed into the wardrobe.

I heard the door open. "Uh, hello!" said Jack, sounding surprised. When I heard the voice that responded, my head jerked up and came into sharp contact with the wooden base of the bed. The resultant pain throbbing in my skull was further aggravated by the childishly sweet voice of the new arrival.

"I came to make sure that you were comfortable. I do hope the room is to your liking," said Queen Amelia.

"It is. Yes. Thank you."

"This is my favorite room. Such a lovely view from the window."

"Indeed. It's a very lovely view."

Queen Amelia laughed, her voice getting louder as she came further into the room. "Why, Jack, you seem almost scared of me. You're not, are you?"

Jack cleared his throat. "No. Should I be?"

"Maybe." She laughed again. There was a sound of scuffling and Jack's feet bounded into view.

"Your Majesty, I must say that I--"

"Come here, Jack. I need to tell you something."

"I'd be delighted to hear what you have to say, but I'm confident that I can hear you quite well from here."

The Queen's pink shoes joined Jack's near the bed ruffle and just as quickly his retreated until I could no longer see them. One of the Queen's little shoes began to tap. "I must insist that you stay in one place."

Suddenly there was a loud crashing sound. "Confound it, Jack, but I really think you must have been fooling me!" It was Ron. I watched as his boots approached the Queen's pretty feet and stopped. "Hello there, Amelia. Jack told me he'd seen a mouse in his wardrobe, but I didn't see hide nor tail of one."

"A mouse in the wardrobe," repeated Queen Amelia. "Really."

"I was probably only seeing things, Your Majesty," said Jack.

"No doubt you were, particularly since I eradicated all mice years ago. Now if you will excuse me, gentlemen, I have some matters of the kingdom to attend to." The pink-shod feet stepped from view and a moment later the bedroom door closed.

"Whew. I wasn't sure if I would live to hear you thank me. Who would've imagined that Queen Amelia would take it into her head to come after you like that?"

Jack sighed. "I know, and thank you. I wasn't sure what I was going to do."

"Hey, it's in my job description to rescue people." Ron paused. "Where did Max get off to?"

"I don't know. Wasn't she in the wardrobe with you?"

"I barely fit in there myself. Max? Where are you?"

I closed my eyes, not wanting to reveal my hiding place. There are some girls who can look beautiful in even the most distressing of situations. Cinderella, for example, had looked breathtaking even while emptying chamber pots. I knew this because I'd gone with Ron when he was traveling around with that impossibly tiny glass slipper looking for her. When we got to her house, there she was, carrying a freshly-emptied porcelain pot. When she saw us she set the smelly thing down and straightened up to greet us. Her eyes glowed a crystal blue, her face blushed a pretty pink and her golden curls spilled in tousled glory down her back. Altogether she looked as fresh and lovely as though she had just come from a stroll in the garden.

This ability of looking elegant, or at the very least *presentable*, has eluded me all of my life. It was a fact that I usually accepted with resignation and some humor. But at this moment I wanted more than anything to look graceful and pretty. Knowing that this wasn't possible, I would have at least settled for getting out of the room unobserved.

I sighed and wriggled out from under the bed. I hadn't taken two steps towards the door when Ron burst out laughing. "You hid under the *bed*?"

"Be quiet. I'm going to my room to freshen up."

"You might want to. You're a mess." Ron was sublimely undisturbed by the nasty look I gave him, as evidenced by his rude snickering. I turned and swept regally from the room.

Chapter 23

Safe in my room, I sat down at the small dressing table and looked in the mirror. My face was flushed and my braid almost completely undone. I shook my head at the view and set to work on taming my hair even while my mind focused on the few moments when Jack and I had been alone together. The fleeting sensation of recognition was gone, but the memory of the look in Jack's eyes as he gazed down at me lingered. I wasn't sure what it meant, but I was relieved when a knock came at my door summoning me for lunch so I could stop thinking about it.

It was only as we went to sit down that I saw that two places were set on either side of the Queen and the fourth was set at the opposite end of the enormous dining table.

Guess who was meant to sit there?

As I settled into my assigned place, it felt as though the others were miles away. It was hard to hear what they were saying but Queen Amelia kept laughing. I picked up my spoon and jabbed it into the bowl of porridge. Having eaten porridge for dinner and breakfast, I couldn't bring myself to take a bite.

Just then someone whimpered. Startled, I glanced down the length of the table. Jack, Ron and Amelia had their heads close together, talking animatedly. I lifted my spoon and the whimpering sound came again. This time I looked down. A little dog, its fur dyed a dreadful pink, gazed up at me with pleading brown eyes.

I glanced at the others again. Jack, Ron and the Pink Queen weren't giving me a moment's attention. I watched with narrowed eyes as Amelia placed her hand on Jack's arm and simpered. If I'd had an appetite before, it was gone now.

I scooped some porridge into my spoon and lowered it to the dog's level. It hungrily licked the spoon clean and wagged its tail for more. "Glad to oblige," I muttered and put my bowl on the floor. In no time at all the porridge was gone. The dog gave the bowl a final lick and then crawled under my chair, settling down with a contented sigh. "Good boy," I said, picking a pink dog hair out of the bowl before setting it back on the table.

The party was progressing at a jolly rate at the other end of the room. I put my chin in my hand and watched the laughing and flirting with disgust. The Queen made no effort to hide her interest in Jack, and more than once I considered picking up my empty bowl and flinging it at her head. Only years of strict training in table manners stopped me. Well, that and the realization that I was too far away to actually hit her.

I was interrupted from my grim musings by the sound of an extremely loud yawn. I looked under my chair to find an exposed view of canine teeth gaping back at me as the dog yawned again and collapsed on its side. I glanced down the table in time to see both Ron and Jack yawning. They tried to cover their yawns politely but it seemed that as soon as one ended another began. The Queen was watching them with an expression of chilly satisfaction.

Something clicked in my mind just as the Queen narrowed her cold gaze down the length of the table at me. Heart pounding, I faked the biggest yawn of my life, stretching elaborately and blinking my eyes as though I could hardly keep them open.

Queen Amelia stood up and Jack and Ron quickly stood with her. "Gentlemen," she said, "I can see that your travels have wearied you more than you let on. Perhaps you should take a short nap before you commence the rescue of my daughter?"

Ron shook his head. "No, I really think it would be best if--" He stopped and yawned so widely that his jaw popped. "If we rescue the princess right away."

"I agree with Prince Charming," Jack said, swaying and blinking slowly. "We really ought to get moving and rescue Princess...Princess..." He looked around as though he couldn't remember what he had been saying.

Queen Amelia smiled and slipped her arms through both of theirs. "I must insist on a nap, my dears," she said. She glanced my way so I faked another yawn. "You too, young lady."

I followed her as she led the way to our rooms. "Sleep well, handsome prince, darling Jack." Looking tiredly bewildered, Jack and Ron went into their rooms, closing the doors behind them. With no other choice than to do likewise, I went into my room. Just in case, I lay down on my bed and closed my eyes.

My mind was racing. Obviously the Queen had laced the porridge with a sleeping potion, but why? Why wouldn't she want her daughter rescued as soon as possible? As I lay pondering, I heard the door open. I resisted the urge to look and instead made my breathing deep and even. After a moment of silence, my door closed again. I waited a little longer and then sat up. It was time to find out what her Majesty of Madness was up to.

I peered out into the hall. Four guards stood against the opposite wall, their faces expressionless. I whistled softly and noted that the only change in their demeanor was that they stopped blinking. Even the Queen walking by wouldn't notice anything amiss unless she actually tried to talk to them.

I slipped into Jack's room. He was lying face down on his bed, fully clothed.

"Jack," I whispered. "Hey Jack, wake up!"

He grunted and opened his eyes with what appeared to be an enormous effort.

"Are you alright?" I asked.

"Jus' really tired," he slurred. He tried to push himself up and failed.

"I think Queen Amelia put some kind of sleeping potion into our porridge. I'm going to go and see what she's up to."

He shook his head. "No, Max."

"What do you mean, no?"

"Too dang'rous."

"I'll be fine." I patted his hand and was startled when he grabbed mine with surprising strength.

"Don't go."

I tried to pull away. "Jack, this is the perfect opportunity. She won't be expecting any of us to come around because she thinks we're all asleep. I've got to see what she's up to."

"Max." Jack propped himself onto his elbows with an effort. "Max, I need to tell you something." His hair was wildly askew and he blinked at me in an endearingly boyish way.

"All right."

"I need to tell you somethin'." His voice trailed off and to my alarm his eyes rolled up into the back of his head. He collapsed onto the bed with a soft thump.

"Jack?" Alarmed, I clambered up onto the bed beside him and pushed him onto his back. Was he dead? Had she given him too much sleeping potion?

Just then he let out the loudest snore I'd ever heard. I looked down at him while he continued to snore, rending the air with explosions of noise that were so comical I had to laugh.

He was fine. It was a shame that he'd conked out when he did, though. I wondered what he had been going to tell me.

I checked on Ron and found him in a similar state. From the looks of things, neither of them would be waking up very soon.

Chapter 24

I made my way downstairs and paused in the main hall, wondering where to find Queen Amelia. The guards didn't react as I walked past them and after the first few I didn't bother to whistle anymore. It was almost like they were there more for ornamentation than for any actual guarding. Then I noticed that one of the guards was watching me, his expression open and friendly. He looked a lot younger than the other guards and I wondered if he would be a good source of information. I strolled over and pretended to admire the pink tapestry on the wall beside him while I tried to think of a way to start a conversation.

"Nasty thing," he said.

"Excuse me?" I asked, startled.

"The tapestry. That's what you're looking at, isn't it?"

I really looked at it. It depicted a group of men being attacked by a hideous sea monster with an evil, almost human grin on its face.

"It's awful."

"Queen Amelia wove it. It's a terrible thing to have to stand guard next to."

"It's better than having to fight the actual serpent, I suppose," I said.

"Luckily for us, our serpent can't leave the water. So provided we get across the moat bridge fast enough, we don't have to fight it." He paused. "Anyway, I shouldn't be talking to you." He straightened up and stared ahead, but I could tell that his heart wasn't in it.

"Why not? Is it against the law to talk to guests or something?"

He gave me a look. "What do you think?"

"The laws in this kingdom are ridiculous," I said. "I'd never be able to stand living here."

"And I'm sure all the laws in your land are perfectly sensible," he said, looking steadfastly forward.

"Most of them are," I said. "The Kingdom of Veiland is known for its—" I stopped. "Is something amusing you?"

"I've heard all about Veiland," he smirked. "They say that the King of Veiland is always planning wars and battle strategies even though he hides at the first sign of an argument. And Prince Charming— of course you know this since you're traveling with him—all he does is go around rescuing a lot of silly girls when he should be paying attention to his own kingdom. And the daughter—Molly or Mable, I can't remember her name--"

"Maxine," I supplied tersely.

"Yes, that's it. I forgot that you would know; you've most likely met her, eh? I've heard that she has no idea how to behave in spite of all of the princess training courses her mother makes her attend."

"I happen to know," I said, "that Princess Maxine is very well-behaved. Just because she doesn't act like an air-headed ninny--"

"I hear that plans are in the works to have Veiland under a new rule by the end of the month," interrupted the guard. "Have you heard about that? Apparently Veiland's army is a joke and even a bunch of untrained farmers--"

"Hold it, hold it! What do you mean that plans are already in the works to have Veiland under a new rule? Do you mean someone is planning on *invading* Veiland?"

I must have looked pretty upset because the guard's face took on, if you'll pardon the expression, a guarded look. "They're probably only rumors," he muttered.

"*Who* is planning on taking over Veiland?" I demanded.

"Look," said the guard, "I would suggest that before you start worrying about your beloved homeland, you might want to consider the fact that you and your friends have gotten yourselves into a whole lot of trouble by coming to *this* kingdom. You do realize that, don't you?"

I felt like I was getting a lot more information than I had bargained for. "What do you mean?"

"Surely you've heard about this kingdom?"

"Clearly there is a whole lot that I haven't heard."

He rolled his eyes and spoke slowly, as though I were a dim-witted child. "We haven't had anyone come to rescue Princess Golden in hundreds of years because most people know to avoid it."

I decided to focus on one piece of information at a time. "You aren't making any sense. Are you trying to tell me that Queen Amelia is hundreds of years old? She couldn't be any older than twenty-five." I paused. "Which now that I think about it is rather strange. How could Queen Amelia have a daughter old enough for Ron to marry?"

"You don't have much experience with curses, do you?" the guard asked. "*Obviously* this castle is under a curse and *obviously* you don't grow any older when you're under a curse. So we will all look the same age we were when the curse was first put into place, now wouldn't we?"

"*Obviously* I don't like you very much," I said. "I'm going to find someone else to talk to."

"Good luck with that. I'm the only one who *will* talk to you, given my gregarious personality. I've always been this way. Mother said that I was the most talkative child she'd ever encountered."

I walked up to one of the other guards. "Excuse me," I said.

"Approaching a guard for purposes of communication is strictly prohibited," the guard intoned.

"But I was just talking to that other guard and no one cared," I protested.

"Pointing out the obvious is also strictly prohibited. If you continue in this unlawful behavior I will be forced to imprison you."

"What did I tell you?" the first guard asked. "Personally, I think that they've all gone a bit batty after all of these years."

I sighed and returned to his side. "Fine," I said. "Talk to me."

"First, allow me to introduce myself. I haven't been able to do that in a long time." He stuck out his hand for me to shake. "The name's Bruce Mathers. You can call me Bruce."

"My name is Ma—uh, Rose."

"Yes, I heard that you were the one chap's sister."

"That's me. Jack's sister."

Bruce raised an eyebrow. "Not a very good liar, are you?" he asked.

"What do you mean?"

"I've never seen a girl blush when she talks about her brother."

"I, uh..."

"Your secret is safe with me, Rosie." He winked. "Best to not tell the Queen, of course. She's chosen Jack for herself, so if she found out that you aren't his sister, she'd put poison in your next bowl of porridge instead of a sleeping potion. Speaking of which, but how is it that you aren't asleep?"

"Well, I sort of fed my porridge to a little pink dog."

"I suppose it wouldn't surprise you to hear that feeding porridge to little pink dogs is strictly prohibited?"

"Not really."

"Why didn't you eat it?"

I wrinkled my nose. "I don't like porridge very much."

"I've been eating porridge for years," he said. "It puts hair on your chest."

"Another reason for me to give it to the dog," I said.

He looked surprised for a second, and then a strange expression came over his face. It took me a minute to realize that it was the beginning of a smile. Slowly his lips came up, his face a mixture of amusement and alarm, as though he wasn't sure how to respond to what he was feeling. Then he started laughing, a strange cawing noise that sounded rough and raw. "Hair on your chest," he gasped, bending over and slapping at his knees. "Guess you should've given it to the dog, now, ha, ha, ha!"

I folded my arms and waited, glancing behind me at the other guards in case laughing was also prohibited. They were watching Bruce curiously but made no move to arrest us. I made a mental note to avoid any other amusing comments, just in case.

Bruce wiped at his eyes. "I haven't had a laugh since, well, let me see; was it in '42? Or '43?"

"I'm glad I amuse you," I said. "Now if you would please tell me who it is that is planning to invade Veiland and why it is that we are in so much trouble by having come here to rescue the princess, I would greatly appreciate it."

He quickly sobered. "Sorry, Rosie, but I don't think I will tell you who it is that's going to invade your homeland. Sometimes it's more comfortable not knowing things that will affect the rest of your life."

"Yes, but sometimes people *want* to know and don't care if it's comfortable or not."

"Trust me, in this case, you'd rather not know."

"Please?"

"Sorry, Rosie, it's for your own good."

"Aaargh! Fine! Don't tell me. Don't tell me anything. I don't know when I've had a less informative conversation." I whirled around and began to walk away. "I'm going to find the Queen, and when I do, I'm going to put in a special request that she put you in a dungeon or the moat or somewhere where innocent travelers like me aren't afflicted by your existence."

"I never said that I wouldn't tell you why you're in trouble for coming to this castle in the first place."

I stopped. Without turning around I said, "Fine. Talk."

"Once upon a time--"

I looked back at him. "You're not really going to start your story that way, are you?"

"Why shouldn't I?"

"It's highly overused. Why not just say two years ago in March..."

"It was exactly three hundred and fifty-four years ago, actually."

"So say, 'It was exactly three hundred and fifty-four years ago," I said.

"I thought that you wanted to hear this," said Bruce.

"I do."

"Then prove it by shutting up so I can tell the story."

I was silent.

"Well?"

"I'm shutting up."

He looked at me narrowly. "Alright. Here's what I know."

Chapter 25

"*Three hundred and fifty-four years ago*, Princess Amelia was a bright-eyed little girl with long golden hair that curled down her back like sunshine."

"Bruce, no offense, but would you mind just telling the story without all of the flowery detail? Just give me the gist of it."

He glared at me. "Who's telling the story here, you or me?"

This was going to take awhile, I could tell. I sat down on the floor, leaning up against the wall. "Go ahead."

Bruce continued. "The princess was so lovely and so bright that soon all of the people were calling her Princess Golden."

"Are you kidding me? Queen Amelia is really Princess Golden? I thought Princess Golden was her daughter!"

"Rosie, if you interrupt again, I am not going to finish the story. Do you understand?"

"Sorry," I said.

"Princess Golden's mother died when she was a baby, so her father raised her by himself. He didn't do a very good job of it, though. He gave her whatever she wanted without consideration of the feelings or even the belongings of others.

"One day this got her into trouble. She went where she had been told not to go, into the deepest, darkest part of the forest. There she found a little cottage. Being tired and hungry, she let herself in. Since she was a spoiled princess, she wasn't used to asking for permission, and after finding porridge on the table, she helped herself. Now the porridge was meant for a family of enchanters, who went about in the guise of ferocious bears by night, and came home during the day to eat their magical porridge and rest from their wicked deeds." Bruce looked at me and sighed. "What?"

"How did you know that I wanted to say something?"

"You looked like you were going to explode. It was kind of hard to miss."

"Well, are you telling me the story of Goldilocks and the Three Bears? Because if you are, I have to say that everyone has heard this story ever since they were little. Do you expect me to believe that it really happened?"

"I don't care if you believe it or not. It's true, and that's all that matters. Now do you want to hear the rest or should I go on guarding this wall like I have been for hundreds of years?"

"I would like to hear the rest, please," I said.

Bruce continued. "So Princess Golden went into the cottage and ate the porridge that tasted just right to her, but this meant that she ate the porridge of the youngest enchanter, which wasn't such a good idea since the youngest enchanter had a terrible temper. Then the princess went and fell asleep right in his bed, so that when he got home after a long night of burning villages and found some smelly little girl in his bed, he wasn't too happy.

"Next thing Princess Golden knew, she was being carted home on the back of the furry bear. He dumped her inside the castle grounds and proclaimed that once she reached the age of twenty-five, she and all those in the kingdom would be trapped timelessly, unable to leave the boundaries of the kingdom and unable to lead normal lives until a prince with a true heart and pure motives came to free her. And naturally the way to do this was to slay the serpent that he put into the moat."

"How come I've never heard this part of the story?" I asked. "In Goldilocks and the Three Bears, all she does is run off in the end and that's it. You'd think that the part about the enchanter and the moat and all that would've been included since it's the most interesting part of the story."

"Yes, but the stories you're used to hearing are usually about sweet, kind maidens who deserve happy endings. In the true version of this story, Princess Golden is a spoiled brat who grows up to be a batty queen. Goldilocks and the Three Bears has been edited enormously to satisfy the desire of people everywhere for their heroines to be good."

"The story of Goldilocks is weird anyway," I said. "Why bears? Why porridge? Why weren't the bears eating meat? It just doesn't make sense."

"The truth doesn't have to make sense. Now let me finish." Bruce looked at me sternly to see if I were going to interrupt again. I mimed zipping my lips and throwing away the key. He shook his head and continued. "The years passed and Amelia's father died, leaving her queen over the land. She married a young man but kept his identity a secret. The couple had a child when Amelia was twenty and they named her Golden after Amelia's old nickname. When Amelia turned twenty-five, just as the enchanter had said, no one was able to leave the kingdom and everyone stopped aging. At about the same time, the Queen's young daughter Golden was taken away by the enchanter and Amelia was left alone."

"What happened to Amelia's husband?" I asked.

"It's been rumored that she got mad at him and fed him to the serpent in the moat," said Bruce. "At first many princes and knights came to rescue the Queen but none of them had true hearts or pure motives. Consequently, they were unable to rescue her and not only that, but a lot of them ended up being eaten by the serpent. The rescuers who survived couldn't go home since once they entered the kingdom they couldn't leave due to the curse. And this, Rosie, is your problem. You'll be trapped here timelessly just like everyone else."

"Not if I have a say in the matter," I said.

"You don't. Anyway, after awhile Queen Amelia began to really lose it. She had her entire castle done up in pink in honor of little Goldie's favorite color and for some reason she became so obsessed with porridge that she decreed that no one could eat anything else. She made up a huge list of laws that made the people of her kingdom more and more miserable while the outside world seemed to forget their existence.

"Now all the Queen wants is a handsome new husband, and she doesn't care about the curse or the fact that we are all tired of living in an enchanted bubble. And that's the story." Bruce folded his arms and looked down at me where I was still sitting on the floor.

I thought for a minute. "Has anyone tried to kill the enchanter?"

"If no one has been able to kill the serpent, what chance would the same individuals have in killing a powerful enchanter?"

Rhetorical questions can be so annoying. "I'm pretty sure that my bro--" I stopped myself. "I mean, I'm pretty sure that Prince Charming has a pure heart. He rescues princesses all the time."

"Yes, but he gets engaged to them, too. Wouldn't that mean that he has an ulterior motive?"

"Not necessarily."

"I don't know." Bruce shook his head. "We've had a few princes come along, and I was sure that they had true hearts and pure motives, but then it turned out that they were only doing it for glory and recognition. No offense, but from what I've heard about your brother, it seems like his heart is pretty set on what the world thinks of him."

"Where do you get all of your information?" I demanded. "For a guy who is supposedly cut off from everything, you seem to have a pretty good source."

Bruce smiled. "Can't tell you that," he said. "Just know that I'm not as isolated as you might think. Now my question for you is: how did your group hear about Princess Golden? We haven't had any rescuers for a long time and those that used to come were coming to rescue Queen Amelia."

"We heard about her from our Royal Wizard." My eyes narrowed. "Who, now that I think about it, has a lot of questions to answer when we get home."

"If, you mean."

"Pardon?"

"*If* you get back home. You realize that not only are you stuck here until Prince Charming proves his true heart, but you're also stuck here with a queen who might or might not tolerate your presence outside of a dungeon at any given moment. I'd hide in your room as much as possible if I were you."

"For hundreds of years? I don't think I can do that."

"At least until Prince Charming wakes up and we see if the serpent eats him or not."

"You're awfully negative."

"I'm a man who has been wearing pink in a pink castle for hundreds of years. It doesn't get much worse than this."

"On the contrary," Queen Amelia's high-pitched voice cut in. "It does indeed get worse."

Chapter 26

"Dragon snot," muttered Bruce as I scrambled to my feet. We turned to face the queen as she came towards us. Her eyes were focused on me.

Not good.

"You're awake," she said in a falsely pleasant voice.

"I sure am."

"*How* are you awake?"

"It's kind of a long story," I said, even though it wasn't.

"Better to not say anything," hissed Bruce, which, unfortunately for him, reminded the queen of his presence.

"Ah, Bruce," she said. "Have you told Rose your story?" She looked at me. "Bruce was a prince about three hundred and forty years ago. He was one of the first who came to rescue me, but when he found out about that hungry serpent he didn't even try. He just put down his sword and agreed to spend the rest of forever as a guard. I can't see why I let him. I abhor cowards."

"Queen Amelia, surely you know by now that I am a better diplomat than a fighter. My heart is true, but I'm afraid that my bravery just isn't up to snuff."

"Then wouldn't you say that, as a guard, you're pretty much useless?"

He swallowed. "Well, now, I—I wouldn't say *that*, exactly."

"And the serpent outside gets hungrier every day. Maybe we ought to give the old girl a snack. What do you think, Rose?" The cold eyes fixed on me.

"I'm sure the serpent would prefer something else," I said. "Maybe some fish?"

"There aren't any fish. She's eaten them all."

"Now, Queen Amelia," said Bruce, wringing his hands together. "You've got to remember that in spite of my cowardly ways I do have other uses. After all, who provides you with all of the news from the other kingdoms? Who tells you when the enchanter is coming?"

She stared at him. "You."

"Right! *Exactly*. Me." He pounded his chest emphatically.

"But what I'm wondering," she said, "is how it is that you know every time the enchanter is coming? How is it that you know outside news? This is what I'm wondering, Bruce."

His eyes grew wide. "Your Majesty! You can't be serious! We've worked together for so many years and now you're suggesting…"

"After three hundred years and the loss of my daughter, I can consider a lot of things that I've never considered before. Guards!"

The witless guards sprang forward. "Put this man into the dungeons," commanded Queen Amelia.

"Wait! Queen Amelia! Don't do this! Don't put me down there! You need me!" Bruce's cries grew fainter as the guards drug him away.

In the following silence, the queen turned to face me. "So," she said. "You never answered my question."

"Which question?"

"Where I asked you why it is that you're not sleeping?" She raised an eyebrow. "Of course, I already know that you're awake only because you fed your porridge to my dog. Do you realize that the dose I put in there was for someone of your size? You could have killed him."

"How was I to know--" I began.

"The point is you shouldn't have been feeding my dog!"

I felt my face grow red. "Maybe if *you* paid more attention to feeding your dog than dying it the right shade of pink, it wouldn't have been begging for food! Did you ever think of that, you porridge-eating prissy?"

The queen's mouth dropped open as she gaped at me. "How dare you?" she squeaked.

"Oh, please. What are you going to do, put me in the dungeons? Allow me to assure you that the dungeons would be preferable to another minute of trying to stomach this nauseating pink décor."

"Max, what are you doing?" Jack stood at the bottom of the staircase, gazing at me with horror.

"I hate bullies," I said.

"There are better ways of dealing with bullies than blatantly insulting them, especially when you know that they're stronger than you."

I eyed the queen. "I could take her."

"If it was a case of hand-to-hand combat maybe you could! But you'll be dealing with her guards, remember?" Jack sounded like he wanted to strangle me.

"I could take them, too. They don't seem too quick on their feet." I glanced over at the nearest guard, who seemed entirely oblivious to our conversation.

"In point of fact," said Queen Amelia, "I believe my guards could certainly subdue you long enough to feed you to the serpent. Don't think--" The sound of the drawbridge slamming down interrupted her. Several guards ran through the hall as though fleeing something too terrible to fight. Immediately thereafter an odd smell of wet fur, rotten fish and most bizarrely of all, men's cologne, filled the air.

Queen Amelia flashed us an irritated glance. "If you had eaten your porridge like good children, you would be sleeping safely upstairs," she said.

I looked at Jack. "You didn't eat your porridge?" I asked.

He shrugged. "I ate some of it. What about you?"

Before I could answer a dark, hairy shape flung the courtyard doors open. "Good afternoon, Princess Golden." The voice was rough and deep as it rumbled across the hall.

Queen Amelia glared at the new arrival. "How many times have I told you to not call me by that name? You know who it reminds me of."

The creature in the doorway laughed. "Why do you think I persist?" The shaggy shape came forward, moving with a liquid smoothness that was at odds with its ungainly form. As it emerged from the shadows, I saw that it was a bear, enormous and terrifying. It stopped before the queen and surveyed us with a snarly grimace that I suppose passes for a smile in evil bear enchanters.

Suddenly the creature's shape began to shift and lurch and I stumbled back to get out of the way. The bear's head twisted and seemed to shrink while at the same time the claws grew out into the long pale fingers of a man. The animal's brown fur knitted into itself in shades of deepening purple until in the next instant a sinister man stood before us, clothed in purple and silver robes. His eyes glinted malevolently, and I saw that they were an odd, yellow-gold color, making him seem somehow less human in his human form.

"Let me look at your visitors, Amelia," the enchanter said. "It's been awhile since the last noble prince." He came towards us and the smell of wet fur and cologne grew stronger. "Well look here: one of them is a girl." He laughed. "Really,

Amelia, are you so desperate now that you have *girls* coming to rescue you?"

While I should have been focusing on the fact that my life was in peril, I was distracted by the sudden realization that the enchanter was trying to combat his bear odor with cologne. It was an odd touch of vanity that made me less afraid of him than I should have been. He stopped in front of me and reached to touch my cheek.

Jack stepped between us. "Don't touch her," he said, glaring.

The enchanter studied Jack leisurely. "You're wearing a mask," he said. "I suppose you think that you have some deep, terrible secret you need to hide?"

Jack's jaw clenched. "My whole life has been made up of secrets," he said.

The enchanter laughed. "Don't be foolish, boy," he said. "Neither your mask nor your secrets can be hidden from me. Now step aside."

"No."

"I will not ask again. *Step aside.*"

"I will not."

The enchanter growled under his breath and then swung his hand, knocking Jack backwards as though he weighed nothing. He fell heavily to the ground and lay still.

"Jack!" I moved to go to him but the enchanter gripped my shoulder. With his other hand he turned my face so I was forced to meet his eyes.

"So," he said, "Has a girl come to slay the serpent?"

"The *serpent* isn't the one causing the problems." I tried to pull free but his grip was like iron.

"How delightful," he growled. "You think you've discovered a better way to break my enchantments. Don't you realize that I have ways to make your life eternally miserable? Ask Amelia about misery. She could tell you."

Just then a voice from the stairs muttered, "I *knew* I would need a sword. Hey there! Guard! Toss me that staff, will you?" A staff flew into Ron's hand and thus armed he strode forward. "Unhand my sister, you rogue!" he ordered, brandishing the staff as though it were made of the finest steel.

I shook my head. A stick of wood versus a monster. Only Prince Charming would think that those were good odds.

Chapter 27

The enchanter loosened his grip enough that I was able to squirm free and kneel at Jack's side. "Jack," I whispered frantically. He didn't respond.

Ron pointed his staff at the enchanter. "I command you to leave this castle at once."

The enchanter rolled his eyes. "And if I don't?"

Ron looked blank for a second. "Eh?"

"I said, if I don't leave? What will you do then?"

"Well..." Ron looked down at the staff in his hands as though finally realizing that it was pretty inadequate in terms of the danger he was facing. "I suppose I will have to...uh...knock your head off with this piece of wood."

The enchanter threw back his head and laughed, startling all of us. "That's wonderful," he said. "You'll knock my head off. I haven't heard anything so blatantly ridiculous in a long time."

"What's so ridiculous about it?" Ron demanded. "You don't think I could do it?"

"No, I do not. My dear boy, I have been attacked by literal armies of experienced fighting men with swords, arrows, and even the most powerful magic. Do you really believe that you, armed with a little twig, could cause me harm?"

"It never hurt to try," Ron said. Without further warning, he swung with all of his might at the enchanter's head. Ron's little twig connected with the enchanter's skull with a sharp cracking sound, knocking him to the ground in a flurry of robes.

Queen Amelia screamed.

"What do you know," Ron muttered as it became apparent that the enchanter wasn't getting up. "It worked."

Queen Amelia rushed over. "Quick, you fool, grab his arms. I'll grab one foot and you, girl, get over here! Get the other foot! We'll feed him to his own serpent and our kingdom will be free of this curse once and for all. Hurry!"

But it was too late. Already the enchanter was stirring, and I had a feeling that he wasn't going to be as easily amused when he came around.

Just then Bruce walked in. "Whoa," he said, his eyes wide as he took in Jack and the enchanter both stretched out across the floor. "What happened in here?"

Queen Amelia was too distracted to notice that her guard was mysteriously free from the dungeons she had just sent him to. She dropped the enchanter's foot and shrieked at Ron, "Hit him again! Hit him again!"

"No," said Ron. "It is not honorable to strike a fallen man."

"Honorable?" she yelled. "*Honorable?* Are you crazy? This is the evil enchanter Dominicus. He kidnapped my precious daughter and ruined my life. *Hit him again!*"

Ron assumed his I-Am-the-Crown-Prince look. "I refuse. No matter how villainous the enemy, you do not strike them when they are already down."

Queen Amelia looked like she wanted to strike Ron. Instead she grabbed the staff away from him and raised it high above the enchanter's still form. Before she could swing, the shape on the floor convulsed. The pale hand lying nearest her foot sprouted dark hairs which quickly thickened into matted fur, while the fingers shortened and long black claws curled from the ends. The rest of the enchanter's body underwent a similar transformation, and in the next instant the bear sprang from the floor, snarling and enormous.

Queen Amelia tried to swing the staff at his head anyway, but he grabbed it from her and threw it across the room. Roaring ferociously, the enchanter picked her up and threw her over his hairy shoulder. She screamed and then fainted, something all titled females, in scary or awkward situations, are taught to do as soon as they are old enough to crawl.

"Wow," said Ron. "I was wondering why you stunk like a wet dog. You're really a bear?"

The bear whirled to face Ron, its lips drawn back in a terrible snarl.

"Not only do you stink like a wet dog," continued Ron in the manner of a man who, seeing that death is imminent, has decided he will have his say, "but there is also a definite aroma of rotten fish. But at least you're trying. I mean, the cologne does help."

There was a short moment of silence as Ron's imitation golden eyes gazed calmly into the bear's blazing yellow ones. Then the enchanter made an odd barking sound and I realized with a jolt of surprise that he was actually laughing. He stretched forth a massive paw and laid it on Ron's head.

I cringed and involuntarily looked away as a loud cracking sound shot through the room. A moment later I heard the bear shuffle away but I didn't look up. I cradled Jack's head in my lap as the crushing realization swept over me that the enchanter had just killed my brother.

"Rosie?" I had forgotten about Bruce. I could tell from the sound of his voice that he was hovering over me. "Rosie, are you alright?"

What a stupid question. Of course I wasn't alright. I swiped the tears from my cheeks with one hand. "Go away, Bruce," I said. "Leave me alone."

"But Rosie, somebody ought to go see where Dominicus is taking Queen Amelia."

How could he be so thick-headed? Who cared about Queen Amelia at a time like this? My brother was dead and Jack wasn't moving. I was about to utter a truly scathing response when something heavy plopped onto my knee. My eyes flew open in alarm. Perched on my knee like it had every right to be there was an enormous, hideously ugly green frog.

To have a huge frog come out of nowhere and land on me in the midst of my sorrows was too much. "Blech! Get away from me!" I yelled and knocked it away. The frog tumbled head over flippers and lay still for a moment, the thin yellow skin on its throat pulsing frantically. Then it rolled to a sitting position, shook itself, and hopped back over to me. It stopped about a foot away and stared up at me with enormous golden eyes.

Talk about creepy.

"Rosie?" Bruce crouched at my side. "I hate to break it to you, but that frog is Prince Charming."

I looked at Bruce like he was insane. "What are you talking about?"

He cleared his throat and glanced in the direction where I knew Ron's body lay. "When that bear laid his paw on Prince Charming's head, it was to turn him into a frog. I thought I should tell you since I noticed you had your eyes closed when it happened."

My gaze flew to where Ron had been. Instead of his body, as I had feared, there was nothing but a pile of clothes. *Ron's* clothes. Which meant...

I looked down at the frog. Its eyes seemed to be pleading for recognition. Those oddly golden eyes. That strangely human expression.

"It could've been worse," said Bruce. "I was expecting Dominicus to tear Prince Charming into little tiny pieces."

"So was I," I said in a strangled voice.

"A frog isn't bad," Bruce continued. "I mean, it severely limits his ability to rule a kingdom, but what with Veiland about to be overthrown, it doesn't matter anyway."

"I really think that you ought to stop talking," I said. "My friend here is unconscious, my brother has just been turned into a small green amphibian, and you're trying to comfort me by saying that since my family's kingdom is about to be overthrown, it doesn't matter?"

"Did you just say your *brother*?"

"Yes, yes, my brother. I'm Maxine Charming. I don't see why it matters if you know." I glanced down at the frog. "I cannot believe this is happening."

Bruce rubbed the back of his neck. "Well, Rosie—I mean—Princess Maxine, I don't know what to say."

"You being speechless is better than the tactless route you were on a minute ago," I said. "As a matter of fact, weren't you just thrown into prison for talking too much? How is it that you're not still locked up?"

Bruce grinned. "Queen Amelia banishes me to the dungeons at least a couple of times a week. I have to put up a good fight so she won't feel bad. And she doesn't ever seem to remember when she sees me that I'm supposed to be locked up."

I bent over Jack, smoothing his dark hair away from his face. "Well, Bruce, as long as you're a free man, go get me a wet cloth for Jack's face, will you?"

"Sure." He left.

Jack was alarmingly still. I couldn't think of anything I could do to help. Except... On a few of Ron's quests, he had encountered enchanted maidens who could only be awakened by a kiss. I had always felt kind of skeptical with the idea of a mere kiss waking someone up from some magical spell, but looking down at Jack's still face, I found myself desperate to try anything that would help. Lifting his head off my lap, I knelt beside him, closed my eyes and puckered my lips.

"RIBBIT."

My eyes flew open to see Ron the frog glaring at me. "Turn around, frog," I said. "I don't want you watching me."

"Ribbit, ribbit, ribbit!" No doubt it was hard for Ron to get his meaning across, given the one-word vocabulary that he'd been reduced to, but it seemed that he objected to me kissing Jack.

"Turn around or I'll lock you into that chest over there. I'm serious."

Ron's froggy eyes glowered at me unblinkingly before he finally flopped around to face the other direction.

It was now or never. Putting my hands on either side of Jack's face, I leaned in.

Chapter 28

"What in the name of gnomes are you doing?" My eyes flew back open to see Jack scowling up at me. I yelped and scooted back.

"Maxine Charming," he said, stiffly sitting up. "Were you trying to look behind my mask again? Because I may as well tell you that it won't come off."

"I, um..."

Jack rubbed his temples like he had a headache. "The *reason* it won't come off is because it's a visual enchantment, not a physical object. So will you please stop attacking me every time I end up unconscious around you?"

I nodded and looked away. A burning red surged over my face as I thought about how close I had been to kissing him. Hopefully he would never know what I had really been up to.

Jack sighed. "I suppose it's only natural for someone of your intelligence to want to know who I am. But please, please promise me that you will stop trying to pull my face off in your quest to discover my identity."

"I promise," I said.

"Ribbit," added Ron, and if a frog could look amused, he managed it.

Jack glanced over. "Where did that frog come from? And where is Queen Amelia and that smelly enchanter?"

It's not often that one is called upon to provide such bizarre answers to relatively normal questions. I cleared my throat. "The frog is Ron. And the enchanter took Queen Amelia away after she tried to finish knocking his head off."

"You're not making any sense," said Jack. "Did you just say that *Ron* is a *frog*? And *who* was knocking the enchanter's head off?"

"Ron hit Dominicus—that's the enchanter—on the head with a staff, and then Amelia wanted to hit him again but Ron wouldn't let her, so Dominicus turned Ron into a frog and carried Amelia off."

Jack was looking at me like I was crazy. "Are you trying to tell me that your brother, Prince Charming, is now an *amphibian*?"

"Ribbit!" Ron hopped over, glad to be getting some attention. "Ribbit, ribbit, ribbit!"

"Whoa." Jack looked at the fat green frog with a mixture of alarm and disbelief. "I'm sorry, Max, but are you sure that this is Ron? I mean, did you actually see it happen?"

"Well, no. I closed my eyes because I thought that the enchanter—he was a bear at the time—was going to rip him apart. But when I opened them, there was the frog and there was the pile of Ron's clothes--" Jack's eyes widened on seeing the discarded clothing on the ground. "And the guard, Bruce--"

"Who is Bruce?"

"He's a guard. I just said. Anyway, he saw it happen."

"And you trust this Bruce?"

"No reason not to trust me," said Bruce, walking into the hall carrying a dripping pink cloth. "Glad to see that you're awake again; Rosie here was worrying herself sick over you."

Jack glanced at me and then back at Bruce. His expression grew cold. "'Rosie?'"

"Oh, well, I know that she's really Princess Maxine, but I started out calling her Rosie and you know how these things go." Bruce offered Jack the wet cloth.

Jack stared down at it and then back up at Bruce. "And what am I supposed to do with that?" he asked in a tone of haughty disdain.

"I asked him to get you a wet cloth because I was going to try to revive you with it," I explained.

"Really." It was clear from his tone that Jack didn't believe me. "And was this before or after you tried to rip my face off?"

Bruce's eyes widened.

"*Before*," I said, glaring at Jack. What was the matter with him all of a sudden?

"I see. I'm glad that you were so efficient at exploring all of the time-honored remedies for unconsciousness. Will another guard be coming in soon with smelling salts?"

"Don't be an idiot, Jack. I was trying to help."

"You have a unique way of being helpful."

Gritting my teeth, I got to my feet and picked Ron up. "Turns out you're better company unconscious," I said. "Next time I won't bother trying to revive you." I turned and marched away.

"Where are you going?" Jack called.

I didn't answer.

"You're in for it now, old chap," I heard Bruce say.

"You stay out of this."

"I'm just saying." Bruce followed me. "Hey there, Rosie, are you looking for something?"

I glanced at him. "Why is it so quiet around here?"

"The guards left. With the queen gone, they decided to head down to the village."

"That was fast. She just barely got carted off."

"They saw their opportunity. She hardly ever lets them go into town."

"So everyone's gone?"

"Everyone but you, your friend and your frog."

Perfect. It would be easier to do what I was planning without a bunch of brain dead guards standing around waiting to put me in the dungeons. "Do you know where the kitchens are?"

"Hungry?"

"Starving. I could even eat porridge."

"You won't have to. Even though the queen made everyone else eat porridge, she didn't always obey her own rules. Follow me."

He led me to the kitchens and showed me a secret stash of food. I didn't bother asking how he knew about it. I grabbed a bite of this and a handful of that, and then I sat down and stuffed my face with ham and apples and bread smeared with butter and honey. I offered some to Ron, who I'd set on the table beside my plate, but he didn't seem interested.

"So tell me again about this curse," I said between mouthfuls.

Bruce bit into an apple and leaned back in his chair. "Well, like I said, the curse can only be broken if the serpent is killed by a prince with pure motives and a true heart."

"Does it have to be a prince?"

He chewed thoughtfully. "No, I expect any man with a true heart and pure motives could break the curse."

"What I meant was, could a *girl* break the curse?"

He laughed.

"That wasn't a joke," I said.

"And yet it was funny." He grinned at me and took another bite of his apple.

It was futile to argue. "Do you have any weapons around here?"

Bruce paused, looking at me thoughtfully, and then he shrugged. He got up and opened a tall cupboard in the back of the kitchen. Inside was a whole stock of wooden staffs.

"Why doesn't Queen Amelia have better weaponry if she's got a man-eating serpent in her moat?" I asked, pulling one out.

"Because the enchanter comes every so often and takes all of the weapons away. I think he worries that if all of the villagers got together they might manage to kill the serpent with or without pure hearts and all that."

"Great. So I'm going to have to try to fight a sea serpent with a stick. This should go well." I swung the staff back and forth to get a feel for it.

"What are you doing?" Jack stood in the kitchen doorway, clearly torn between keeping an eye on me and keeping an eye on the food still spread out on the kitchen table.

"Nothing. I mean, I was just bored and decided to swing this staff around for fun."

"You are a terrible liar."

I didn't say anything.

He sighed. "Max, will you please tell me what you're planning on doing with that staff?"

"She's going to try to kill the serpent."

"*What?*"

I glared at Bruce. "Thanks a lot."

"You're more than welcome," Bruce said. "You'll get yourself killed if you try to fight that beast alone."

Jack rubbed his forehead wearily. "Maxine, I can't let you risk your life facing a monster who has killed who knows how many experienced fighting men."

"So what are we going to do, stay here forever?"

Jack looked confused. "What does killing the serpent have to do with staying here?" he asked.

Bruce began to explain again about the curse while Jack piled food onto a plate and began to eat. Bored, I watched as a fly buzzed over a smear of honey on the table. Suddenly a long narrow tongue shot out and wrapped around the fly. There was a slight zipping sound as the tongue returned into the mouth of its owner in nearly the same instant.

I gagged and covered my mouth with both hands while Ron smacked his green lips, a look of pleased satisfaction on his face.

"What's wrong?" asked Jack.

"Trust me, you don't want to know," I said.

He shrugged and turned back to Bruce. "So killing the serpent is the only way to break the spell?"

"That was quick," I said. "It took him a lot longer to tell me."

"That's because you kept interrupting," Bruce said.

"They were pertinent questions."

Jack leaned back from the table and patted his belly. "I will never take real food for granted again," he said. Then he stood up and went to the cupboard, pulling out two more staffs. He took three kitchen knives from a rack and handed one to each of us. Jack tied his knife to the end of his staff with some twine, and waited while we did the same.

Bruce looked rather pale as he worked on his makeshift spear. "I want you both to know that I'll do my best to fight bravely, but when I get eaten, don't be surprised."

"You aren't going to get eaten," Jack said. "If we work as a team, we should be fine. Right?"

"Right," I said.

"Hopefully," said Bruce.

"Ribbit," said Ron, and he burped.

Chapter 29

Looking out over the murky moat waters, I barely suppressed a shudder. The possibility of being sunk under that forbidding surface within the confines of a serpent's stomach was a highly unpleasant thought, even if I wouldn't be alive to notice.

"Are you *sure* we have to kill the serpent to be able to leave the kingdom?" I asked Bruce, setting Ron on a stone bench inside the courtyard.

"Positive," said Bruce. He tightened the knots of twine on his homemade spear. "Either that or the serpent has to leave the enchanted boundaries herself, but she's so hungry that she'll probably eat everyone in the kingdom first, which kind of defeats the point."

"I thought you said that the serpent couldn't leave the moat," I said.

"That was only when Queen Amelia was still in the castle," said Bruce, as though it were perfectly obvious. "Now that Dominicus has taken Amelia away, the serpent isn't bound to the water anymore."

"Does the serpent know that?" asked Jack.

"We'll find out soon enough." Bruce straightened his pink uniform. "Right, now here's the plan. We'll go out one at a time and each take a turn wearing her down. That way all three of us aren't instantly killed, and whoever goes last will stand a greater chance of being able to slay her. Then that person can go on to rescue the Queen, or maybe just go on home; whichever they'd like."

We stared at Bruce.

"What?" he asked.

Jack shook his head. "I've heard a lot of so-called plans this past week," he said, "and based on that I never thought that I would say this, but that is the absolute *worst* idea that I have ever heard!"

"It was just a suggestion," said Bruce.

"I don't know about you guys," I said, "but I want to get this over with."

"Alright, let's go," said Jack.

We took a collective deep breath and walked out onto the middle of the drawbridge. The sun shone down and the only sound was the gentle lap of moat water against the castle walls.

"Where is it?" I asked, after several minutes went by with no sign of the beast.

"Maybe it's hiding," suggested Bruce.

Jack was drenched in sweat. "Perfect," he growled, unable to hide a slight tremor in his voice, "A *shy* sea serpent. What are we supposed to do now? Dive in and wrestle it out?"

"Look!" Bruce pointed to the bank across from the castle. Near the moat bridge a chunk of earth was missing as though a very large creature had hauled itself out of the waters, clawing the soft embankment as it went. The grass beyond was flat and sodden, showing plainly the path that the animal had taken. "I think she's already left."

"Great. Just great." Jack stomped off, following the serpent's trail without bothering to see if we were following. I knew that he was being rude because he was scared to death, but it was still annoying. Muttering under my breath, I retrieved Ron, and then Bruce and I began to walk side by side towards the village with Jack marching ahead.

"Do you really think that we're going to be able to kill this serpent?" Bruce asked. "Not to discourage you or anything, but I've seen the old girl at work and she's pretty deadly."

"I don't know," I said. "I suppose I could try whistling, but if it wouldn't work on the trolls I doubt it would have any effect on a sea serpent."

Bruce shot me a puzzled look. "Do you mean if you whistle some peaceful song you'll be able to lull the serpent to sleep? Because I can tell you right now that she doesn't like music."

I paused. "Not exactly."

"So what are you talking about?"

"Well." I decided to tell him the truth. "My fairy godmother gave me a rather unusual gift."

"Unusual in that it wasn't one of those fairer-than-them-all kind of deals?"

I glowered at him.

"What?" he asked.

"Just because I am obviously not the recipient of a gift of beauty--" I began.

His eyes widened. "That's not what I meant at all. You're a very nice-looking girl--"

I waved my hand to cut off his blathering. "Look, why don't I just show you what I mean about the whistling?"

He looked grateful for the opportunity to change the subject. "Sure."

After a glance ahead to make sure that Jack was out of range, I whistled softly. Bruce stood unmoving, and I was about to give him the time to come out of it when he blinked.

"If that was your attempt at music, you might want to work a bit on the melody," he said. "I don't think that one note counts as a song."

"You didn't freeze."

"What do you mean?" He eyed me warily. "Were you trying to turn me into a block of ice?"

"Er, no. Let me try it again." Jack was even further ahead, so I hazarded a louder whistle this time. A little bird that had been chirping happily in a tree behind Bruce stopped mid-note. Bruce turned his head and looked at it.

"What happened to that bird?" he asked. "Look, it's not even moving."

"Ten seconds," I said, ignoring him.

"It's just sitting there with its beak hanging open."

"Four, three, two, one," I said, and on cue the bird twitched, let out a feeble squawk and then fluttered weakly to the ground where it just lay there, panting.

"Oops," I said. "Poor little guy."

Bruce faced me again. "You did something to that bird," he accused.

"I was trying to do it to you. Obviously it didn't work."

"So you actually *freeze* things?" He took a step back.

"Well, not literally. They don't freeze as in turning cold, they just stop moving for as long as I want whenever I whistle. Only with you it had no effect at all." I studied him thoughtfully. "It's strange. The only other person it hasn't worked on is my evil aunt."

"Are you saying that I'm evil?" Bruce grinned.

"No, of course not. I'm just saying that you seem to be immune to my power."

He shrugged. "I guess."

"Are you people coming?" Jack called from far ahead.

Bruce and I looked at each other and then hurried forward. We were on the village road by now, and it was easy to see by the trail of slime that the serpent had gone this way not too long before.

I caught up to Jack. "Do you hear that?" he asked.

I listened. There were people screaming not too far away, interspersed with the roaring of what could only be a very large and very ferocious creature.

"The sea serpent," I breathed.

"Come on!"

We ran into the village, rounding the corner into the town square in time to see an enormous, hideously ugly monster lifting several villagers to her mouth. All around us people were yelling and scrambling to get out of the way. I hurriedly set Ron safely behind a tree and followed Jack as he ran towards the serpent.

The noise was deafening, but somehow Jack managed to get his voice to carry over it all. *"Halt!"*

The beast paused, glancing down at Jack with an expression of almost human surprise. Jack drew back his arm and threw his spear. It hissed through the air and in the next instant buried itself in her flesh just below the ribs. The serpent roared and dropped her squirming lunch. The erstwhile captives picked themselves up and ran away. Soon everyone was gone from sight, leaving us to face the monster alone.

She was a truly ugly creature, far worse than the illustrations of sea serpents that I had seen in books back home. Her small red eyes glared from a yellow-brown face that was coated with slime from the moat. Her long, snake-like neck was covered in spikes that ran down her back and her thick, powerful tail whipped back and forth.

"Throw your spear!" Jack shouted as the serpent began to advance towards us, a string of drool trailing from her mouth.

I brought my arm back to throw the spear just as the creature swung her tail, knocking Jack and I off our feet. The spear tumbled from my grasp as the sea serpent grasped me and lifted me high into the air. I looked into the inky black depths of the serpent's gaping mouth and realized that I was about to become lunch. "Jack!" I screamed.

In that instant the monster's entire body shuddered. I looked down from my lofty height to see Jack's hands grasping one end of my spear, the head of which was buried in the creature's belly. She gave a shriek of pain and dropped me. Seconds before I hit the ground, Jack's strong arms caught me. He set me aside and pulled his dagger from his vest, lifting the blade high to finish the job.

"*Stop!*" Bruce ran up behind us. "*Don't do it!*" The frantic note in his voice made Jack pause. Bruce grabbed the dagger out of Jack's hands as above him the serpent threw back her head and roared. The two homemade spears were still buried in her body and she swiped at them ineffectually.

"You fool," Bruce said, smiling at Jack. "You listened to me." He threw the dagger aside and looked up at the serpent, who was bellowing from pain and rage. "Hush now, darling. Give me just a moment and I'll get those nasty pin pricks out." Jack and I stepped back as the friendly guard in pink transformed into an enormous, hairy, hideously ugly bear.

Chapter 30

My legs refused to support me any longer. I sat down and put my head between my knees, breathing deeply so as to not disgrace myself by fainting.

Jack knelt beside me, putting his arm around my shoulders. "Are you alright?"

"I've been better," I said. "But thanks for saving my life." I could hear Bruce the Bear talking to the serpent in a growly bear-voice that I could tell was meant to sound soothing. I was having a hard time wrapping my mind around the sudden knowledge that Bruce was a bad guy. He had seemed so likeable.

"I can't believe that I listened to him," Jack said. "I should have stabbed it when I had the chance."

"He was desperate to stop you," I said. "You could hear it in his voice. Anyone would have turned back to see what he wanted."

"Let's get out of here while he's busy trying to get the spears out," said Jack, pulling me to my feet.

Bruce's voice stopped us. "I would prefer to have you two stick around for the moment, actually." He waved his paw in our direction and instantly we were surrounded by a see-through, greenish bubble that extended about a foot around us on all sides.

For a moment neither of us said anything. "I cannot believe this," Jack said finally. "Things just keep getting worse and worse."

"Don't worry," I said. "It will work out. We're the good guys, right?"

"Your naive trust in happy endings is endearing," said Jack. "But we're facing a bigger problem than you realize. Haven't you figured out yet who those two are?"

"A really, *really* ugly couple? I can only imagine what their children will look like."

"We already know what a child of theirs looks like," he said. "Think about it, Max."

I paused as my mind began to put together what Jack had already figured out. "Wait a minute. Goldilocks..."

"And the three bears," said Jack. "Exactly. Meet the other two bears."

"Except that one of them is a serpent."

"I would guess that her being a serpent is only a temporary arrangement."

"Fine, I could go along with that, but how could Bruce only look a few years older than we do?" I protested. "Aren't you suggesting that he's Papa Bear from the story?"

"Max, he's got magical powers. I would imagine he can look however old he wants to look. Besides, everyone in this village is already older than we are by over three hundred years. We're infants compared to everyone here, but their age just doesn't show."

An enraged snarl interrupted our conversation and I jumped. Bruce was tugging on one of the spears with his hairy paws while dodging the serpent as she tried to swipe him out of existence. "Darling, if you kill me, who will get these out?" he asked her reasonably.

The serpent's shape began to alter, only the transition for the monster was not as smooth as Bruce's had been. Her terrible form lurched and shivered, becoming first a beautiful woman with long, curling black hair and then morphing into a sleek, powerful-looking bear.

"That's better, my dear," murmured Bruce, "Stay as you are for only a moment longer, and....there!" He pulled the remaining spear free with a quick yank. The enchantress-bear roared so ferociously that chills trickled down my spine. Her eyes glowed red, flashing as though they were lit from within. For all that she'd just had two spears sticking out of her side, she didn't seem too weakened. Bruce gave her furry shoulder an affectionate pat and then turned back to us.

"Forgive me for placing you in this restrictive bubble," he said, "but I couldn't have you sneaking away while I was otherwise engaged. I will take it away now if you promise not to run."

"We promise," said Jack.

"Speak for yourself," I muttered.

A soft breeze wafted across my face as the hazy green shield disappeared. Bruce smiled, which wasn't all that pleasant of a look given that he was still in the form of an evil bear. "Allow me to introduce you to my dear wife Sira, who is the cruelest, most terrible and most wicked enchantress in the world." He looked at his wife with a strange mixture of pride and distaste.

"You call her your 'dear wife' now," I said, "but earlier you kept telling us that the only way to break the curse was to kill her. Why would you tell us something like that if all along she was your wife?"

He shrugged. "It was the truth. We arranged the enchantment so that the only way the curse could be broken was for someone to kill the serpent. Either that or she had to leave the kingdom herself, but how was that to happen if she couldn't leave the moat? Although now, of course, she is able to roam freely since my son took Amelia away."

"It seems to me that your enchantment is a little too complicated," said Jack.

"Of course it is. The more complicated the enchantment, the more interesting it keeps things. Although this one did backfire a bit." Bruce shook his head ruefully. "I didn't expect to get stuck for so many years with next to nothing happening. Who knew that young men with true hearts and pure motives are so rare?"

"But no one's killed the serpent," I said. "So even now you still haven't found someone with a true heart or pure motives."

"Not so," said Bruce. "Jack has already fulfilled that part of the enchantment. The very fact that his spears were able to enter the thick skin of the serpent proved him, for only one whose heart is truly pure could have an effect on someone whose heart is truly black. It has to be an equal contrast, you see."

"Not really," I said, watching as Jack picked up his dagger from the ground where Bruce had tossed it earlier. He dusted it off and returned it to the sheath inside his vest, seeming unimpressed by this analysis as to the quality of his heart. "Anyway, you stopped him from killing the serpent."

"Yes, but he still has the necessary qualifications. Not only was that enough to break the curse, it's also a point of interest." He yawned, exposing an impressive set of bear canines. "Anyway, I suppose I'd better take the wife home since the game is over. No doubt she'll start trying to eat people again if I don't hurry."

A terrible growl came from behind him. It was clear that Sira was not enjoying the conversation, not that I could blame her. It must have been galling for her to hear her husband casually pointing out that her death was necessary to break a curse, not to mention the fact that he had been the one to arrange the curse to work that way.

"Now, now," said Bruce, patting her furry arm. "I stopped him from stabbing you with the dagger, didn't I? I know for a fact that that would have killed you."

In answer she lunged forward with a flash of sharp canines and black claws, swiping at Bruce's head. He barely ducked in time. Sira lifted herself high on her hind legs to claw at him again and I knew that this time Bruce wouldn't be able to dodge her quickly enough.

"Get back, Max!" Jack shouted, grabbing several stones from the ground. He threw one the size of an apple, hitting the side of Sira's head. She snarled and turned on Jack just as he threw the second stone. It hit her between her eyes with a dull thud. She lashed out with an enormous paw, striking Jack across his chest even as she crumpled to the ground.

Jack swayed and fell to his knees. The front of his tunic was slashed open and four white lines across his chest bloomed a violent red. "Jack!" I knelt beside him, feeling sick. There was too much blood for me to be able see how deep the gashes were. I ripped off the lower portion of my skirt and pressed it against his chest.

"She got me," he gasped. "I can't believe it."

"Please don't die," I said, my voice trembling.

"I have no intention of dying," he muttered. "It's just the shock of her getting me. I thought that I was out of range, but I forgot to take into account that she's no ordinary bear." He grinned at me weakly, his eyes sparkling with mingled amusement and pain.

Without warning, a strange, tingling feeling washed over me, burning my skin and robbing me of my breath. Jack's mask was still there; it was still his face looking back at me, but I now knew with an indefinable assurance who it was sitting before me. The color in my face drained away, and it was all I could do to keep pressing the cloth against his wounds.

Bruce knelt beside me and pulled the fabric away, studying Jack's chest. "Superficial scratches," he announced. "The excessive bleeding makes it seem worse than it really is. You'll be fine." He patted Jack's shoulder and before my eyes the wounds faded until I could hardly tell where they had been. Only the torn fabric and bloodstains on Jack's tunic remained as evidence that he'd had a run-in with a bear. Bruce grunted with approval and went to check on his unconscious wife.

"He could have at least said something about my stoic endurance of pain," said Jack, stretching experimentally. "Or maybe let me bleed a little longer so I could feel like a true hero. This instantaneous healing of battle wounds isn't very satisfying." He glanced at me when I didn't respond. "Max, what's wrong? You look like you've seen a ghost."

I had been so stupid. Even with his face masked and his voice disguised, there were still his mannerisms, his behavior, and especially, his personality. The easy camaraderie that I had felt with him from the beginning had indicated all along something more than an acquaintance of only a week.

I wasn't up to anymore surprises, but as I sat there looking at him, his appearance began to alter itself. The bushy eyebrows thinned and faded, leaving brows that were still thick, but well-shaped and defined. His enormous nose seemed to shrink while at the same time his lips grew firm and fuller than the thin lips I was used to seeing. Only his eyes remained the same: a warm brown with flecks of gold.

My mind struggled to process what it was seeing even though the revealed face was more familiar to me than my own. Freed of the enchanted disguise, he was startlingly good-looking. How was it that I had never noticed how handsome he was? I searched his face, somehow missing Jack's ugliness.

"Max, you're scaring me. Why are you looking at me like that?"

He didn't know his mask was gone. I remembered that he had said that his mask was a visual enchantment, which meant that since it wasn't an actual physical object, he would have no way of knowing that I could now see past it. "Jack, I..." I stopped. He wasn't Jack. He never had been. A tear coursed down my cheek. I swiped it away quickly but I wasn't fast enough.

"Max! You never cry." Looking alarmed, he scooted closer to me and put his arm around my shoulders. "Hey, I'm fine. Really. Didn't you hear what Bruce said? He said that they were superficial scratches."

"That's not it." I wiped at my eyes impatiently. Taking a deep breath, I looked at him. "I'm sorry. I didn't realize it was you. I should have, but I didn't."

He grew still. "What do you mean?"

"I don't understand how I could have been so blind. I've known you almost my whole life. How could I have not known who you were, even with that stupid mask and your disguised voice?"

He stared at me. "You know me?"

"Yes, I know you, Connor." I took a shaky breath. "Suddenly I knew it was you even though the mask was still there. Then everything went all weird and your mask just…faded away."

"Maxine." His voice sounded strained, only now it was easily recognizable as Connor's voice. "Do you realize that you're the first person who has ever seen past my mask?"

"That's not true," I said. "Dominicus knew."

"He knew that I was wearing a mask but he couldn't see past it."

"But why couldn't you tell me? Why didn't you trust me?"

"You don't understand—I do trust you. I trust you more than anyone in the world, now more than ever. But I couldn't tell you because--"

Sira's return to consciousness involved roaring so loudly that I couldn't hear what Connor said. She came to her feet in a swirl of dust, shoved her husband away from her, and in the next instant pushed away from the earth, soaring into the sky and out of sight.

Chapter 31

Bruce watched his wife's retreating form and then he walked back to where we were still seated on the ground. Leaning down, he clasped Connor's shoulder with an enormous paw. "Thank you. My wife would have killed me if you hadn't intervened. Given that I am an evil enchanter, I wonder why you bothered?"

"It just sort of happened," said Connor. He seemed a little relieved at the interruption.

"I see. Well, I appreciate what you did for me."

"Um…You're welcome."

"That said, I've decided that I would like your company for a bit longer. I've been growing rather bored over these last few centuries and I've found you both to be terribly entertaining individuals. I'm taking you home with me."

We looked at him in dismay. "Thank you, but we really do have to be on our way," said Connor.

Bruce tsked and shook his head. "The truth is, I'm not the sort of person who cares about what other people want," he said. "It's been a long day and I'm tired. Get your frog, Rosie, and let's get going."

Shakily I got up and swiped the remainder of tears from my eyes. So much had happened in the last few minutes that it was almost a relief to be told what to do, even if that meant I was cooperating with a kidnapper. I found Ron waiting by the tree, zapping insects expertly with his long, sticky tongue. I picked him up and he croaked a greeting around the unidentifiable mass of twitching legs in his mouth. Shuddering with disgust, I turned around to find Bruce towering behind me. He picked me up with his massive paws and threw me over his shoulder.

"Hey, put me down," I protested. Ron let out his own squawk of dismay, but that may have been because I was squeezing him too tightly.

"Settle down, Rosie, or I'll have to put you under a spell," Bruce said mildly. Seeing as how he had just admitted to putting his own wife under a pretty rotten spell, I settled down immediately. Bruce picked Connor up and tossed him over his other shoulder and in almost the same instant Bruce sprang into the air. I watched in terrified dismay as the ground seemed to fall away underneath us. The enchanter flew straight up and then began to fly towards one of the eastern peaks. My stomach lurched and I closed my eyes, trying desperately to imagine myself anywhere but where I was.

After a few moments I heard a small croak. I opened my eyes to see Ron's froggy face wearing what can only be described as a look of pure enjoyment. His eyes were intently scanning the ground below us as though he wanted to memorize every moment of our flight. Watching him, I realized that Ron was taking the opportunity to appreciate doing something we never in our lifetime could have expected to do: fly.

There was something unreal about being so far above everything, soaring through the air. The wide valleys and peaked mountains were like a beautiful painting in shades of blue, purple and green, and Queen Amelia's white castle looked like a little toy, with the village around it appearing idyllic and serene.

Slowly my heart settled down and my breathing evened out. Somehow, witnessing my brother's joyous appreciation for the beauty of the view made my fear seem foolish. I realized that I shouldn't let the risk of falling stop me from enjoying the thrill of the journey.

This was an amazing moment. I decided that the only thing lacking was friendly conversation. "So Bruce," I began.

"*Not* a good time for talking," interjected Connor. I peered over at him and noticed that he looked a little green around the edges as he hung over Bruce's other shoulder.

"You don't even know what I'm going to say," I said.

"I don't need to," Connor was clutching the enchanter's furry coat with both hands. "I just know you and that means that this is not a good time for talking."

"I don't mind if she wants to talk," said Bruce.

"Well," I said, "I've been thinking about things and I was just wondering how you ended up in Amelia's castle in the first place? I know that you arranged for Sira to be the serpent in the moat, but where do you fit into the story?"

"Excellent question," said Bruce.

Connor groaned. It was hard to tell if it was because of our conversation or our current mode of travel.

Bruce ignored his other passenger and continued. "You see, all along Queen Amelia thought that I was just another prince who had failed, only I was really there to keep an eye on things."

"Of course," I said.

"Then, without even telling me, my son changed the enchantment." Judging from his tone of voice, it was still a sore subject.

"What do you mean?"

"Dominicus changed it so that I was stuck too. At first I could leave whenever I wanted, but he rearranged things. I can't tell you how demoralizing it was to have my only son turn on me! After all of my work in raising him to be a terror, I never expected that he would use it against me like that."

"It's a real shame when children grow up the way they were raised," I said dryly.

Bruce's furry head bobbed in agreement. "You will understand, then, why I was willing to be helpful when the three of you came along after so many years. Finally there was a chance that I would be freed! You may recall that the curse required someone who had a true heart and pure motives to kill the serpent. While I certainly wouldn't *want* to kill my own wife, I admit that I had thought about it from time to time. But I didn't fit the bill, what with me being an evil enchanter and all."

There was really nothing I could say to that.

Bruce continued. "I saw right away that the three of you were different, but I admit that I rightly placed my hopes on Jack here."

"And why was that?" Connor spoke up for the first time.

"You were the only person to come to the castle with an entirely unselfish motive."

"What about me?" I asked. "My reasons for coming weren't selfish."

"I hate to contradict you, Rosie, but you came because your brother's choices were adversely affecting your life. So even though your motives were good, you still had a strong self-interest in the outcome."

"I don't see why Dominicus was so intent on keeping all of you trapped in the kingdom," said Connor. "What do you suppose he was up to?"

"While I pride myself on the wicked workings of my mind," said Bruce, "I cannot claim the ability to fathom the intentions of my son. Frankly, he's bewildered and confused me ever since he was young. I thought that it would get better as he grew older, but I'm afraid that we still don't see eye to eye on a lot of things."

"What I don't understand," I said, "is why you even *want* to be an evil enchanter. I'm sure that pillaging has its perks, but after awhile it seems like it would get pretty boring."

"I am sure I don't know what you mean," said Bruce, sounding offended.

"Think about it," I said, ignoring Connor's fierce looks that indicated he wanted me to stop talking. "You burn down villages and terrorize people and the next day those same people—or the survivors, anyway—get up and rebuild. So you go back and burn the village down again, and then they rebuild again. It's this never-ending cycle. You're fighting a losing battle. I'm going to be perfectly honest with you here, Bruce—"

"Not a good idea," muttered Connor.

I ignored him. "I think that the reason you feel so restless and bored is not because you were stuck in a pink castle for hundreds of years, but because you need to alter your purpose in life. You seem like a nice enough enchanter-bear...um...thing, aside from your moments of cruelty and sheer evilness. So why not give up the whole wicked lifestyle and, I don't know, spread cheer and warmth throughout the world instead of terror and misery? Plant a garden. Get a dog. Learn ballroom dancing."

Connor groaned. "Please just stop talking, Maxine. Do you want to die?"

"No, no; go on," said Bruce. He sounded interested.

"And have you thought about grandchildren?" I asked. "Maybe it's time for Baby Bear, a.k.a. Dominicus, to settle down. I've heard that spoiling the grandkids is even better than raising your own. And Dominicus seems like he must have been a real handful to raise."

"You're telling me," growled Bruce. "From day one he was getting into trouble. It might be fun to see him with some little monsters of his own. Of course, we'd have to put an extension on the cottage..."

"Yes, exactly! There's nothing more rewarding in your retirement years than puttering around the house," I said.

"So all we have to do is find my son a wife to produce these grandchildren," mused Bruce.

I blinked. That hadn't really been what I was getting at. "Uh, yes. That too. There are any number of girls out there who would love to marry a hairy, yellow-eyed, evil enchanter like your son." Sadly, this was really true. I knew of at least twenty different princesses who would be delighted to marry Dominicus...under one condition. "As long as he's rich, of course."

"Oh, we're very well off. You don't raid and plunder villages for centuries and not come by some financial security in the process." Bruce pondered the matter for a moment. "Yes, I think that this is a very good idea," he said.

"Great! I'll make you a list of all of the girls I know who are mercenary enough that the smell of fish won't throw them off."

"I appreciate the offer," said Bruce, "but don't waste your time."

There was something in his tone of voice that made me pause. "Why? Do you already know of a nice, evil girl for your son to marry?"

"I do, although I'm not sure 'evil' is the right descriptive term."

A foreboding tremor ran up my spine. "Dare I ask who the...lucky girl is?"

"Of course you may, since it involves you. You're feisty *and* smart, which is exactly what my son needs. Of course, we will have to work on your evilness, but that's nothing that a few years with a mother-in-law like Sira won't cure. And you already have a talent for magic, which you demonstrated for me earlier with your little whistling trick."

I was having a hard time catching my breath. "But, Bruce, you can't think that *I* would make a good candidate! I'd make a terrible wife!"

Connor snorted.

"The wedding will be tomorrow," growled Bruce. "Now hush up. I've got some planning to do." He sighed. "Grandkids. What a great idea."

The rest of the flight passed in a weighty silence.

Chapter 32

Located in thick forests atop the highest mountain, the enchanter's cottage was not at all what I had expected. It wasn't surrounded by bones and carnage, nor was it a forbidding, scary-looking place that would indicate to a passerby that evil people lived there. In truth, it was a charming little house with ivy climbing the walls and flowers growing in the well-tended gardens around it.

Bruce landed on the front lawn and set us down. Sira was already there and it was clear that she had been waiting for us. She had transformed into her human form, which I recognized from when she had been fluctuating back and forth while at the village. Connor and I hardly had time to orient ourselves with being earthbound again when she stepped up to us, a look of cold fury on her face, and slapped Connor.

Hard.

"That's for throwing rocks at me," she snarled. "And I can't wait to repay you for stabbing me with those pathetic sticks." She snapped her fingers and ropes appeared, twining around us like serpents until our arms were effectively bound to our sides. I was still holding Ron in my hand and he gave a small croak of protest as a rope wrapped around him as well.

Sira then turned to me, coming uncomfortably close.

"No offense or anything," I said, "but I'm really not comfortable with people getting into my space like this."

She sneered, her full lips curling back to reveal startlingly yellow teeth. I suppose when you're stuck as a sea serpent for hundreds of years you don't have a lot of opportunities to practice good hygeine. "The feelings of my meals has never interested me, little girl," she hissed.

"I ought to tell you right now, Sira," interjected Bruce, "that you simply cannot eat your future daughter-in-law. It just isn't done. So how about I go fix you a nice bowl of pasta instead?"

"What?" Sira stared at her husband.

"Pasta, my dear. You've always liked my spaghetti."

"Did you just say something about a *daughter-in-law*?"

"I did! Isn't it the most brilliant idea?"

"Have you gone completely mad?"

"You and I both know that Dominicus isn't getting any younger," said Bruce. "And this maiden is the only one in the last five or six hundred years that hasn't fainted at the sight of him. Plus, she has magical abilities. We can have her trained in the family business in no time."

"Where on earth did you get such a moronic idea?" Sira demanded.

Bruce flashed me a happy grin. "Well, from her, actually."

"*She* suggested that she marry Dominicus?"

"Not in so many words, I suppose, but she mentioned grandchildren and retirement, so I thought--"

"Retirement?" Sira growled. "Why would people in the prime of life retire?"

Bruce clasped his paws together in a pleading way. "Haven't you ever thought about grandchildren? I would *love* to be a grandfather. Imagine having the precocious little ones gather around while I teach them how to ransack villages and terrorize entire communities! We aren't going to live forever, Sira. You never know when you or I might--"

"*Stop.*" Sira held up one hand and then spoke slowly and deliberately. "I have been soaking in a moat for over three hundred years. Do you have any idea how badly that dries out the skin? I am not in the mood to discuss ridiculous, unutterably horrifying ideas like grandchildren. I need moisturizers and I need food, in that order." She marched across the lawn and into the cottage, slamming the door behind her.

"That went well," said Bruce.

We looked at him.

"No, really. If she truly had been against the idea she would've just eaten you both to stop further argument. She's developed a real appetite for humans after all of those years as a sea serpent." He chuckled, as though his wife's cannibalistic tastes were a cute little quirk. "Ah, I can't tell you how good it is to be home." Bruce stretched and all of a sudden his form shifted and shrunk. In the next moment, Bruce as a human stood before us, only instead of his pink guard uniform he wore dark blue robes embroidered with what looked like tiny green dragons. "Now then," he began, when a piercing scream rent the air.

"Oh dear, sounds like Queen Amelia. Please excuse me." Bruce hurried into the cottage, leaving us alone on the lawn.

An instant later, Queen Amelia burst out of the cottage, shrieking and carrying a little girl who looked about five or six. The child had her arms wrapped around Amelia's neck and her golden curls bounced as Amelia ran. Dominicus ran behind them, growling even though he was in his human form. He caught them before they got past where we were standing.

"Stop that dreadful screaming, Amelia," Dominicus snapped. "You're going to scare her!"

"Since when do you care about scaring others?" Amelia sobbed. "It's always the same thing with you, isn't it, Dominicus?

You just love to blame other people for the exact things that you do best."

"Well, I don't know why you keep screaming," he retorted. "You always were a drama queen."

She stopped sobbing and glared at him. "And you always thought that you knew everything. Some things never change!"

Connor and I glanced at each other in confusion.

"Just hand Goldie back," said Dominicus. "I'll take you to your castle if that's what you want."

"I won't leave without her."

"You can't take her back there."

"Why?"

"Amelia, haven't you figured out yet why I brought her here in the first place?"

"I have no idea why you do half of the things you do. I do wonder that hundreds of years have passed since she left the kingdom boundaries and yet she hasn't aged a day. Do you have her under a spell too?"

"I was planning on bringing her back to you eventually. I never intended to deny you the joy of raising her. To that end I have prevented her from growing up."

My mind was racing. If I was interpreting things correctly, Amelia and Dominicus were married. And if they were married, that meant that the scheduled wedding for tomorrow was definitely off. I breathed a sigh of relief.

The little girl lifted her head from her mother's shoulder. "Let me down!" she ordered.

"Goldie, what have I told you?" Dominicus asked sternly.

Goldie stuck a finger in her mouth. "Let me down, pwease."

"Very good." He nodded at Amelia and she reluctantly set Goldie down. The child ran over to where Connor and I stood.

"Why are you tied up?" she asked us, still sucking on her finger.

"Well, because..." I wasn't sure how to tell her that her grandma was most likely going to eat us later and that she had tied us up so we couldn't get away. It just didn't seem suitable for a child's ears. "Because we're playing a game."

"Can I play too?"

"Goldie, come back over here, please," said Dominicus, holding out his hand. She ran to his side.

"Is this because I wouldn't let you tell your parents that we were married?" Amelia asked, resuming their argument.

Connor looked at me with a raised eyebrow. I flashed him a grin and whispered, "That was my shortest betrothal yet."

He laughed shortly and shook his head. "I think we were safer when you were the fiancé," he said.

Dominicus growled again. "It had nothing to do with that, Amelia. It was because you wouldn't let us raise our daughter in a healthy environment. You were spoiling her as rotten as you had been as a child, and I couldn't let that happen. So I brought her here."

"Yes, a fabulous improvement, bringing her here with your crazy parents."

"My crazy parents have been at *your* castle this entire time, making sure that you couldn't get away until you were willing to change your ways."

She looked startled. "Are you serious? Where were they?"

"You may recall Prince Bruce, who came to rescue you at the very first? Meet your father-in-law. He was keeping an eye on you for me, letting me know how you were. It was awfully obliging of him, given that he didn't even know that you were family."

"*Prince Bruce? He's your father?* But he looks younger than I do!"

"Amelia, my parents are enchanters. They look how they want to look."

"And your mother? Where was she?"

"Mother wasn't really in on the why of things. She was just delighted to have a shot at being an evil serpent in your moat. Although she was stuck there a lot longer than any of us anticipated. She isn't very happy about that."

"The evil sea serpent is my mother-in-law?" Queen Amelia shrieked, looking like she might faint.

"Hey, she may have a few eccentricities, but she's good at what she does," Dominicus said, clenching his jaw angrily.

"She was actually *eating* people, did you know that?"

"Like I said, she's good at what she does."

"I can't believe this." Amelia paced back and forth on the lawn for a moment. "But didn't your parents know that we had a child?" she asked.

"Of course not. They didn't even suspect that we were a couple since you wouldn't let me tell them. They only thought that I was tormenting you and your kingdom for the fun of it."

"We know now," interjected Bruce. He and Sira emerged from the doorway of the cottage where they had apparently been standing for some time. "You two are really married?" he asked. He was watching Queen Amelia with an expression that could only be defined as resignation and some dismay.

"We eloped," Dominicus said.

"When?" demanded Sira.

"Well, Golden--"

"Amelia," Amelia interrupted.

"Right. Sorry. *Amelia* and I fell in love and secretly married not long after her twentieth birthday." Dominicus glanced at Amelia and she blushed bright pink to match her hair.

"Then that means that little Goldie here is my granddaughter," exclaimed Bruce, a wide grin splitting his face.

"What? What? Do you mean to tell me that I'm *already* a grandmother?" gasped Sira. "*I'm* a grandmother? I'm too young to be a grandmother!" Running her hands over her face as though she were feeling for wrinkles, she ran back into the house.

"I'll cancel the wedding then," said Bruce, kneeling in front of Goldie. With a wave of his hand he conjured a toy serpent out of the air. The ugly little toy looked exactly like Sira had as a sea serpent. Goldie laughed with delight, snatching it and hugging it to her chest as though it were a pretty porcelain doll.

"What wedding?" asked Dominicus.

Bruce looked sheepish. "I was going to have you marry Princess Maxine," he said.

"*Who?*"

Bruce pointed over to where Connor and I stood as silent witnesses to this touching family drama.

Dominicus glanced over, only then noticing our presence. "Why are they tied up?" he asked.

"Because they don't want to be here, I suppose," said Bruce distractedly. His focus was on his newly discovered granddaughter. "You have to tie people up if they aren't willing to stay put."

Dominicus ran his hands through his hair. He was clearly having a taxing day. "Does Mom know that they're here? Because if she does, she might try to eat them. You do realize that."

"Yes, yes. It's a nasty habit we'll have to break her of."

There was a pounding sound and everyone looked down to see Goldie smashing her new toy's head in with a rock.

"Oh, isn't that cute," gushed Bruce. "That's how you used to play with your toys, Dom."

Queen Amelia took a step back. She looked slightly unnerved, as though finally realizing what sort of family she had married into.

"Time for supper!" yelled Sira from the doorway. She was brandishing an enormous knife. Connor and I stiffened, each of us thinking the same thing: what, or more specifically, *who*, was for supper?

Chapter 33

"Oh, relax," said Sira when she saw our faces. "We're eating porridge. Red meat bothers my stomach after a stressful day."

"What is it with people around here and porridge?" muttered Connor.

"And why she would need that huge knife to prepare it?" I asked.

Dominicus walked over to where we stood, followed by the rest of his family. Even little Goldie managed to look sinister as she carried her mangled toy serpent.

"Run along and eat," I said, smiling brightly. "We're perfectly comfortable right here all tied up on the lawn."

"I don't know if *I'm* comfortable leaving you two out here," said Bruce. "Who knows what kind of trouble you could get into?"

"We'll be good," I assured him.

"I doubt that's possible. Perhaps we should bring you inside."

Connor sighed. "What is the point in bothering with us anymore?" he asked, sounding irritated. "You have your family all together again, you found out that you have a daughter-in-law *and* a granddaughter, supper is ready, and you're hungry. So why don't you go eat and let us go on our way?"

"It's not really in our nature to be accommodating," said Bruce. "We are evil enchanters, you know."

"And my stomach might settle down later," added his wife with a terrible smile.

"Besides which, if I'm going to stay here, I'll need servants," Amelia simpered, fluttering her eyelashes at Connor.

Dominicus looked at his wife and then at Connor. "I say we let them go."

His family stared at him like he was crazy.

"But I want them," Goldie said. "Give them to me!"

Dominicus glanced down at his little daughter. "What?"

"I want to keep those peoples," she said, pointing at us. Her voice had the age-old whine echoed by spoiled children everywhere. "Give them to me now!"

"That's *it*," snarled Dominicus. He glared at Amelia. "Now do you see why I took her when I did? Look how spoiled she is! There is no way I'm letting these two stay here. Our daughter needs to learn that she can't just *keep* people like they're toys."

"Don't be ridiculous," said Amelia. "She's a princess. She can do anything she likes."

Dominicus' face turned a deep shade of red and his nostrils slowly flared in and out. "I will put up with a lot of things," he began, his voice rising with each word. "My mother as a sea serpent who would eat me if she had half the chance, my father being friendly and agreeable even though he's *supposed* to be the most evil enchanter in history, my wife decorating the entire castle in pink—but I will not—*will not*—tolerate a spoiled daughter! *Do you hear me?*" He was roaring. Everyone within a thousand mile radius could hear him. Even Sira's mouth was hanging open, and I had the feeling that not many things surprised her.

After a stunned silence, Bruce cleared his throat. "Whatever you say, son," he said. He turned to us. "Run along, you two. No more dawdling."

"But--" I began, gesturing with my chin to my tied-up arms. Ron was growing slippery in my hand and I could only imagine how uncomfortable he was.

"No arguments! Get out of here right now or I'll set my wife on you!"

"And I thought that *Maxine's* family was dysfunctional," said Connor, turning to leave.

"My family isn't dysfunctional," I protested. "Just because my father is a little war-crazy and my mother only cares about her beehives and Ron--"

Ron had been remarkably quiet given all that we had been through, but at the sound of his name he spoke up. "Ribbit," he said.

Connor shook his head and turned to walk down the steep trail that led back to Amelia's kingdom, apparently not caring that he was still tied up.

Amelia looked at me distastefully. "Why is that dreadful girl holding a frog?"

"It's that prince from your castle," said Dominicus. "I turned him into a frog."

"Prince Charming? Whatever for?"

Dominicus scowled at her. "He hit me on the head with a stick. And as I recall, you were about to repeat his action."

Before they could pursue that line of contention, Goldie wailed, "I want it!"

"What do you want, sweetheart?" asked Bruce.

"I want the fwoggie!"

"No." said Dominicus. "Keeping the frog is the same thing as keeping a person."

"Not really," said Bruce. "Prince Charming *used* to be a person. Now that he's an amphibian, it's completely different. For pity's sake, Dom, let the child have a pet."

"Hey," I said. "This is my brother you're talking about! And he's still a person even if he doesn't look like one."

"Your brother?" asked Amelia. She shook her head as though deciding to not bother with determining our true familial status. "Whoever he once was," she said, "There is no trace of him remaining. All that's left is a repulsive frog, and while there's no accounting for my daughter's tastes, if that's what she wants, then that's what she will get."

Connor returned to my side. "What's the delay?" he asked, gesturing with his head for me to get moving.

"They're trying to keep Ron," I said. My voice was shaking.

"But I thought we already covered the whole not-keeping-a-person thing." He strained at his ropes to no effect.

"We did. But now they're saying that Ron isn't a person since he's a frog, and that little-"

"I want the fwoggie," whined Goldie, stomping her foot.

"Not good," said Connor, looking worried.

During this exchange Ron had begun to ribbit over and over as though he were so panicked that he forgot that no one could understand him. Unfortunately, this only seemed to egg Goldie on in her desire to own a frog. She threw herself down and began shrieking and kicking her legs in a full-fledged tantrum while the others sent Dominicus reproachful looks.

"Fine!" Dominicus snarled. He turned to me. "Listen, whatever your name is. I'm taking the frog."

"No!" Given that I was tied up, I couldn't do much to stop him as he removed the rope that had tied Ron to my hand. Dominicus carried Ron over to his daughter and handed him to her.

Goldie clutched Ron and sniffed. "*My* fwoggie," she said. Ron croaked miserably, his golden eyes wide with terror.

"Now that that's settled," began Dominicus, when another argument erupted as to whether they should just turn Connor and me into frogs to simplify matters.

"We'd better go," Connor whispered.

"But what about Ron?" I asked. There was a terrible feeling in the pit of my stomach as I watched Goldie with her new pet. Having just witnessed her care of the toy serpent, I feared that my brother would not last long in her hands.

"We'll come back for him, I promise. But we need to leave before they turn us into frogs, too. Come on."

I followed Connor towards the forest. It was starting to get dark and the shadows of the trees loomed darkly overhead. "Connor, let's try to get your dagger out to cut these ropes off," I said.

"We will in a minute. I want to get as far away as possible before they change their minds about letting us go." He sounded tense. "But we'll definitely want to get untied before we go much further into this forest, in case..." His voice trailed off.

"In case what?"

He hesitated. "There's a chance that this forest has the same infestation as the Miraysian Forest you were lost in a few days ago. You remember those creatures, the Maligios?"

I felt a prickling of dread at the base of my skull. "I wish I could forget. Are you trying to tell me that there might be more of those...*things* around here?"

"Yes, unfortunately." Connor glanced back to see how far we had gotten from the cottage. "There might be a lot more of 'those things' around here."

"Why doesn't somebody do something to get rid of them?"

"The Maligios have proven difficult to kill. Ordinary methods like arrows or swords don't seem to work too well, in part due to their unusually thick skin. And it would be easier to get rid of them if someone wasn't deliberately creating them."

"What do you mean?"

Connor ducked under a low-hanging branch as we entered the first of the trees. "Max," he said slowly. "How much do you know about your Aunt Regina?"

"Basically that she's evil and scary," I said. "But what does she have to do with any of this?"

"Well, I hate to be the one to tell you," said Connor, "but your Aunt Regina is the creator of the Maligios."

Chapter 34

I was speechless for a moment. "I know she's a terrible person," I said finally. "But I don't think she's capable of creating man-eating monsters."

"She's capable of a lot of things that might surprise you," said Connor.

Memories of past encounters with Regina came to mind; one awful cruelty after another, committed against myself and others. "You're probably right," I admitted. "But how do you know so much about Aunt Regina, or the Maligios, for that matter?"

"I've heard things," he said vaguely.

"Sorry, but that isn't going to work, Connor," I said. Now that we were finally alone, the questions that had been building up inside of me ever since I realized who he was came pouring out. "You have a lot of explaining to do, starting with the fact that you somehow have the power to wear an enchanted mask, and ending with the whole not-telling-me-who-you-are thing. I mean, what did you mean by letting me call you Jack for a week, and for telling me that I have never known you? I've known you since I was a little girl."

Connor's pace slowed. "Max, there's a lot about me that you don't know," he said.

I waited, but when it became apparent nothing more was forthcoming, I said, "Yes, and that's what bothers me so much. You were my best friend growing up. And now you're telling me that you have this whole secret life?"

He shook his head. "Look, let's get these ropes off before we do anything else," he said. "It will be too dark to see soon and we're going to have to find a place where we'll be safe from the Maligios."

I didn't answer.

"Max, please?" Connor looked at me entreatingly. "You have to trust me." The look in his eyes reminded me of Jack and I felt disoriented. Now that I knew that he was Connor, it was like I was having to merge two different people into one. Maybe Connor was right: maybe I *had* never known him. Perhaps all along I had taken my friendship with him for granted. Sometimes when you've known someone for a long time, you don't give them room to change. You keep them in the little, comfortable place you've assigned them to, and never bother to delve any deeper into who they've become. I had learned more about Connor in the last week than I had known about him in the last ten years, all because I hadn't known it was him.

"What's wrong?" Now Connor looked concerned.

I shook my head and forced a smile. "I'm fine," I lied. "So, how are we going to get untied?"

Connor studied my face for a second before answering. "Well, I have a dagger in my boot," he said. "I was thinking if we both sat down, you could maybe reach it with one hand and pull it out."

"I thought your dagger was in your vest," I said. "The one the Troll King left you? He took your boot dagger. I saw it in his hands."

He flashed me a mischievous grin. "That was my *other* boot dagger. The Troll King left me better armed than you thought."

"Apparently so." I couldn't help smiling back.

Connor had me sit down and after some effort, I was able to retrieve the dagger from his boot. Holding it awkwardly in one hand, Connor cut through the ropes around my waist. I then turned and did the same for him. By then it was completely dark. We got to our feet and looked around. The night was thick and silent around us and I edged closer to Connor.

"So now what?" I asked.

"Do you see those rocks against the mountain over there?" he asked. I couldn't, but I nodded anyway. "Let's head over there and see if maybe there's some kind of cave or something we can hide in."

It seemed like a pretty sketchy idea but we had made it surprisingly far on sketchier ideas than that. "Follow me." Connor said. He turned and made his way through the trees.

I wondered how he could even see where he was going. The darkness seemed to press against us from all sides. I followed him closely, trying to see where I was putting my feet.

"So what do you know about Prince Torstein?" Connor asked.

I stumbled over a tree root and he turned and took my hand. The warmth of his hand holding mine was distracting and I had to concentrate to remember what he had just asked me. "Not much. I just met him last week."

"No, you didn't. Don't you remember how he came to visit when we were kids? And he got your boat for you out of that pond?" I felt him shiver.

"What's wrong?" I asked.

"What?"

"You just shivered when you were talking about Torstein getting my boat back for me."

"I did?"

"You did."

He didn't answer for a minute. "Don't worry about it," he finally said.

I stopped walking. "Tell me," I said.

He tugged on my hand to get me moving again. "It happened a long time ago, Max. Now keep moving."

"Please tell me?" I used my most beguiling tone.

He sighed. "Fine. When your toy floated away, I swam out first to get it for you."

"You? But you don't know how to swim!"

"Actually, I do. I learned before I came to live with your Aunt Marge. Anyway, Torstein swam up behind me, and he... well, he was bigger than me then. He grabbed my shoulders and pushed me under the water. Then he got the boat for you. I barely made it out of the pond. Ever since then..."

"Ever since then you've been afraid of deep water," I said slowly. "Connor, that's terrible! Why didn't you tell anyone?"

He shrugged. "I was just a penniless boy that your Aunt Marge took in. No one would have believed me over a *prince*. And it didn't matter so much since Torstein didn't come around after that."

"But why didn't you say anything the other day, back at Uncle Philip's castle?"

Connor made a scoffing sound. "Like what? 'Hey, Max, your fiancé tried to drown me when we were kids?' I don't think so."

"I would have listened to you."

"It's not like you could change things," he said. "You have to marry the guy. That's the life of a princess: a never-ending duty to be sweet and obedient."

It was my turn to scoff. "You might have noticed that I don't exactly fit the descriptions of sweet and obedient. In fact, I think I've disappointed everyone with my absolute lack of princess-like qualities."

This time it was Connor who stopped walking. "Don't say that," he said, turning to face me. "You think for yourself, you're smart, brave, funny-" He still held my hand.

"A nuisance, a troublemaker, incapable of following the traditional patterns of behavior-"

"Original, kindhearted, feisty-"

"You know, not too long ago you were lecturing me on becoming more ladylike."

"There are reasons why I said what I did." Connor spoke quietly. "The truth is that I like you as you are."

I felt strangely shy. "And I like you as you are."

"Oh yeah?"

"Yeah."

Connor moved closer, making my heart jump in my chest in the oddest way. He put his fingers under my chin and lifted my face to his. I could just see his expression in the surrounding darkness, and there was something about the way he was gazing down at me that caused a tingling warmth to spread over my body.

"Technically," he whispered, "I could be beheaded for what I'm about to do." He kissed me, his lips soft and warm against mine, and the world faded completely away. All that mattered was now, with Connor's gentle kiss and the touch of his hands holding my face.

After a moment he pulled away, his smile barely visible in the darkness. "Max, I've been wanting to tell you for the longest time—" He stopped and lifted his head. "Wait. Something's not right."

I wanted him to kiss me again, but I tried to focus on whatever it was that he was sensing. As I listened, I realized that a strange quiet had fallen over the forest; a crystallized silence that seemed to weigh down all of the usual sounds of the woods at night. Then I heard something infinitely more troubling: the dry whisper of countless small bodies moving through the trees.

"They're coming," Connor whispered. "We've got to hurry." He took my hand again and led me swiftly through the brush.

Chapter 35

We came to the rock outcropping Connor had seen and he began to poke around, trying to find an opening where two people could hide. As I stood waiting, I heard an odd, asthmatic rasping in the tree right over my head. I looked up and realized with horror that one of the Maligios was crouching in the branches watching us. Judging from its laborious breathing, it was either out of breath from its hurried journey to come eat us, or there was something wrong with its lungs. I really, really hoped it was the latter.

"Connor?" I called as quietly as I could. Actually, it was more of a muted shriek. It brought him back to my side with comforting speed and I pointed upward frantically.

"Ignore it," he whispered.

Yeah, right. How do you ignore something that's about to drop onto your neck and start eating you? The rasping grew louder as more of the Maligios jumped into the trees around us. I tried to remain calm. "Connor, they're everywhere."

"How did they gather so quickly?" he muttered, more to himself than to me. "It usually takes them longer--" He stopped. A glowing ball was floating towards us through the trees.

I swallowed hard and clutched Connor's arm. "What is that?" I asked.

"I have no idea," he said, sounding unnerved. We backed up as the yellow-white orb drew closer, blinding us with its brilliance. Soon we were up against the rocks and had nowhere to go. Connor pulled the dagger from his vest and stepped in front of me as the floating light reached us. We shielded our eyes from the light and readied ourselves for attack.

The glowing orb floated harmlessly up overhead, and now that the light was out of our direct line of vision, it illuminated the scene before us like a powerful lantern. Even so, I blinked several times, wondering if I were seeing rightly. Prince Torstein sat on a white horse holding a drawn sword. There was a look of concern on his handsome face. "My darling Maxine," he exclaimed. "It is such a relief that we have found you!"

I gazed at him speechlessly as my bewildered mind pieced together the realization that my fiancé had just come to rescue me. But who was he rescuing me from?

"Are you well, my love?" he asked.

Before I could answer, another voice cut in. "She's fine. Maxine is used to trouble." I turned my disbelieving eyes from Prince Torstein to the second newcomer.

Aunt Regina? This was even more unexpected and my mouth dropped open. What was she doing all the way out here? Aunt Regina is the kind of person who thinks having to wait for the servants to serve her is roughing it. The idea of her *outside*, *riding a horse*, boggled my mind.

"What are *you* doing here?" I asked.

Prince Torstein glanced at Aunt Regina. "Why, my dear, we came to rescue you," he said. He turned and made a gesturing motion behind him. Out of the darkness the soldiers of Treagal stepped forward, their expressions anything but pleasant. Or maybe it was the fact that their arrows were pointing straight at us that made them seem so unfriendly.

"Prince Torstein, I respectfully request that you command your men to lower their weapons," said Connor. "There is no need to have them threatening us in this manner."

"On the contrary," he said. "I suspect that there is every need."

"I do not understand your meaning," Connor said, his voice steely.

Torstein swung off his horse. "My meaning is perfectly clear," he said. "And if you wish to remain alive, you will not move."

I considered trying my whistling trick, but what good would that do if it didn't work on Aunt Regina, the most dangerous one in the crowd? My best chance lay in acting the part of an air-headed ninny. I just hoped that Connor would understand what I doing.

I put a hand to my forehead and tried to look pale and helpless. "Prince Torstein, how glad I am to see you!"

Connor and Torstein snapped their heads in my direction, their faces mirror images of surprise and suspicion. I fluttered my eyelashes, hoping it actually looked right for once. "It is so nice to have my own prince come to my rescue. I was terribly afraid of those nasty monsters." It was easy to give a realistic shudder with the red-eyed beasts lurking in the trees above us.

Torstein laughed. Sheathing his sword, he held out his arms. "Come here, sweetheart. I'll take care of you, don't you worry." His condescending tone made my self-imposed role a lot harder to perform. Avoiding Connor's eyes, I made my way to Torstein's embrace. He put his arms around me and pulled me close. "See, Regina, I told you that your little beasts were going to be trouble."

"Nonsense. They are as trustworthy as myself."

Torstein raised his eyebrows.

"Well, *I* can trust them, anyway," Regina said.

Connor cleared his throat. "As good as it is to see a happy couple reunited, I find that I am anxious to get back home. If you will excuse me..." He turned to leave.

"Stay where you are," ordered Torstein. "I am placing you under arrest."

"What?" asked Connor, swiveling back around. "On what charges?"

"Yes, what did he do?" I asked.

"As soon as we discovered your absence, my dear, we feared that you had been kidnapped." Torstein slanted a hard look at Connor. "Obviously our suspicions were correct."

"That's ridiculous," said Connor. "I found Princess Maxine wandering in the Miraysian Forest and accompanied her in order to protect her."

"So you claim," said Torstein, eyeing Connor with open skepticism.

"But it's true," I said. "He came just in time to save me from these Maligios things."

Torstein ignored me and waved his hand to his men. Two soldiers stepped forward and tied Connor's arms behind his back.

"I would advise tying up Maxine as well," said Aunt Regina.

I stiffened as Torstein looked at her quizzically. "Why should we bind her?" he asked.

"We discussed this," Aunt Regina said with exaggerated patience. "I know that you think this whole situation was due to a kidnapper, but I'm telling you, Maxine was more than likely an active participant in whatever's been going on here."

"Perhaps," said Torstein, looking down at me. "Yet even if she were inclined toward foolish action, what harm could a girl do against so many men?" It was starting to annoy me how they were talking about me like I wasn't even there.

Regina rolled her eyes. "Don't be a fool," she said. "I know her. She's only acting docile to get us to let our guard down. Let's tie her up before she tries something."

One of the most frustrating things about relatives is their complete lack of discretion. Because they have known you since birth, they think that it's their exclusive right to dish out all the dirt they can. They will happily dredge up something you did before you were even old enough to crawl, and act like it is a clear foreteller of how you are going to be the rest of your life. Just because I accidentally shattered a magical mirror of hers when I was a little kid, she's never forgiven me. Of course, there may have been a few more incidents in the intervening years, some which were possibly intentional, but the point is, I was trying to present a kind and gentle version of myself, and Aunt Regina was destroying my reputation faster than I could construct it.

I gazed up at Torstein with wide, innocent eyes. "I am so happy you came to my rescue," I said sweetly, and snuggled closer into his embrace.

It worked.

"I will not allow her to be bound," he announced. "Mount up, men. It's time to go."

Aunt Regina made an exasperated noise. "You're going to regret this," she warned.

I resisted the urge to stick my tongue out at her and asked instead, "What about my brother?"

"Prince Charming?" asked Torstein. "Where is he, now that you mention it?"

"He's in a cottage at the top of this mountain, being held captive by these terrible, evil enchanters--"

"He's with Bruce and Sira?" interrupted Regina, sounding amused. Trust her to be on a first name basis with them. "And he's still alive?"

"Yes," I said, glaring at her. "At least, he was an hour ago. Only he's not, uh, quite himself, exactly. He's sort of a… a frog." It's an embarrassing thing to have to admit about one's brother.

They both started laughing. "How perfect is that?" asked Regina. "Things are coming together so well." She spurred her mount forward.

I looked at Torstein desperately. "But we can't just leave him up there! What if he gets hurt?"

Prince Torstein had been speaking in a low voice to one of his soldiers. He turned to me. "What if who gets hurt?"

"My brother! We were just talking about him, remember?"

"Oh yes, of course." Torstein lifted me onto his horse and swung himself up behind me. "There's no need to worry, my dear. All will be well in the end."

I felt a sinking sensation in the pit of my stomach. My previous confidence in happy endings for the good guys was unexpectedly being challenged by someone whom I suspected wasn't all that good of a guy in the first place.

Chapter 36

Regina's monsters followed us at first, snarling and quarreling amongst themselves, but after awhile they seemed to get bored with our steady pace and went off to do whatever it is that evil things do in their spare time. I alternated my thoughts between worrying about Ron to wondering if Connor was going to be put into prison when we got wherever we were going. And when I thought about Connor, I couldn't help but remember the kiss we had shared. Even thinking about it now made my heart beat faster, which is a strange sensation to experience when it involves your childhood best friend.

I realized that my feelings for Connor had been changing into something more than a friend for some time; I just hadn't admitted it to myself until now. While there was a lot I didn't know about Connor's true identity, I knew enough about him to see what an amazing person he was. He was everything any girl hopes for: kind, brave, intelligent and honorable.

Hopefully he understood what I had been trying to do in my effort to get into Prince Torstein's good graces. Seeing Torstein appear in the middle of a forest in the middle of the night had been entirely unexpected and most definitely unwelcome. I felt uncomfortable riding along in his embrace and I went through a dozen escape plans in my mind. The problem was that although my fairy godmother gift would allow me to freeze my fiancé and his soldiers, I would still have Aunt Regina to contend with. Knowing as I did now that she was the creator of the Maligios was further proof to me that as an adversary, she was more than formidable.

As the night wore on my thoughts grew jumbled as the lack of sleep began to catch up with me. I dozed fitfully in Torstein's arms before finally falling into a deep slumber.

I awoke as the morning sun began to break over the horizon. I was lying on a blanket under a tree while the soldiers milled about preparing breakfast and tending to their horses. Torstein stood nearby, conversing with some of his men. On seeing that I was awake, he concluded his conversation and joined me.

"Good morning, my dear," he said.

"Where are we?" I sat up and ran my hands over my hair. It felt like it could use some serious attention.

"Just outside the Kingdom of Lost Souls."

"The Kingdom of Lost Souls?"

"It is called so because those who enter it are never seen again," explained Prince Torstein. "I'm surprised that you did not pass by this area on your way up the mountain. There's some kind of curse where those who travel into the actual kingdom boundaries are never seen again. Everyone knows to avoid the place."

He meant Queen Amelia's kingdom. Who knew it had a reputation? My eyes narrowed as I realized one person who undoubtedly would have known: the Wizard Marvelonius.

Torstein continued. "We're waiting to meet up with my younger brother, Prince Jaspien, and then we will join up with the rest of my army."

"Prince Jaspien?" I asked, instantly distracted from thoughts of the conversation I planned to have with Marvelonius once I got home. "As in, Prince Jaspien of the Kingdom of

Denitri? Prince Jaspien of the royal-decree-to-put-all-visitors-to-death? *That* Prince Jaspien? He's your *brother*?" Torstein's credentials were already pretty smudged with his close association with Aunt Regina. Hearing that he was related to the arrogant guy that threw me into prison only days before really didn't help matters.

Torstein raised his eyebrows. "I don't really concern myself with Jaspien's methods in ruling his little kingdom, but yes, he's my brother—technically more of a stepbrother." Torstein waved his hand impatiently. "But none of that is important right now. I wanted to ask you about the spell your kidnapper placed us under on the evening of the ball. I don't know if you were aware of this, but we were unable to move for *several hours*! I need to know how he does it."

I swallowed. "You know," I said, "a person can feel pretty stiff after being under a spell like that. Although there are worse spells. I once knew this girl who was turned into a warthog--"

"I am not interested in hearing about your warthog friends. I would like for you to answer my question."

"What was your question?" I asked, stalling.

"How was it," he asked through gritted teeth, "that your kidnapper immobilized us?"

"Oh, *that* question. Well, first of all, I wasn't kidnapped, as I mentioned before. You might remember. So based on the absence of a true kidnapper, we must conclude that there is someone out there who, for reasons of their own, didn't want any of you moving for awhile. It's not unknown for vindictive magical persons to arrive in the midst of happy celebrations with intentions of revenge. And everyone knows that my Aunt Regina has a lot of enemies, so doubtless someone was upset about something she did and--"

"And nothing," he snapped. "I want to know how it was done!"

Have I mentioned that I find short tempers extremely unattractive in fiancés? "I'm not sure how it was done," I said, which is true. I have no idea how the sound of whistling causes people to be unable to move. "All I know is that I left the ball and then I got lost in the Miraysian Forest. I was trying to find my way home when you, uh, rescued me."

He watched me with narrowed eyes. "I see. And I am so glad that you are unharmed."

"Yes, me too. And it's great to see you again and, um, everything."

A soldier approached us. "Your Highness, the lookout says that Prince Jaspien is approaching."

"Excellent. Tell the men to mount up and be ready to leave at a moment's notice."

"Yes, sir."

Torstein turned to me. "We will continue this conversation at another time, Princess Maxine." It sounded like a threat. I wanted to tell him not if I could help it, but I was still trying for the whole trick-him-into-thinking-I'm-sweet plan.

He lifted me onto his horse. "And I have some exciting news," he said, looking up at me and forcing a smile. "With your marriage to me, not only will Treagal and Veiland become one kingdom, but plans are underway to unify all of the countries in the area into a single great empire. My dear, you will be an empress over a realm the likes of which has never been known in the history of the world!" His smile became genuine even as my fake one faded.

"I can see how that would be a lot of...fun," I said. "But let's back up a little. *How* are Treagal and Veiland going to become one? Because my understanding was that my brother, Prince Charming, would be the king of Veiland and that *you* would be the king of Treagal. And that's not even mentioning your idea about an empire."

Torstein looked disappointed with my reaction. "I can see that it's going to take some time for you to fully understand the scope of my plans."

"And what about my father?" I continued. "What has he said about the whole empire, Treagal/Veiland being one thing?"

"I have been unable to secure your father's blessings," he said shortly. I could see from his face that this was a sore point. "However, since we are to be married it is hardly a matter of concern." Torstein put his hand on my knee and I resisted the urge to lift it back off. "Maxine, you are missing the point of this conversation! *You are to be the queen of an empire!* No other lady in the history of the world will have the power, wealth and prestige that you will have at your fingertips. What a wonderful thing for you, as well as for the sons that you will someday bear me."

My eyes widened. *Sons?* Now there was a horrifying thought. The conversation couldn't possibly get any worse. Then Prince Torstein looked forward and smiled. "There's Jaspien now."

Wait, I take that back.

Chapter 37

Prince Torstein stepped forward to greet the small entourage of men who rode through the trees towards us. Jaspien dismounted and the brothers greeted one another by clasping arms.

"Jaspien," said Torstein warmly. "How fair you?"

"I'm a bit stiff, actually," said Jaspien. "My men and I had an inauspicious encounter with a sorceress."

Uh oh. I hunched down in the saddle, trying not to be seen. If I could only figure out how to handle Aunt Regina, now would be the perfect time to escape.

"I'm glad to see that you and your men are unharmed," Torstein said.

"I wish that were the case. However, many of my men remain as though frozen under the dreadful spell which she cast. The kingdom has been invaded and we have only just managed to escape, thanks to the assistance of my wizard."

Torstein's eyes narrowed. "This spell: did everyone stop moving, becoming as though they were statues?"

"Yes, exactly," said Jaspien. "How did you know?"

"I experienced this same phenomenon last week. It appears that a terrible power is afoot. Only—you say it was a *female* who placed you under this spell?"

"Yes. My sources tell me it was a red-headed she-devil."

Aunt Regina rode up in time to hear this last comment. "I've already told you who the culprit is," she snapped.

Before either of them could comment, a soldier rode up leading a horse with Connor mounted on it. His hands were tied in front of him and he looked as though he had spent a sleepless night. Prince Torstein glanced at Connor, looking confused.

"Not him, you fool," snarled Regina. She pointed at me. "*Her.*"

Jaspien hadn't noticed me up to this point but now his eyes widened as he recognized me. "You!"

I offered a weak smile and waved. "Hello again."

Suddenly the sound of galloping hooves and shouting filled the morning air as a band of masked horsemen thundered through the trees and into the camp. We turned in time to see Connor fling the already-severed ropes from his hands, gather up his reins and wheel to follow them. Soldiers yelled and scattered before their determined approach and in another instant both the mysterious rescuers and Connor himself had disappeared into the trees.

"You idiots! Follow him!" screeched Aunt Regina. This order seemed a bit unnecessary since the men were already turning their horses to pursue the escaped prisoner.

I decided my moment had come. Tilting my head back, I whistled louder than I ever have in my life. A pure, piercing tone came from my pursed lips, high and clear and ringing. It seemed to rise above the noise and tumult for a moment before it settled on the unsuspecting scene below. In an instant the charging horses, shouting soldiers, and sword-wielding guards appeared as though they were carved of stone. Torstein and Jaspien wore identical expressions of anger and surprise, their mouths open in silent shouts of indignation. The sudden shift from ear-deafening noise to deep silence was wonderful.

There was only one problem.

"I wish you would stop doing that." Aunt Regina slid off her frozen horse. "Do you have any idea how long it takes me to revive everyone?" She sighed. "At least now I know *how* you do it; no one would tell me. It's hard to stop someone from performing their little tricks if you don't know what you should be watching for."

I leaned forward and whispered into my unmoving mount's ear while Regina began to roll up her sleeves. The horse's ear twitched.

"Now then," said Regina. "Before I get to work on this mess that you've created, I think I need to do something about you so we aren't working against each other."

"Aunt Regina, please," I said. "I'm your niece. Doesn't family count for anything with you?"

She looked at me quizzically. "Darling, it has long been established between you and I what sort of person I am. Why would you expect me to show you any kindness now?"

I shrugged. "I didn't. It just seemed like I ought to give you a chance." I kicked my mount's sides and charged towards Regina in a burst of speed. Eyes wide, she scrambled backward while raising her hands as though to perform a spell. She was too late. I leaned over one side of the horse just as I came up to her and swung my fist into her nose.

It was a good hit. She crumbled to the ground like a broken porcelain doll. I wheeled my mount back around and watched her carefully. She didn't move and I couldn't help a little smirk. It was nice to see that while my magic had no effect on her, my fist certainly did.

Speaking of my fist…I looked down at it. It was bright red and throbbing like mad. "*Ow,*" I muttered, cradling it in my other hand. Hopefully nothing was broken. Aunt Regina had a hard nose.

After tying my wicked auntie up, I turned my mount in the direction of the Kingdom of Lost Souls. Now that Connor was safe, the next item of business was to go and rescue my brother, but I needed to see about getting some food and other supplies first.

As I rode, I contemplated Connor's escape. It had all the signs of a pre-planned effort, from Connor sitting pathetically on his mount, pretending to still be bound, to the rush of riders through the camp while Prince Torstein was distracted greeting his brother. What I didn't understand was who Connor's rescuers were. Where had they come from, and why didn't they come to our rescue in all of the troubles we'd gotten into before now?

What bothered me more than anything else was why Connor hadn't made sure I was galloping away by his side. I couldn't understand why he had left me to fend for myself in a group of scheming, power-hungry people. With troubling thoughts like these, I made my way down the narrow trail, back into the Kingdom of Lost Souls.

Chapter 38

The atmosphere in the village was in stark contrast to my last visit. Before it had been like a funeral, now it was more like a festival. A crowd of people stood laughing and talking in front of the inn while several pigs roasted on spits nearby. The innkeeper's wife saw me ride up and she elbowed her husband. They both turned to face me and I swallowed uneasily, unsure as to what kind of reception I was going to get.

"Sorry to interrupt," I said. "I was hoping that you might have some food I could purchase. Maybe some bread if you have any, or even porridge."

The innkeeper and his wife watched me with eyes that were strangely bright, and I wondered if they were well. Suddenly the innkeeper's wife swept into a low curtsy before me, bowing as though I were, well…royalty. To my dismay, the innkeeper followed his wife's lead, and it all went downhill from there—literally—as the group of men and women in front of the inn lowered themselves into curtsies and bows until I was the only one who remained upright.

You might think that since I'm a princess I would be used to this kind of treatment, but in my family Ron is the one who gets the attention, not me. People who bow low as my brother rides by are usually rising up by the time I come along.

It was so quiet I could hear the sizzle and pop of the pigs on the spit. "Your food is burning," I finally said. "Somebody should check on that. It would be a shame to ruin it after all of this time of eating porridge."

The people straightened up and gazed at me as though I were already legendary.

I shifted uneasily and then reined my horse to ride around them. "I'll just be on my way. Thanks for, um...everything."

The innkeeper stepped in front of me. "I don't think you understand," he said. "You freed us from the enchanter's curse. You broke the spell that had bound us for many long years. At last we are free to live as we choose, and for that we honor you. For that we bow before you in true gratitude."

"But you've got it all wrong," I protested. "I had nothing to do with the spell being broken. I was just there. So thanks for the nice gesture and all but--"

"Nonsense," said the innkeeper's wife. "We saw how you and that handsome boy fought the serpent! As soon as they flew off we found that we were able to leave the kingdom as we wished. And we are free at last from Queen Amelia. If it weren't for you, we would still be under the enchanter's curse and Amelia's terrible reign."

"Where is the young man who was with you, by the way?" asked the innkeeper.

"He rode on ahead," I said. "I'm surprised that you didn't see him come through, maybe with a bunch of other people?"

They shook their heads. "We haven't seen anyone," the innkeeper said. "Just you. By the way, my name is Thomas and this here is Dolores."

"I'm Maxine."

"Three cheers for the lady Maxine!" someone cried out. The whole crowd began to shout, "Hip, hip, hooray," and then they closed in around me, pulled me from my horse and carried me above their heads.

Orders of "Put me down," and "It wasn't me who rescued you," were lost in the sea of rejoicing people. I washed up at a table where a plate piled with food was placed in front of me. While my back was pounded by the exuberantly grateful people, the tantalizing smells of pork and freshly baked bread drifted into my interested nose.

I realized that in situations of misplaced heroism, there is only one thing that you can politely do: accept their thanks, eat the meal, and *then* ride away.

As I was eating, Dolores handed me a package wrapped in brown paper. "This is a little something that I put together for you in case I saw you again," she said. Inside was a pair of trousers and a white tunic elaborately embroidered with gold and green thread. "Hope they fit," she said, smiling at me.

"Wow. Thank you." I would be able to ride the horse astride now without showing an indecent amount of leg like I'd been doing. And then when I got my motorcycle back...

Then Dolores handed me my traveling bag.

"Oh, hey, I forgot that here the other day," I said, taking it with a smile.

"Yes, it was under the bed," said Dolores. "We found it when the food in it began to spoil." She wrinkled her nose at the memory. "I put a fresh supply of food into it for you."

"We've heard talk about uprisings in the kingdoms, miss," added Thomas. "You'd best find your other friends and head home where you'll be safe."

"I'll do that," I said, deciding not to mention that my home wouldn't be all that safe of a place with my aunt and fiancé on the rampage. After changing into my new clothes, I followed Thomas and Dolores outside. "Thanks for all of your help," I said, swinging into the saddle.

Thomas smiled at me. "Anything for the girl who saved us from the scourge of endless porridge."

"Amen to that," said Dolores.

I waved and then reined the horse towards the enchanter's mountain.

Chapter 39

I made it to the enchanter's cottage by early afternoon. A pale wisp of smoke drifted from the red brick chimney and the paned glass windows sparkled in the sunlight. Hidden behind a leafy bush, I watched as Sira walked out of the little house. From my vantage point I could hear her humming peacefully as she gathered flowers and put them into a basket hanging from her arm.

Sira was not the sort of woman to pick flowers merely because she thought that they were pretty. It was therefore safe to assume that she was gathering the flowers to brew a poison or some awful spell. Either way, a person would have to be either really dumb or really naive to not realize that this idyllic scene was too good to be true.

I was about to settle down to wait for Sira to go back inside when I heard a voice say, "Pardon me." My head popped back up and I watched in horror as a young lady emerged from the trees opposite me and approached Sira. "I have been lost all morning in this awful forest," the young lady said. "I'm so glad I found you!"

I snorted. It was doubtful that anyone with a bit of sense had ever been *glad* to find Sira.

"It's terribly frightening to be lost," Sira said, sounding a lot like a sweet, kind lady gathering pretty flowers instead of a wicked enchantress gathering poisonous flowers. "Why don't you come inside to rest and then I'll help you find your way?"

Great. Sira was going to try to eat this girl, I just knew it. Now I'd have to rescue my brother *and* her.

"I couldn't possibly rest yet. I have to find him." The girl sounded like she was about to start crying.

"And how was I supposed to know that you were looking for somebody?" growled Sira. For all of her skills in sounding sweet and nice, she would do well to work on learning patience.

The girl didn't seem to notice. "I'm looking for my fiancé," she said. "Well, technically he's more of an ex-fiancé."

I straightened up and peered through the bush's leaves, trying to see the girl's face. What were the chances that a girl would come looking for an ex-fiance in the very cottage Ron was being held captive in?

The young lady continued, "He's the one who decided to end things; I still don't know why. I thought that he loved me. I know I love him."

Sira interrupted. "My dear child, I am not at all interested in your romantic woes."

The girl went on as though Sira hadn't spoken, "I keep getting this uneasy feeling that he's hurt or in trouble. I haven't slept for days. You didn't happen to see him walking by here recently, did you? I was told that he might have come this way."

"There are a lot of ex-fiancés in this world," Sira snarled, all pretense of being nice completely gone. "You might not realize that, being as young as you are. So how am I supposed to know if your particular ex-fiancé walked by, particularly since I don't even know his name or what he looks like?"

"Oh. Well, his name is Ronald Charming," said the girl, taking a step back as though finally realizing that something about Sira wasn't quite right. "And I couldn't give you a description because he's always changing how he looks. But he is the most wonderful man in the world and I love him with all of my heart, even though he's also a swine and I can't stand him. Please, have you seen him?"

"Prince Charming?" Sira paused. "Uh, no. No, I've never heard of him."

"But I didn't say that he was a *prince*," said the girl. Maybe she wasn't quite as dumb as she seemed. "I just said Ronald Charming. How did you know that he's a prince?"

"Lucky guess." Now it was Sira who took a step back.

"The trolls told me that he was up here in a cottage. Only I got lost and wasn't sure if I had found the right one."

"The cottage that you want is on the other side of this mountain. If you follow that path up and walk for two days, you'll find it, easy as pie. Now if you'll excuse me, I have some important things that I need to get done right away." Sira turned and practically ran into the cottage, slamming the door behind her.

The girl stared after her for a second. Then she put her hands over her face and ran, conveniently right towards where I was hiding. "Hateful woman," she sobbed. "Why is everyone around here so strange?"

I stepped out from my hiding place. "Don't scream," I said.

She screamed.

"I should've expected that. Cinderella, look, it's me." I held my hands out towards her.

Cinderella gaped at me with tear-filled blue eyes. "Princess Maxine?"

"Yes. What are you doing here?"

She started to cry again. Really, it was amazing that she'd made it so far on her own.

…Wait a minute.

"Cinderella, how did you get here?"

"What do you mean?" she sniffled.

"I mean, how did you get from Veiland to here? And don't try to tell me that you walked, because there is no way that you made it all the way here in those shoes." I gestured towards her dainty satin slippers that, aside from a little dust, showed no signs of a long journey.

She wiped her nose on her sleeve. "The wizard took me. He dropped me off at the bottom of the mountain because he said he had some urgent business to attend to. So the trolls carried me most of the way, but then they said they couldn't go any further and I had to go alone. I was awfully frightened but I knew that I would do anything for my love—I mean, for Ronald—so here I am. Only I think I must be lost because the trolls told me that Ronald was in a cottage at the top of this mountain and that awful woman just told me she's never heard of him."

"Did you just say that *Marv* brought you here? Marvelonius the wizard?"

"Yes, and it was terrible! We rode on this frightful contraption with only two wheels. It was all wobbly and it made this horrible roaring sound, and I had to wear *trousers*. Of course, I changed into my gown as soon as possible as it isn't appropriate for a lady to wear..." Cinderella's voice trailed off as she realized what I was wearing. "Oh."

"Don't worry about it." I resisted the urge to pat her on the head and thought for a minute. "I wish I could say that I'm glad you're here, but it really makes things much more complicated. It's strange that Marv sent you up here alone—or brought you along at all, for that matter. Did he say what his urgent business was?"

"No, and I did not ask, for it is not proper for a lady to delve into the business of others if they do not desire to tell her."

"I really wish my mother hadn't made you take all of those princess training courses," I muttered. "You've been corrupted."

A flash of fire came into her eyes. "You try fitting in with a bunch of mean princesses who treat you like you're beneath them!" she snapped.

"Yikes. Sorry. I didn't mean..." My voice trailed off under the intensity of her glare. "Cinderella, you don't need princess training courses to be a true princess. And anyway, Ron loved you for you."

She put her hands on her hips. "Then why did he break our engagement?"

"I don't know," I said. "Because he's an idiot? How about we go rescue him and then you can ask him for yourself? Unless you already did ask him?"

She looked away. "No. I was so sad when he told me he wasn't going to marry me that I couldn't think of anything to say. I just went and mopped the floors of the third and fourth stories of the castle to work through my thoughts. I do my best thinking when I'm mopping."

"I'll keep that in mind."

"So we need to rescue Ronald?"

"Yep. The lady that you just spoke to was lying to you. Ron *is* in that cottage and he's currently being held captive by a very fierce, very determined five-year-old."

Chapter 40

Cinderella just looked at me as though she were waiting for me to finish. When I didn't say anything else, she said, "Princess Maxine, sometimes I can't tell when you are jesting. This is one of those times. How could a child hold a grown man captive?"

I hesitated, not sure how to tell her that her beloved Prince Charming was now a frog. "Ron isn't exactly how you remember him," I said. "He isn't quite as strong as he used to be. And, er, his coloring is a little off..."

"Was he ill?"

"Not really."

"What exactly are you saying, Princess Maxine?" She sounded a bit snappy.

"Look, could you stop with the Princess Maxine all the time?" I asked. "Just call me Max."

"I cannot. It would not be proper."

"What about your current situation strikes you as proper?" I demanded. She was starting to get on my nerves. "It's not proper for you to have traveled with Marv without a chaperone, it's not proper that you wore trousers while doing it; it's not proper that you climbed a mountain in broad daylight *without a parasol*. Soon you will be going to rescue someone, which is *very* improper. Rescuing often involves running and yelling and sometimes even behaving aggressively. So why don't you just forget everything you learned in those princess training courses for a little while so that we can actually get things done?"

She bit her lip and gazed at me thoughtfully for a minute. "Well, if you put it that way," she said, and started to dig in the large handbag she was carrying.

"What are you doing?"

"Getting ready to rescue Ronald, of course. If I am to be running and yelling and behaving aggressively, I need to get those trousers back on. It's impossible to be mobile in these lovely, yet very restrictive gowns."

"Uh, good," I nodded. "Excellent."

She retreated behind a bush and began to change.

"So what's the matter with Ronald?" Her voice came to me sounding muffled in folds of cloth. "You said that he is now weak and his coloring is off?"

I grimaced. "Yes."

"Is there anything else wrong with him?"

"It depends on how you look at it. He's perfectly healthy, he just isn't in his usual form, exactly," I stopped, trying to figure out what to say. "It might be easier to understand what I'm talking about when you see him. Or maybe not." I was starting to sweat. How could I prepare her for the shock of discovering that Ron was a frog?

"You're saying that he isn't himself right now."

"Yes, exactly."

"Odd coloring, weaker than he used to be, not in his usual form... Did someone put him under a spell?"

"Yes—that's *precisely* what happened." I felt relieved. Maybe she wouldn't be so alarmed with Ron's new look after all.

"A common dilemma in the rescue business, I've learned. I'm sure a remedy will easily be found."

"Since when did you get to be such a professional in the 'rescue business'?"

"Oh, I've been reading about it in *Your Prince, Your Rescue: How to Orchestrate a Happily-Ever-After*. It's a very informative book that teaches a princess all she needs to know about being a damsel in distress. You should read it."

"Uh, sure. Remind me when we get home."

"Of course. I have to say, Maxine," she emerged from behind the tree wearing trousers and a loose-fitting peasant blouse, "I really think that you would benefit from this book. It helped me realize that I went about my relationship with Ronald all wrong. For example, I let him have every dance at the ball. *Every dance!* I have since learned how important it is to let the prince know that he isn't the only man in your life. A girl needs to flirt with a lot of young men and ignore her prince until he comes to rescue her. Then, after their first kiss, he will propose and they will live in happy bliss for the rest of their lives." She paused. "And that's another thing: I didn't let Ronald rescue me. All he did was return my shoe! I just don't think that's very romantic, do you?" She gazed at me earnestly.

I just stood there looking at her.

"What?" she asked.

"Everything that you said is completely ridiculous," I said. "You're blaming yourself for things that you had no control over."

"What do you mean?"

"Maybe the reason things didn't work out is because Ron is a dimwit."

"Oh no, not at all. My book clearly states--"

"Your book is wrong if it's teaching you to not be yourself, among other things. We can talk about it more later, but we really need to go find this dumb brother of mine. And let me assure you, the condition he's in is definitely *not* romantic." I explained to Cinderella as briefly as possible the situation that we were facing, making sure to leave out key details that would possibly cause her to faint (like the fact that Sira had a taste for human flesh or that Ron was an amphibian).

"So what's the rescue plan, Princess Maxine?" Cinderella whispered as we began to creep through the trees and brush towards the back of the cottage.

"Call me Max, remember? And I don't have a plan." Since I was in the lead it took me a minute to notice that Cinderella had stopped walking. I glanced back. "What's the matter?"

"You just told me that the people who live in that cottage are the most evil enchanters in history. And now we are going to confront them with no weapons and no magical powers and *no plan*? Are you crazy?"

"Not that I know of. I just couldn't think of anything because we have no weapons and no magical powers. I was hoping that a plan would present itself by the time we get there."

"And if nothing comes to mind?"

I resumed walking.

"*I said*, if nothing comes to mind?"

I gritted my teeth. "I don't know."

"Well! I have to say, *Max*, it's a good thing that your brother is the one in the rescue business and not you, because you obviously don't have a clue what you're doing!"

I whirled to face her. "Listen, I was going to do this by myself when you blundered your ninny-headed way in and clued Sira in to the fact that people are going to be looking for Ron, which means they're going to be on their guard now! So I don't need to have you nagging me because I don't have a plan! *You* are the liability in this rescue! And if you don't stop talking, I'm going to leave you here so I can attempt this without someone jabbering on in my ear and criticizing me! Got it?"

Her blue eyes were wide as she stared at me. She nodded. "Fine. Good. Great." I paused. "Shall we continue?" Another nod.

I turned and started walking again. In a moment I heard her footsteps following. Then I heard a little sniff. I ignored it. She sniffed again. I turned around in time to catch her wiping her nose on her sleeve. Someone needed to get this girl a handkerchief. "Why are you crying?" I asked through clenched teeth.

"I'm not crying." She glared at me through her tears.

"Oh really. So your eyes are just watering all of a sudden."

"Yes. My eyes are sensitive to sunlight."

I closed my eyes and concentrated on breathing for a minute. Then I said, "I am sorry for yelling at you. Maybe you should go back and wait with the horse."

"No. I'm coming with you. Besides, I don't know where it is."

"You don't know where the horse is?" I repeated incredulously. "But we just left it five minutes ago!" I stopped as fresh tears welled up in her eyes. "Never mind. Let's just keep going."

The trees began to thin out, and soon I gestured for her to crawl behind me through the bushes to a vantage point where we could see the back of the cottage. The sun was high overhead, shining down and causing beads of perspiration to run into my eyes. I swiped my forehead with my sleeve. "Alright, so what we need to do now is determine who is home and who isn't--"

A high-pitched wailing interrupted me. "Nooooo!"

Startled, Cinderella and I pressed ourselves into the uncomfortable embrace of a large bush as a tangled mass of golden curls emerged only a few feet away. "Fwoggie, come back!" shrieked Goldie, her face red and dirty. "Gwamma, my fwoggie is trying to get away again! Catch her for me *now*!"

My heart jumped into my throat as Sira emerged from where she had apparently been crawling on all fours. Her long black hair was a mess, with twigs and leaves jutting out of it, and her lovely face was as smudged and red as her granddaughter's. She came to her feet, her expression a mixture of weariness and despair. "Maybe this time the frog has gotten away for good, Goldie," she said, putting both hands on the small of her back and wincing. "Why don't we play with that nice little dolly I made for you?"

"No! I want the fwoggie! Get it for me, Gwamma, or I'll scweam!"

Clearly this was a threat that had been used to advantage before as Sira's face blanched and she hastily dropped on all fours again. "No, no, darling, please don't scream. You know how that hurts Grandma's ears."

"Now, now, now!" Goldie stood with her hands on her hips, looking very much like her mother as she scowled down at her filthy grandparent.

Sira crawled around peering under bushes. "Why did you let go of the string I tied around its neck?" she demanded after a moment, baring her teeth in a show of her old spirit.

Goldie's answer was to draw in a deep breath.

"Alright, alright! Don't scream, you nasty little brat; I'll find your hateful frog!"

Goldie started screaming. I immediately understood why Sira hated it so much; it was the most piercing, awful, shattering sound that I had ever heard. Clamping my hands over my ears, I glanced over to see how Cinderella was taking it. To my surprise she just looked irritated. Before I could stop her she came to her feet, marched over to where Goldie stood, and picked her up from behind.

Chapter 41

The screaming stopped as Goldie hung limply for a moment, her face reflecting her surprise at this unexpected development. It didn't take her long to recover. "Let me go, let me go," she shrieked, squirming and kicking. "I'll scweam!"

"If you scream again, I'll scream too and you'll see how it is," said Cinderella. "I have never seen such an ill-mannered, terrible little girl in all of my life!"

Goldie kept struggling for freedom. "I am *not* ill-mannered!" she yelled. "Gwamma, save me this instant or else!"

I had forgotten about Sira. I looked to see where she was, worried that she would be upset that her granddaughter was being treated so unceremoniously. Sira was still crouched on her hands and knees, staring at the unlikely scene with a mixture of amazement and relief.

"You are too ill-mannered," scolded Cinderella. "A true lady stays clean and treats her grandmother kindly and, most of all, does not scream unless her life is in peril! You should be ashamed of yourself!"

Goldie stopped squirming for a minute to consider this. "But I like to scweam. Everyone does what I want when I scweam."

"I'm not doing what you want," Cinderella pointed out.

Goldie started screaming again. Sira and I both cringed and put our fingers in our ears.

Then a strange thing happened: we could no longer hear Goldie's screaming. The sound that drowned out Goldie's terrible shriek left me in no doubt as to who had the greater lung power. I stared at Cinderella as she stood with her mouth wide open, screaming in a pitch and tone that reverberated through the entire mountain. When she finally stopped I removed my fingers from my ears to a ringing silence.

Goldie's eyes were wide.

"Now do you see how unpleasant that is?" asked Cinderella.

Goldie just hung in her arms.

"I would like for you to go now and apologize to your grandmother for treating her unkindly. Afterwards she will see about getting you a proper pet. Ladylike little girls do not own frogs. Do you understand?"

Goldie nodded. Cinderella set her down and Goldie walked a trifle unsteadily over to where Sira still crouched in the dirt. "I'm sorry for being unkind, Gwamma. I would like to go inside now, please."

Sira came slowly to her feet, brushing twigs and leaves from her hair and skirt. I tensed, wondering what was coming. Sira walked forward and held out her hand to Cinderella. "Thank you," she said.

Before I could shout a warning, Cinderella took Sira's hand. Her eyes widened in surprise.

I don't know what I was expecting; maybe for Cinderella to melt before my eyes or for her to be turned into a frog herself, but nothing happened. Sira let go of Cinderella's hand and walked back to her cottage, followed by a subdued Goldie. The door to the cottage closed.

I turned to Cinderella. "Wow," I said.

"What?" She looked a little defensive.

"I didn't know you could scream like that. And for so long, without drawing a breath. I mean, that was *amazing*."

"Yes, well, it turns out that some of the things that I learned in *Your Prince, Your Rescue*, are helpful in real-life situations."

"That book teaches about screaming?"

"There's a whole chapter about screaming, with training exercises to practice tone, pitch, stamina, everything. Of course, these screaming abilities are supposed be used for when a dragon carries one away or something along those lines. The book didn't say anything about having a screaming match with a spoiled child."

"Hey, whatever works." I grinned at her. "Now we just need to find that frog!"

Cinderella gave me an odd look. She glanced down at the hand Sira had grasped. In it was one end of dirty white string. The rest of the string trailed off into the bush near where Sira had been crouching. "She put this in my hand," she said. "It was as though it was her way of saying thanks." She shuddered and tossed the string down.

I leapt towards the string just as it began to snake away into the bushes. "What are you thinking?" I yelled, catching the end of it just in time.

"What are *you* thinking?" she demanded. "Why on earth would you want to keep a nasty frog?"

I ignored her, following the length of filthy string into the bushes. Parting the branches, I scooped out a very dusty, very scared-looking, very beloved frog. "Poor guy," I said, lifting him up. There was a pink ribbon tied around his neck along with the string. "It's alright, Ron," I said as he stared up at me with traumatized golden eyes. "She probably didn't remember that you were a boy."

He croaked weakly.

"Hey, Cindy," I said, turning around. "We need to find some flies, fast. He most likely hasn't been fed in awhile."

Her face was pale. "Did I just hear you call that revolting little animal 'Ron'? As in *Ronald Charming*?"

Upon hearing himself described as a 'revolting little animal,' Ron closed his eyes.

"Hush," I said. "He's been through enough without you insulting him." I began to walk away. "We'd better get moving before they change their minds. I have found enchanters to be very fickle people. And keep an eye out for some flies or other bugs, will you? We need to get some food into him as soon as possible." Cinderella looked slightly green but she didn't say anything else as we made our way back to where the horse was tied.

While we traveled I caught a few insects and fed them to Ron. I heard a gagging sound behind me and turned to see Cinderella holding her stomach. "Please, if you're going to feed that thing, can you try to do it where I can't see you?"

I glared at her. "Don't call him 'that thing,' alright? His name is Ron and you know it. Try to have a little compassion here."

We journeyed the rest of the way down the mountain in silence. Cinderella rode the horse while I walked ahead on foot, carrying Ron. I led the way to the small meadow that I had gone through only days before with Ron and Connor. The sun was starting to set and I could tell that both of my companions were exhausted.

"I think that we ought to camp here for the night," I said. "The switchbacks are terrifying enough in the daytime."

"Camp?"

"Yeah, you know, sleep out under the stars? Build a fire? Tell ghost stories?"

"Ghost stories?" Cinderella's voice trembled.

"We'll skip the ghost stories. Let's go back to the forest before it gets dark and get some wood. Then we'll get as far away from the trees as we can, build up a nice, big fire and get some sleep."

"Why do we need to get as far away from the trees as we can?"

I hesitated. Obviously her journey here with Marv had been a lot easier than mine if she hadn't yet encountered the Maligios. "Because we don't want to start a forest fire, of course," I lied.

We carried as much wood as we could to our chosen campground. I wanted to have plenty of firelight in case the Maligios ventured out of the forest. Although Connor had told me that they were attracted to light, I couldn't help but want plenty of it to get me through the long night ahead.

And besides, maybe he was wrong. Aren't all animals afraid of fire?

Chapter 42

Setting up camp is easy when you don't have any supplies. Cinderella stacked the wood and I started the fire and tethered the horse where it would have plenty of grazing. After we ate there was nothing else to do. We sat staring into the fire, thinking our own private thoughts.

Cinderella's eyes kept straying over to where Ron lay sleeping in the grass, his arms and legs splayed out and his soft frog belly rising and falling with each breath. Swallowing hard, she whispered, "Is that really Ronald?"

"Yes."

"What happened?"

"He was trying to protect us from one of the enchanters and ended up getting turned into a frog." I gave her the details.

"He really is brave, isn't he?"

"Yes," I said. "He really is. I just hope that Marv will know what to do to restore him to his human self."

Cinderella looked away. "I already know what to do," she mumbled.

"You do?"

"Good grief, Maxine, don't you ever read?"

"Sure I do. I was reading this great book about exploration before I left--"

"That's not the kind of reading that I mean. Don't you know anything about being a princess, or about rescues and princes and spells?"

"Well...no. Not really. My mother forces me to go to those princess training courses, but I admit I don't pay much attention. I don't see the point in learning how to faint or sing like a nightingale."

Cinderella rolled her eyes. "Maybe if you had learned all of that then you would also know what needs to be done in this situation."

"Why don't you *tell* me what needs to be done?" I suggested, annoyed. "That way, instead of spending so much time fault-finding, we can restore Ron to his human self."

"It might not even work," Cinderella muttered. "It might only be a story."

"If I knew what it was I could at least offer my opinion."

She cleared her throat. "Well, see, there's a frog, and...and then there's a lady. And the lady has to... She has to..." Cinderella closed her eyes and swallowed. "The lady has to kiss the frog to turn him back into his true self."

I stared at her. "Kiss? As in *kiss*?"

"Yes."

"On the frog's actual *lips*?"

"Yes."

"Why?"

"What do you mean, why?"

"I mean, why would anyone have to *kiss* the frog to turn him back into his original self? I've heard of kissing to wake maidens who claim to be under a spell, but kissing amphibians? That's disgusting! Who comes up with these things?" I was genuinely horrified. It was one thing to kiss someone under a spell; after all, I had been close to kissing Connor not too long ago when he'd been lying unconscious in Amelia's castle, but kissing any animal, especially a frog, was wrong in so many ways.

"I don't know." Cinderella looked a little startled by my reaction.

"Can't we just tap the frog on the head three times or something tidy like that?"

"I think the spell calls for a kiss because kissing a frog is more of a sacrifice than tapping it on the head," said Cinderella. "It's showing that you care so much for the person that you're willing to do whatever it takes to help them, even if it's not something that you want to do."

In the bizarre world of princesses and spells, this actually made sense. "Alright, I could see that," I said. "But all grossness aside, what good will a measly kiss really do?"

She blinked. "Kisses aren't measly," she said. "Haven't you ever heard of Sleeping Beauty?"

"Sure. She was going to be my sister-in-law not too long ago. What's your point?"

"She was awakened from a powerful enchantment with a kiss." Cinderella sighed, clasping her hands in front of her and gazing dreamily into the fire.

I raised my eyebrows. "You're kidding me. You really believe that? She was *pretending* to be under an enchantment so that my doofus brother would 'rescue' her."

Cinderella glared at me. "What about Snow White? If she hadn't been kissed she'd still be lying in the glass case with that poisonous bit of apple lodged in her delicate throat."

I made a scoffing noise. "Sure she would. It's a good thing my brother has such magical lips, or we'd have unconscious damsels scattered around all over the place. Or maybe you should consider the fact that while he's been riding around kissing girls across the land, you've been crying into your mop bucket, believing in ridiculous fairy tales."

"You're being mean."

"Maybe I am. I just don't think that kissing a frog is going to accomplish anything. Pardon me for exercising a little logic."

She ground her teeth together. "It *would* work," she said. "It's probably the only thing that would."

"Fine. So kiss the little green guy if you're so convinced of it."

"I...can't."

"You've just been at me for the last five minutes trying to convince me that a magical kiss is our only solution. And now you're telling me that you can't? What's the problem?"

"What's the problem?" She looked at me incredulously. "He's a *frog*! He's been eating bugs all day! He's green and he's cold and he's got little suction cups on his fingertips. That's the problem!"

"Well, *I* can't kiss him," I said.

"It wouldn't work with you anyway," she snapped. "It has to be a kiss of true love."

"Doesn't it always?" We glared at each other. "Do it," I said.

"No."

"*Yes*. You kiss him or I'll..."

"You'll what?" she asked, jumping to her feet and putting her hands on her hips. "*Scream*?"

I couldn't think of a suitable threat.

She smirked at me. "That's what I thought. I'm going to bed." Flouncing over to where she'd spread her gown across the grass, she stretched out to sleep.

"Oh, that's *it*," I said. I walked towards her.

She scrambled to a sitting position. "Wait. Wait, Maxine," she said. "Don't do anything hasty, will you?"

"Too late for that," I said. Before she knew what I was about, I shoved one of Ron's leftover crickets between her lips and then held her mouth closed. "Good news, Cindy, now you won't have to worry about Ron being the only one with bug breath!"

Eyes wide, she screamed through her closed mouth, kicking until she managed to knock my legs out from under me. She spat the mangled cricket out, gagging a little. In the next instant she landed on me. It took me a minute to catch my breath and that was all the time Cinderella needed to find her own leftover cricket to shove into my mouth. The flat, bitter taste of it coated my tongue before I choked and accidentally swallowed it.

I grabbed her shoulders and twisted violently to the side, knocking her flat. "I've had it with you," I hissed, holding her down. "You don't deserve my brother. I'll find him a *real* princess who will love him enough to kiss him. Then they'll live happily ever after while you read your wretched books that won't do you any good because you're not brave enough to do as they instruct."

She stopped struggling and then, predictably, started to cry.

"You with the tears!" I let go of her and stomped over to the fire. "I've never met such a crybaby!"

She didn't answer. Her crying seemed different this time: quieter and somehow more profoundly sad. After a moment I took a deep breath. "I'm sorry," I muttered.

"You don't understand." She sat up and wiped her eyes.

"Yeah, I do. You're scared of frogs and their cold, green lips."

"It's not that." She stopped. "Well, it kind of is, but also, I just don't think…"

"What?"

"It's supposed to be a kiss of true love," she whispered.

"Right. So what's the problem?"

She flashed an irritated glance my way. "I don't think *my* kiss would help him. I don't think he'll turn back into himself. It's supposed to be a kiss of *true love*."

"You keep saying that. I thought you did love him."

"I do!"

I realized what she was trying to say. She didn't think that *Ron* loved *her*. And why would she? After all, hadn't he been the one to dump her and then turn around and get engaged to another girl the next instant?

"Oh," I said. "I get it."

"Took you long enough." She wiped the tears from her eyes. "Anyway, we should get some sleep--" Just then a large green frog landed on her knee and gazed up at her soulfully.

Chapter 43

Trust me, while I have never seen a frog look soulful before and certainly never expect to again, that's exactly how it was. Ron's golden eyes seemed to be trying to say all of the things that flowed from his heart: love, devotion, apology, and a whole lot of other feelings that would be hard to define, especially since I am not an expert in reading the emotions in a frog's eyes. I'm pretty sure that Cinderella figured them out; her expression softened and her own eyes filled with a gentle glow.

"Ronald," she whispered.

Feeling as though I was intruding, I took a step back, but there was nowhere to go. I froze as ever so slowly, Cinderella bent towards him. He tilted his head back. Her eyes closed. His lips puckered. He put one of his suction-cup-tipped fingers gently on her cheek and they kissed.

I'd forgotten that Ron had left behind a pile of clothes when Dominicus turned him into a frog. It came forcibly to memory now as Ron-as-a-human abruptly sprawled into view, wearing all that a frog generally wears.

Meaning: he was stark-naked.

"Aaaaaah," I screamed, thus shattering what was no doubt a very romantic moment. I snatched up Cinderella's gown and threw it over Ron just as Cinderella opened her eyes.

"Aaaaaah," yelled Ron as he realized his predicament. He scrambled to his feet and wound the gown around his waist. Cinderella alone seemed untroubled by his sudden appearance into nakedness. She gazed at him, obviously still enchanted by The Kiss of True Love, even though they had already kissed before, but whatever.

Ron finished securing the gown around his waist. Then he grasped Cinderella's hands and pulled her to her feet. "Cindy," he croaked. He cleared his throat. "Oh, Cindy, how I've missed you."

"Then why did you break our engagement?"

He looked down. "I was afraid. You were so genuine and amazing—none of the other girls were like you. They pretended to like everything that I liked, but you were just yourself. And you're the only girl who has ever taken the time to see the real me, and I was terrified that you wouldn't like what you saw. I didn't know how to handle it, so I ran. Can you ever forgive me?"

Her answer was to throw herself into his arms.

"Alright kids, break it up," I said. "Let's wait until Ron has had a chance to recover from being a frog."

"I feel fine," he said. A moth fluttered by and he eyed it hungrily.

"Sure. I can tell," I said. "But maybe we should get some sleep and then tomorrow we can get you some clothes--"

"Cindy, will you agree to be my betrothed? Again?"

She hesitated. "Ronald, I can't agree to marry you unless you promise to be done with these ridiculous quests. I need a commitment that won't end next week."

He got down on one knee, which in my opinion was a little risky given his current attire. "I swear to never go to the rescue of a damsel in distress again, unless said damsel is you. You are the woman of my dreams, and I hereby commit myself to you for the rest of my life."

It really would have been a touching scene if he had been properly dressed, but Cinderella seemed to find it everything that she had hoped for as she began to cry (no comment) and threw herself into his arms.

After I fashioned a relatively modest covering out of my cloak for Ron to wear around his waist (for the time being he was obliged to go shirtless), I threw some more wood on the fire and took first watch while they settled down to sleep.

I stared into the fire, thinking about everything that had happened. Nothing had gone at all like I'd expected. While my original quest to stop Ron from his endless rescues of princesses had been accomplished (thanks to Cinderella), now a whole new set of problems had cropped up in the form of Prince Torstein with his plans for an empire.

Sitting there in the flickering light of the fire, surrounded by an ocean of darkness, I found myself missing Connor desperately. I wondered where he was and if he were alright. And most of all, I wondered why he had left me behind.

It was close to midnight when I caught myself dozing off. In a few hours I could get Ron up to take his turn at keeping watch, but in the meantime I needed to stay alert in case the Maligios came. I fumbled in my bag, looking for something to help me wake up. My fingers brushed against the silver jug of never-ending water. Maybe a drink would help. I uncorked it and took a few sips.

I woke suddenly, my heart pounding as I tried to remember where I was. My cheek was pressed into the grass and I was cold and soaking wet. It took a minute of disoriented contemplation to realize what was wrong with the situation: *I was wet.*

I sat up and pushed my dripping hair from my eyes. I was sitting in a pool of water several inches deep. Sloshing around in the darkness, I determined that the pool extended around me on all sides. Where had it come from?

As the fog of sleep cleared from my mind, I noticed that I was clutching a small, hard object in my hand. The cork! I had forgotten to re-cork the silver jug of never-ending water. I splashed about me, trying to find the jug so I could plug it back up, but it was too dark to see.

Giving up on the search for the moment, I looked over to where Ron and Cinderella had settled down for the night. The fire had burned down to a glowing mound of coals and I couldn't see if they were still asleep.

"Ron?" My voice sounded overly loud in the predawn stillness. "Hey, Ron, wake up!"

Silence.

A prickling sense of unease made the hairs on the back of my neck stand up. The silence was as thick and heavy as the darkness around me. The last time I'd heard this void of sound was right before the Maligios showed up.

Sure enough, a few moments later I heard a dry rustling as small, wiry bodies began to make their way through the grass towards me. I struggled to not succumb to the debilitating fear that was roiling deep in my stomach. "Ron, *wake up*!" I hissed. "I need you! Ron! Cinderella!" Nothing moved in the area where they had been.

I got to my feet, realizing as I did so that I had been sleeping in a small depression in the ground. The water had pooled in the small hollow while everything around it was perfectly dry. I wrung water from my dripping hair and stepped out of the puddle.

Instantly one of the Maligios leapt through the air and landed on me, gripping my forearm with its sharp claws. I screamed and fell back into the water, adrenaline coursing through me as I waited for its teeth to sink into my flesh.

But it was gone. As quickly as it had appeared it vanished.

Had it jumped away? Was it lurking behind me? I splashed around in the water, searching for it, but it was no longer there. My heart was pounding as I came to my feet. I could hear them out there, sounding like they had lung problems, but for some reason none of the others tried to attack me. Didn't they know that they could easily bring me down; that there were more of them than of me? Why were they hesitating?

I stepped forward. Nothing happened. I took another step. Instantly there was a rush as four of the Maligios jumped on my arms and shoulders. They were hissing terribly, their breath rancid and foul, and their sharp claws dug into my skin. I couldn't seem to draw breath to scream again; all of my energy was devoted in trying to get them off of me. I managed to pull one away, but another three leapt into its place, jostling for room. Their weight caused me to stumble and I fell again, landing hard in the water.

One of the Maligios made an odd screaming sound which abruptly cut off. The remaining five were clinging to my shoulders and back, their malevolence thick around me. Then one of them sank its teeth into the curve where my throat and shoulder met. The pain was incredible; a searing, burning sensation like a thousand stings from a wasp contained in one small location. I yelled and pulled it away, holding it down so it couldn't bite me again.

As soon as its body touched the water it began to writhe and twist in my grasp. I realized with a jolt of horror that its arms and legs seemed to be shriveling away. Giving a cry of disgust I lifted my arm to throw it when the first rays of the morning sun broke over the horizon.

I stared at the creature in my hands, my mind spinning. What had just happened? I had been holding a monster one moment, and now I held a small, red and white striped snake.

The snake writhed in my hands, no longer interested in anything but freedom. I tossed it into the grass and watched as it slithered away. Had Regina formed her army of monsters by enchanting ordinary animals? And was water somehow the key in restoring them to their natural forms?

Eager to see what would happen to the other Maligios when exposed to water, I grabbed one of the monsters clinging to my shoulders, no longer troubled by the feel of its wiry, dry-skinned little body. As soon as it touched the water, its form shifted and altered, reverting finally into a large rat. Experiments on the rest of the monsters clinging to me resulted similarly, with the Maligios returning to their original forms as a variety of small animals.

Without hesitation I stepped out of the water. I didn't have to wait long for five more Maligios to jump hissing through the air and land on me. I tossed them into the water and watched as small animals crept back out, wet but unharmed.

In spite of their cunning, the Maligios weren't very intelligent. They knew to avoid the water, but they weren't able to use any reasoning powers as to why they should avoid it. They sat and watched me plunge their kind into the water, but as soon as I stepped out onto dry land, more of them immediately jumped onto me. Once restored to their natural bodies, they lost their uncanny, evil aggression and became again wild animals, intent only on escape.

The silver jug continued to faithfully spill more and more water so that my little pool was undiminished by all of the splashing. I kept sloshing back and forth, carrying the Maligios in and watching the animals crawl back out. My shoulder throbbed at first where I'd been bitten, but after awhile I couldn't feel it anymore. There comes a point in moments of desperate necessity where you do what you have to do beyond your physical strength. There is a place deep inside your mind that makes sure you don't give up until the necessary work is done. Only then can you collapse.

The monsters waiting on the bank of my little pool slowly dwindled in number from several hundred to a small handful. A few more bit me as I worked and I was covered in scratches from their sharp claws, but I kept going, destroying my aunt's self-made army a few at a time.

I staggered from the pool one last time and waited while the remaining monsters jumped onto me, hissing and aggressive and totally oblivious to their fate. In my exhaustion I stumbled and fell into the water. I felt the monsters melt away from me but I hardly cared. Lifting my head onto a rise in the grass, I drifted into unconsciousness.

Chapter 44

"Maxine? Max, please, wake up." The note of concern in the voice addressing me penetrated the thick shroud of exhaustion enveloping my brain. I opened my eyes. I was lying on a bed in a large, well-lit room. Judging from the light spilling through the multi-paned windows, it was still morning. A group of people stood around my bed, their faces a jumble of features that I couldn't seem to sort out.

I wasn't sure how they'd managed to get me to this comfortable bed so quickly, but it struck me as rather inconsiderate that they were already trying to wake me up. I had worked hard all morning destroying Regina's monsters; you'd think they would at least let me sleep a little longer.

"How do you feel?" One of the faces on my left allowed its features to merge into a recognizable identity.

"How do you think I feel, Marv?" I asked. My voice sounded hoarse and rough, as though it had been rusting in the rain for weeks. I cleared my throat. "I've been fighting off the Maligios all morning long. So why don't you all run along and let me sleep?"

"But you've been sleeping for days!" Cinderella stood next to Marv, looking fresh and lovely in the morning sunlight. I could only imagine how I looked in comparison.

"And where were you?" I demanded grouchily, prompting Ron to put a protective arm around her shoulders. "I really could've used your help, you know."

"The Maligios carried us away while we were sleeping," she said. "Marvelonius thinks that they put some kind of sleeping spell on us. We didn't wake up until we were too far away to warn you and by then we couldn't get away because there were too many of them."

"We kept expecting the little beasts to bring you along too," said Ron. "But instead more and more of them left until after awhile even the ones guarding us went away. So we came back and found you lying in a pool of water, covered with scratches." He paused. "The weird part is that even though the footprints of the monsters were everywhere, there's no trace of them. They seem to have disappeared entirely."

Marv leaned forward. "What happened out there, Max? What did you do?"

"Maybe we should ask her these questions later," said a voice on my right. "She needs to eat and then rest a bit more."

It was Connor. He sat in a chair pulled up close to the other side of my bed, watching me with open concern. His hand was resting on the covers near my own and I wished I were brave enough to reach out and hold it. "Connor," I said, feeling so glad to see him that if I were Cinderella I would have started crying. "How did you get here so quickly?"

"I don't know about quickly," he said, looking amused. "You've been here for over a week, sleeping the entire time."

"But-" I tried to push myself into a sitting position when a searing pain ran from my shoulder down into my arm. I gasped and collapsed back against the pillows.

"Max!" Connor stood up and grabbed my hand. I would have smiled if I hadn't been hurting so badly. As it was, I waited for the dizziness to pass.

"She'll be fine. The danger is over." Marv looked down at me. "You've been very sick, Maxine. You sustained several deep bite wounds, the most serious ones being on your neck and your lower leg. The Maligios had some kind of venom in their bite. Or at least, some of the wounds looked like they were administered with venom; others were merely bite marks."

I nodded. "That's because some of them were snakes," I said. "Poisonous ones." I felt a deep weariness seeping up inside of me. All I wanted to do was go back to sleep.

"What do you mean, some of them were snakes?" asked Marv. "I thought you were dealing with the Maligios."

"I was. And some were snakes, some were lizards, and some were rats. There was even a fox. It bit my hand." I waved my hand in the air and noticed distantly that it was covered in a thick white bandage. The effort of all of this talking was exhausting me and I wondered when they were going to leave. Except for Connor. He could stay.

"So there were animals attacking you as well as the monsters?"

"No," I said. I felt too tired to explain, but I tried one last time. "The monsters *were* the animals."

I heard their voices through a haze. "She's fading out again, obviously a bit delirious. But she's going to be fine."

"Thank goodness."

When I next awoke, it was dark outside. Connor lay sleeping with his face pillowed in the blankets beside me and I wondered how long he had been there. I reached out tentatively and put my fingers in his hair. It was good to know that he was here, and safe. I had been worried about him.

Then my fingers moved to my own hair. I was immediately horrified. By feel alone I could tell that it was going every which way. I doubtless looked awful.

It's a clear sign that you're feeling better when you have a return of vanity.

I moved to slip off the bed as quietly as possible. I didn't want Connor to see me like this. Or rather, given that he obviously already had, I didn't want to see him seeing me like this.

His voice stopped me. "Where do you think you're going?"

"Um…out?"

Connor looked at me closely. "Are you alright?" he asked. I could tell from the shadows under his eyes that he hadn't had a good night's sleep in a long time.

I nodded, biting my lip.

"Then what's the matter?"

I looked down at my hands, resisting the urge to smooth my hair. "I need a bath," I blurted.

He laughed. "I'll let someone know." He leaned in abruptly and kissed me on the cheek. "I'm so glad that you're safe, Max."

He left, closing the door behind him and I put my hand against my cheek where he had kissed me. I felt torn between hope and doubt. There was no mistaking his genuine relief at seeing me alive and well, but were there deeper feelings than those of a concerned friend? And if he did have feelings for me, why would he ride off with his mysterious rescuers and leave me behind with another man? Thoughts like these kept my mind busy while the servants helped me bathe and dress. The effort of moving around took more out of me than I expected and I collapsed into a chair by the window and watched as the sun slowly rose into the sky.

There was a knock at my door and then Connor poked his head in. "You should be in bed," he said sternly, shaking a finger at me.

"Actually, I'm pretty sure I should be sitting in this chair." I retorted, and grinned up at him. "Where am I, anyway?"

"We're back in Denitri." He settled into the chair beside me.

I looked at him with alarm. "Denitri? But what about Prince Jaspien?"

A new voice chimed in. "This isn't Jaspien's castle, nor is Denitri his kingdom." Marv stood in the open doorway. "And he won't be returning, not if he knows what's good for him."

"What do you mean this isn't his castle?" I asked.

Marv walked into the room and looked out the window, clasping his hands behind him. "Jaspien launched a surprise attack on Denitri six months ago and King Charles barely escaped into the forest with his people. Since then Jaspien and his men have been living here, turning what was once a beautiful kingdom into a slovenly pit."

"Who in dragon's scales is King Charles?"

"We met him not too long ago," said Connor. "He's the one who kept an eye on your motorcycle for you, remember?"

My mouth fell open. "You mean *Charlie*? The guy who was there that night we escaped?"

"Yes."

"He's a *king*?"

"Yes."

"Wow. Seems like everybody has a secret identity these days." I slanted a pointed look at Connor and he looked away.

Marv winked at me. "Luckily for King Charles, about two weeks ago a small group of travelers somehow immobilized Jaspien and his men by causing them to remain as though frozen in place for days. This enabled Charles to recover his kingdom without shooting an arrow or bloodying a single blade. And even though Jaspien later managed to escape, overall things worked out quite nicely."

"What a lovely story," I said smugly. "Those travelers must have been pretty amazing people."

"Or arrogant," said Connor. "And if there's one thing I can't stand, it's arrogance."

"You're just jealous because your fairy godmother didn't give you any powers."

"I don't have a fairy godmother," he said. "And even if I did, I wouldn't want an ability like yours. Seeing the havoc you wreak with it is enough to convince me that fairy gifts of any kind ought to be strictly avoided."

"That's a bold thing to say, Connor," said Marv with a sly grin. "Particularly since you use *your* gift quite frequently."

Chapter 45

Connor shot a dark look at the wizard. "Be quiet, Marv."

"Wait a minute." I sat up straighter in my chair. "Connor's got a gift too?"

"Don't tell her *anything*," growled Connor.

"This is amazing." I looked back and forth between Connor and Marv. "I didn't even know that boys *had* fairy godmothers."

"They don't have fairy godmothers," said Marv, smirking.

"I don't get it," I said. "What else would they have? Fairy god*fathers*?"

"More or less," Marv said. "Only, please omit the word 'fairy.' We godfathers do not like the term 'fairy' as it implies a fluttery, grandmotherly type with wings and glitter and sugary sweetness." He shuddered. "'Godfather' goes alone. It's more rugged that way."

"*We godfathers*?" I asked, staring at him. "*You're* a godfather?"

Connor groaned and put his head in his hands. "Marv, please stop talking?" he asked, his voice muffled.

"Yes, I am Connor's godfather," said Marv, ignoring Connor and puffing out his chest a little. "You just don't hear about godfathers as often as godmothers since we tend to be a bit more modest about our work."

That was debatable. I didn't say this, of course. I didn't want to antagonize my informant. "So what gift did Connor's rugged, modest godfather give him?" I asked.

"One would think that you'd be able to guess," said Marv, ignoring the glare Connor was aiming at him.

"Wait. You mean...do you mean when Connor was *Jack*?"

"Precisely."

"Incredible." I leaned back in my chair. "So the *mask* is Connor's fairy--" Marv cleared his throat and I amended, "I mean *rugged* godfather gift? How does it work?"

"Ah, well." Marv looked pleased by my interest. "His mask is a visual enchantment that he can use whenever he wants, and he can adjust his features to whatever he wants others to see. For you, as I understand it, he made himself look particularly unappealing." He grinned. "I hear you let him know in no uncertain terms how unsightly you found him."

I blushed. "Well, he was really ugly. Or I mean, his mask was."

"Do you realize that you are the first person who, without the aid of magic, recognized that he was wearing a mask?" It was obvious that Marv thought that this was significant. "You are also the only person who saw past his mask to the true face underneath, which of course--"

"That's enough!" We both jumped at Connor's sharp tone. "Marv, will you please stop rambling? We have a lot of things to discuss."

Marv looked at Connor with a strange gleam in his eyes. He seemed awfully pleased about something. "Of course. What should we start with?"

"Let's talk about why Connor wore his fancy mask around me instead of just being himself," I suggested.

"That's not important," said Connor.

"It is to me."

He rolled his eyes. "*Fine.* I wore my mask because I'm told that I resemble my late father a great deal. Until I am restored to my kingdom, it's extremely dangerous for me to go outside of the Charming kingdoms looking like myself."

"Yeah, but Marv just said that you can adjust your features to whatever you want other people to see. And remember how Ron saw a totally different face than I did? Why couldn't you just let me see your real face and disguise it from everyone else?"

"Because—" began Marv, the strange gleam still present in his eyes.

"*Because* I didn't want to put your life in danger," interrupted Connor. "If you had fallen into the wrong hands, it was better for you to not know who I was."

I shook my head. It was obvious that there was another reason, one that didn't have as many holes in it. I decided to pursue a slightly different topic for the time being. "Do you wear your mask only when you travel?" I asked.

He looked relieved by the change of subject. "Around certain people I wear it all the time. For example, your Aunt Regina has never seen my real face, even when I was a child. You can't trust somebody that evil."

"What about when she saw you in the forest the other day? Was she seeing the face she'd always seen on you or a different one?"

"She was seeing Jack's face then."

I would never have been able to keep track of what faces I was supposed to wear around what people. "So how many people have seen your real face?"

He shifted impatiently. "Queen Marge, Marv and you. Oh, and my parents, and people who knew me when I was a baby. That's it. Are you about done with the questions?"

"Not even close." I leaned back in my chair and folded my arms. "Now I need to know why you abandoned me and rode off with your mysterious rescuers."

Connor looked away. "I didn't want to, but that's how it ended up. Anyway, I figured that you'd be safe with your fiancé."

"You could have at least given me a choice in the matter," I said.

"I was sort of in a hurry at the time. Besides, as I remember it you were having a cozy little chat with your sweetheart. I didn't want to spoil the romance with escape plans."

Was he jealous? It was an intriguing thought.

"Connor's life was in peril," said Marv. "Yours was not. And he didn't have a lot of time when his rescuers showed up."

I directed my attention at the wizard. "As for you, why on earth did you haul Cinderella all the way out here?"

He raised an eyebrow at me. "I had a feeling that she would prove useful. Didn't she?"

"Well, yeah, but she was kind of a pain in the neck, too," I said.

Connor looked amused. "From what we hear, you were busy shoving crickets down her throat. So maybe *you* were a pain in *her* neck."

She'd told them about that? What a snitch.

Marv took advantage of the lull in the conversation. "Maxine, what happened out there? Where did all of the Maligios go? There were hundreds of them attacking our men and carrying them off. Swords and arrows did nothing to lower their numbers and yet in one morning, you seem to have wiped out nearly every trace of them."

I told them what had happened that night. "So all of the monsters my aunt created must have originally been wild animals," I concluded. "Somehow water restored them to themselves."

"That would explain the unusual number of snakes and rats that the villagers have been reporting," Connor said.

Marv nodded. "It also explains why some of Maxine's wounds were life-threatening," he said. "The creatures who were poisonous as animals were also poisonous as monsters. It's a wonder she lived."

"But how did you get them all into the water?" asked Connor.

"I carried them." They stared at me. "It's not that big of a deal," I muttered.

"Yes, it is," said Connor. "Those monsters were killing people. Now that we know about the water, we won't have to worry even if Regina creates more of them."

"I only found out about the water by accident," I said.

"And you acted on it," said Marv. "You may have saved our cause by that display of courage."

Chapter 46

Aunt Marge arrived at the castle the next day. She made it clear the moment she walked in the door that her new life's mission was to force me to stay in bed and eat broth. Unfortunately for her, I was sick and tired of being treated like I was sick and tired and I made it *my* new life's mission to thwart her efforts.

I didn't see Connor, Ron or Marv much because they were working with King Charles on their plans for the upcoming war. Whenever I tried to join them they sent me away with a variety of ridiculous reasons, the main one being that I wasn't fully recovered from my illness. Naturally this only strengthened my determination to know what was going on. I resorted to listening at doors and interviewing the servants and soldiers alike.

I also kept busy mapping King Charles' castle, which was a large and ancient structure full of passages and rooms whose existence no one remembered. My luckiest discovery came early one morning about a week after my recovery. I'd been exploring a back stairway when I noticed that there was a landing halfway down that was much narrower than the other landings. This indicated a possible passageway.

I spent awhile poking and prodding before I finally found what I was looking for: a small knob disguised as a part of the stone wall. When I pushed the knob a door swung outward a few inches. The stone of this door looked identical to that of the wall around it, but it seemed to be made of a different material, light enough for me to pull it open without much effort.

I lit the candle that I kept on hand for just such situations and slipped into a room about the size of a linen closet. There were no passageways or shelves, and the only thing of interest was that the inside of the door had a thick metal handle designed for pulling the door closed.

Then I noticed a faint beam of light shining through a narrow gap in the stones on the far wall. I put my eye against the opening and realized with a jolt of surprise that I was looking down into the very room that King Charles and the others used to discuss their war plans.

Marv and Ron entered as I watched and seated themselves at a table strewn with papers and maps. Marv was sorting through a stack of letters while Ron picked up a map. Ron's eyes were back to their natural blue and he had assured me that he would not be changing his appearance anymore. I hoped that he meant it.

"We've received word from your father that the armies of Veiland are ready," said Marv, looking up from the letter he held.

"Good," said Ron. "Do you know, in all of those years of watching my father in his war room, I never actually thought that he knew what he was doing."

"No one did. It must have been a nasty surprise for Regina and Alex. I think that they were counting on Veiland being an easy conquest."

I bit my lip. Who in the name of trolls was Alex?

"Sorry to disappoint them," muttered Ron. The room fell silent as they both applied themselves to their separate occupations.

"Connor should be here any minute," said Marv after a moment.

"Is Charles coming?"

"No, he had to go to the northern border. They found a small number of Regina's monsters there, but that should easily be resolved." Marv put the letter down and rubbed his chin thoughtfully. "You know, we're lucky that Maxine discovered the solution to the Maligios when she did. They were one of Regina's strongest weapons against us for this new empire they're hoping to build. With the threat of the Maligios handled, we actually stand a chance. Not to mention Max's little trick of whistling that aided King Charles in regaining his kingdom."

"Yes, about that—what would you think to having her whistle at the enemy army? If we were to freeze them all then we could--"

"Won't work. Now that they know about Max's gift, they'll be sure to outfit their men with some kind of spell that will leave them unaffected by it."

"I suppose you're right." Ron sighed. "What's taking Connor? He was supposed to be here by now."

The door opened. "Sorry I'm late. Has anyone seen Maxine?"

"You may as well give up on trying to keep track of that girl, Con," said Marv. "Not only has she charmed all of the castle staff and gained the loyalties of every one of Charles' soldiers, she has also taken to sneaking out on her bike to discuss battle strategies with his captains. I suppose you've heard about that."

Connor tried to suppress a grin. "Yes, well, some of the ideas that she's given them aren't half bad."

"That being the case, maybe we ought to invite her to our meetings," suggested Ron. "That way we can spare her the trouble of listening at the door."

My eyes widened. They knew about that?

"Yes, but she does seem to enjoy pulling one over on us." Marv paused. "Is she out there now?"

"No," said Connor. "I have Oswald watching the doors. If she comes, he's to stick his head in and tell us that the shipment of arrows have arrived from Veiland."

I *knew* I couldn't trust that sneaky Oswald.

"Good. So we may speak freely for now at least," said Marv. They began discussing details of the various methods of war that they would be employing. I was growing a bit bored when Ron said something that got my complete attention. "When are we going to reveal your true identity to your people, Connor?"

"I don't know. There are some of my people who even now are unaware that the throne has been usurped. If they hear that I, an obscure ward of Queen Margaret, claim to be the true prince of Treagal--"

I gasped.

Immediately the trio below froze. Marv got up and went to the door. "Oswald?"

"Yes, sir?"

"Have you seen the shipment of arrows yet?"

"No, sir. There has been no sign of it."

"Thank you." He closed the door. It was fortunate for me that at that moment a gust of wind blew against the windows of the castle.

"I think that we're getting a little jumpy when we hear the wind and immediately think that somehow Max has infiltrated our private meetings," said Ron. There was a short silence as the wind continued to throw itself at the panes of glass.

"Still, it wouldn't hurt..." said Connor. They got up and began to look everywhere a girl my size could be hiding.

I hardly paid attention to their futile search. My mind was still reeling with the information that Connor was Prince Torstein. I had known, of course, that he was a prince whose throne had been usurped, but all along I'd assumed that his kingdom was one of the far-reaching ones that I hardly knew anything about. I shook my head and forced myself to concentrate as the conversation below me continued.

"It must have been the wind," said Marv. "Remind me why we don't want her to know about you yet?"

"Because I don't know how she would react," said Connor. "When she finds out that I'm the one she's actually betrothed to, she might agree to marry me only because she doesn't want to hurt my feelings. Plus, she really seems to like Alex. What if she's disappointed that she can't marry him after all?"

"Don't be ridiculous," Ron said. "How can you think that she likes that insincere, pompous idiot?"

"You didn't see her in the forest. She was so relieved to see him—she latched onto him like he was her true hero. And I--" He looked down. "All I did was let myself get tied up again."

"Well, there is the matter of the gift I bestowed upon you at your birth," said Marv. "You remember how I promised that your kingdom would be restored to you only after a princess saw past your enchanted disguise to the true face underneath?"

"How could I remember that," growled Connor. "I was a baby at the time."

Marv gave him a reproving look. "And I've reminded you of it every day since, as you know very well. I also promised you that this princess would hold your heart—"

"Look," snapped Connor. "Just because you meant for your little spell to ensure a happily ever after for me doesn't mean it's guaranteed to work. And I don't want to discuss it any further."

There was a slightly awkward pause. Ron cleared his throat. "Why don't we go over our strategies for the western front?"

They resumed their previous discussion but I was no longer interested. I closed the door to the secret room and went back upstairs in a daze.

Chapter 47

"There you are," Aunt Marge exclaimed. She stood outside my bedroom door. "I've been looking everywhere for you."

I pushed past her without answering and sat in my chair by the window.

"Max? What's the matter?"

"Why didn't you tell me, Marge?"

She joined me by the window. "You might need to be more specific."

"I just found out that your adopted ward, whom I knew as Connor, is really Prince Torstein. Why didn't you tell me?"

Aunt Marge looked down at her hands. "I see," she said slowly, twisting a ring on one of her fingers. "I think it is time that you hear the story about how Connor came into my life." She paused as though to collect her thoughts and then began.

"Twelve years ago, I was a nineteen-year-old beauty: spoiled, self-centered and overly confident in my life as a queen. As you know, I became queen at quite a young age. I thought I knew everything.

"Late one stormy night—aren't they always stormy?—after I had only just returned from a travel abroad, a knock came at the castle door. One of my trusted servants answered it while I stood at the top of the stairs, out of sight.

"A man stood on my doorstep holding the hand of a small boy. He asked my servant if he could speak with me. My servant, per my prearranged instructions--for I had many suitors who came day and night and pestered me no end-- told the man that I was away and that it was not known when I would return.

"The man was obviously disappointed. He turned back out into the rainy night, leading the little boy. There was something about them that touched my selfish young heart. I stepped to the foot of the stairs and told the servant to tell the man that I was Queen Margaret's lady-in-waiting and that I had authorized that they be let in. The servant did as I ordered and the man and the boy were brought into the hall, where they stood dripping all over my carpets. I studied them carefully. The man was young, I would guess only a few years older than I, and the boy I judged to be about five or six.

"'Who are you and why have you come?' I asked.

"The man looked at me with the most penetrating eyes, and for a moment I feared that he knew who I was. But he merely said, 'I have come from Treagal and I have a favor to ask your queen. Do you know when she will be returning?'

"'No, I do not,' I answered. 'It is not my place to know the plans of my queen. What is your business with her?'

"'If it is not your place to know Queen Margaret's plans,' the man observed with infuriating insolence—or so I thought at the time, 'Then it is not your place to know my business with her.'

"I felt such anger then! No one had ever spoken that way to me in my entire life. I was about to order them back out into the night when the little boy sneezed. I noticed then that he was shivering. He was adorable, with dark, curling hair and enormous brown eyes. I forgot about the impudence of the man in my concern for the child.

"I brought the boy up to my sitting room where I had a fire burning and ordered my maid to bring me towels. I proceeded to dry the boy while ignoring the dripping stranger, who had followed us.

"Finally I asked, 'What do you mean by taking this poor child out into such weather?'

"Ignoring my question, the man said, 'It has been said that in spite of her cold manners, the queen has a warm heart.' Startled, I looked up at him and saw that he was watching me with an amused look in his eyes. He continued. 'My Queen, I would request your kindness in hearing me out.'

"The man proceeded to tell me a story of murder and intrigue. The boy's parents had been poisoned several years ago and the murderer, a chancellor named Roger Dublin, had been methodically putting to death all of those who would recognize the boy as the heir to the throne while hiring new servants who would be loyal to him in his scheming. At last only one servant remained, and he had been kept alive due to his prowess as a wizard and his declarations of loyalty to the chancellor.

"Of course this wizard was Marvelonius, only in those days he was known as Marvin Trenton. He explained that it had become too dangerous for the boy to remain at Treagal. Marvin had heard of me and thought that I might be his best option.

"By this time the young prince of Treagal was asleep on my couch. My heart swelled with sympathy for him as he lay there, so pale and small, and when Marvelonius requested that I adopt the boy, I agreed without hesitation. We decided that I would claim him as an orphaned ward from my travels abroad. With me the child would receive the upbringing that he needed to rule his own kingdom one day. Marvin hoped to find employment somewhere nearby under an assumed name and identity. In that way he would be able to provide protection and additional guidance in raising Connor.

"It was at this time that Marvelonius revealed that he was also the young prince's godfather. He explained that the child had been given the rather unusual gift of being able to wear a visual enchantment to conceal his identity from others as he chose. This ability of Connor's, which very few know about, saved his life by giving him the ability to disguise his true looks from his enemies.

"Chancellor Dublin was enraged over the disappearance of the true prince, yet he played the situation to his advantage in every possible way. He introduced his own son, Alex, to the visiting dignitaries as Prince Torstein. He sent out spies in efforts to locate Connor even while he planned to murder him if he were ever found.

"As the years went by, rumors surfaced time and again that a switch had taken place, and the wavering loyalties of the people caused the chancellor a great deal of trouble. The people were weary of his tyrannical rule and knew that they could hope for little better when the purported Prince of Treagal assumed the throne. They hoped that the true prince would come to rescue them from the tyranny and oppression that had been their lot for too many years.

"When Chancellor Dublin passed away, he left as his legacy a cruel and despotic young man with designs to build an empire. Alex was assisted in his endeavors by one of his father's good friends, Queen Regina, who promised him her loyalty and assistance in exchange for the opportunity to rule her husband's kingdom in her own name." Aunt Marge stopped. She was staring out the window as though gazing on the past. Then she shook her head and sighed. "Anyway, that's everything."

"So Alex knows that he's an impostor," I said.

"Yes, and he's recently received word confirming that the true Prince of Treagal is alive. This, among other things, is what prompted him to seek to marry you so abruptly. If he became your husband, even if he were revealed as a commoner, he would still have ties to a royal family. Furthermore, plans were laid to murder Ron, which would have made Alex the future king of Veiland. What Alex did not plan for was your intelligence and ability to think for yourself. If it had been any other princess, she would have already been married to him and a puppet in his hands."

"Why didn't you tell me all of this before?" I demanded. "What if I had gone along with things and ended up marrying him?"

Aunt Marge laughed. "Maxine, I've known you your whole life. I have every confidence in the world that the only way you will marry someone is if you want to. And it was obvious that you didn't want anything to do with the false Prince Torstein. Then when you showed such stubborn determination to follow your brother on his latest quest, we decided that it might be the safest course for you. Knowing your propensity for getting into trouble, we sent Connor to accompany you. We felt that it would be safer for the three of you to face unknown perils than to be home in the company of Regina and Alex."

I was not pacified. "*Safer*? Did you know I was almost eaten by a sea serpent?" I shook my head. "In the future, please credit me with a little intelligence and let me in on things from the start."

To my surprise, she nodded. "I agree with you that it would have been better all around if everyone had known what they were facing, but as it is things have worked out better than we had hoped. For example, your father has turned out to be one of our unexpected strengths. Certainly no one, especially Alex, thought that your father would be capable of organizing his armies so quickly and effectively. Imagine their dismay when they discovered that he was more than ready to fight off an invasion.

"In fact," she continued, "Regina and Alex have been receiving blow after blow in their efforts to gain an empire." Aunt Marge leaned forward, her eyes sparkling. "Marv had a few trustworthy spies who kept him well-informed as to the activities of Alex Dublin. Assassins have been sent multiple times to murder Prince Charming, but Marv kept Ron well-informed of various princesses in need of rescuing. Ron would leave only days before the assassins came and be safe even as he was out battling dragons and rescuing fair maidens."

I stared at Aunt Marge in amazement. "That's why Marv instigated Ron's travels? To keep him out of the way of killers?"

She nodded. "That's also why he gave Ron the idea to change the color of his eyes and hair. While Ron was doing it to please the princesses, it also served as a disguise. In the meantime, Marv traveled the country in various disguises of his own, encouraging the rumors that were already thriving that the man claiming to be the prince of Treagal was an impostor and that the true prince would soon be coming to claim his kingdom. The people of Treagal, as a whole, were more than ready to receive this news. Alex was not proving himself to be a very wise or kind ruler."

I thought of something else. "Has Connor, or I mean, has Prince Torstein--"

"It would be safer for you to continue to address him as Connor," Aunt Marge said. "At least until he assumes the throne."

"Well, has he always known that he is the prince of Treagal?"

"Yes. He came to my home when he was five and he remembers his life before surprisingly well. In addition, I have never attempted to hide anything from him."

"I wish you had done the same for me," I muttered.

Aunt Marge looked at me reprovingly. "Maxine, we've never been sure if Connor would even be able to claim his throne. We knew there was a chance that he would have to find a new path to follow. His future was undecided and dangerous and we decided that the less anyone knew the better."

She could give me all the logical reasons she wanted, but I still felt that they should have told me.

I pondered what else I wanted to know. "Wait, who is Prince Jaspien, then?" I asked. "Alex said he was his stepbrother."

"Prince Jaspien is actually Alex's real brother. Chancellor Dublin intended for both of his sons to gain power and raised them to build an empire."

I had another question ready for her. "So you said that Marvelonius used to work for the Kingdom of Treagal?" I asked.

Aunt Marge nodded.

"Well, Alex saw Marv at the engagement ball not that long ago. Don't you think he would have recognized him as their old wizard?"

"Probably not," Aunt Marge said. "You forget that Alex was only five when Marvelonius left. And no doubt Marv has a few of his own enchantments in place to prevent his being recognized by any of his old acquaintances."

I leaned back in my chair, thinking fast. The way everyone was planning it, we would soon be in the middle of a terrible, bloody war. Yet from the sound of things, the majority of the people of Treagal were in support of Connor as their true ruler. It didn't make sense to have men who were essentially on the same side fighting against each other. If things were going to work out for the best, I realized that I would have to take control. And that meant handling things very carefully in the present moment.

"This is a lot to take in," I said. "And I really don't feel all that well. I'm going to get some sleep, if you don't mind." It was easy to give the appearance of exhaustion since I still looked thin and pale. If I had looked like my usual healthy self, Aunt Marge would have immediately suspected that I was up to something.

"I'm glad to see that you're finally going to give your body a chance to rest," she said. "Rest is vital to achieving a full recovery."

I nodded meekly and climbed into my bed fully clothed, pausing to kick off my shoes even though I would be putting them back on again in five minutes. I could tell that Aunt Marge wanted to say something about me getting into bed without putting on my nightgown but she didn't. She turned to leave and then stopped and turned back. "I forgot—the reason I came was to bring you a letter from your parents." She handed it to me. "Sleep well, Maxine."

I pulled the covers up to my chin and watched Aunt Marge close the door behind her. Feeling a little guilty for the deception I had just played on my aunt, I read the letter from my parents. It was full of apologies (for betrothing me to a power-hungry man) and concern (because of the power-hungry man's hunger for power). Apparently my parents didn't know yet about the whole Connor/Alex switch.

Setting the letter aside, I nestled under the covers and waited. Sure enough, the door to my room opened as someone, probably Aunt Marge, stood there watching as though to make sure that I really was asleep. I made my breathing as even as possible and finally the door closed.

I waited a moment longer before throwing back the covers. I would be long gone before anyone came to check on me again.

Chapter 48

"Every time I turn around, you're trying to sneak off somewhere."

I whirled around. Connor stood in the doorway to the stables with his hands on his hips. "Where are you going this time?"

I turned back to finish tying my traveling bag onto the back of my bike. "If you must know, I'm going to see the enchanters."

He overreacted, as I'd known he would. I waited while he stomped around shouting and waving his hands over his head. "Why?" he finally demanded. "Why on earth do you want to go see those evil people?"

"I think that they can help us."

"How? By making things worse?"

"Maybe, if it's to our advantage."

"Max, don't you realize that your betrothed is out there looking for you? What if he finds you?"

I narrowed my eyes. "Correct me if I'm wrong," I said, "but I'm pretty sure that my *betrothed* already knows where I am."

He stopped pacing and looked at me. "What do you mean?"

"I just had a nice long conversation with Aunt Marge."

His expression grew wary. "What did she tell you?"

"Well, I know that you're Prince Torstein, if that's what you're wondering." Connor's face clearly reflected his dismay. I continued. "She told me the whole story about how you came to be her ward, and about Alexander Dublin and Marv and everything." I shook my head. "All of which are things that *you* should've told me a long time ago."

"I couldn't tell you. It wasn't safe."

"I'd rather know the truth than be safe," I said. "In the meantime, I'm tired of sitting around while you and the boys sit in your war room and scheme. I'm going to take care of things before they escalate out of control." I got on my bike and revved it up.

"Max, wait." Connor hesitated. "Let me come with you."

"Are you serious?"

"Yes. I trust you. And while past experience has taught me that you're not the best planner, you have good instincts. Let me come with you in case you need help."

I thought about it. "Alright. But I'm driving."

"I expected that." He waved his arm and a soldier stepped into the stables. Connor took a scrap of paper and a small pencil out of his pocket and scribbled something on the paper. "Please give this to the Wizard Marvelonius."

"Yes, sir." The soldier left.

"Well, Maxine," Connor grinned. "I hope you know what you're doing."

"Of course I don't. That's half the fun."

An hour later, we roared up to the base of the switchbacks. "We should leave the bike here," said Connor. "There's no way we'll make it up that mountain on it."

We parked the bike behind a stand of bushes and were preparing to begin the ascent on foot when the Troll King appeared in front of us, his orange eyes sparkling. Even though I'd been half-expecting him, his sudden appearance about gave me a heart attack. "You scared the dragon snot out of me," I gasped. "Would you mind just walking up to us next time? You know, like ordinary people do?"

"But it is much more entertaining this way," the Troll King said. "Personally, I love a good surprise."

"Maybe you do, but I'd prefer to not have my heart give out at my tender age."

His lips twitched. "That would be a tragedy. I'll keep that in mind the next time I decide to say hello." He looked at Connor. "And how fares it for you? Have you yet obtained what you seek?"

"It's a work in progress," said Connor, not meeting my eyes.

"I see. And today, instead of traveling to rescue a princess, you travel to rescue kingdoms, is that right?"

Where did this guy get his information?

"I know many things," the Troll King said, glancing at me. "It can be a burden to have so much knowledge, especially when those whom I could assist refuse to heed my words. It pleased me greatly when you followed my advice on your quest to rescue Princess Golden."

"We did?" I asked. "When?"

"You looked to see the heart underneath the professions of evil when you saved the life of the enchanter Bruce. And you recognized that it was not Queen Amelia or her daughter that needed rescuing, but her people. These things proved your willingness to listen to my counsel. Remember this: the souls of men are in constant turmoil. Few are perfectly evil, or perfectly good. You must be wary of making both condemnations or commendations."

"That sounds a lot like the advice you gave us last time," said Connor.

The Troll King's laughter sounded like rocks tumbling down a mountainside. "That's because it *is* a lot like the advice that I gave you last time. But there is one key difference in my advice to you now, so heed it well." He paused, watching us with his glowing eyes, and then said, "You may not know until the moment comes if another will choose to aid you or aid your enemy. Be cautious in your expectations."

I attempted to translate what he was saying. "So basically, we can't trust anyone? Is that what you mean?

"Perhaps," he said. "I am only telling you these things to prepare you for the *possibility* of their occurrence. There is no guarantee that anything will happen."

Connor could see from my face that I was getting frustrated and quickly intervened. "So what is the price this time for us to go up the switchbacks?" he asked.

"There is none," the Troll King said. "The service which you have chosen to render will be helpful to all people." He nodded his head and a weight settled on my side.

"My sword," I exclaimed, irritation forgotten. "Thank you!"

Connor was patting various pockets and grinning. "Yes, thank you," he said. "It was rough having only two daggers."

"Why did you take our weapons to begin with?" I asked.

"I knew that you might use them where you shouldn't," he said. His smile revealed large, pointed teeth and I decided that now was not the time to mention that we'd made do with kitchen knives. "I wish you the best of luck in finding all that you seek," continued the Troll King. "And now, as my final favor to you, I will send you to your destination with no further delays." The Troll King clapped his hands twice and then disappeared as suddenly as he came.

"He's weird," I said.

"I like him," said Connor. "It's nice having him on our side."

I didn't get a chance to respond. The trees and sky and grass all began to smear together in a dizzying blur. I grabbed Connor's hand as the earth seemed to fall away from under my feet. In the next instant we tumbled to the ground and lay there, waiting for the world to stop spinning.

"What just happened?" I asked after I got my breath back.

Connor sat up, rubbing one of his knees. Then his eyes widened. "The Troll King wasn't kidding when he said he'd send us to our destination with no delays."

I pushed myself up. We were sitting in the trees right outside the clearing of the enchanter's cottage. "How did he know where we were going?" I asked.

"He seems to know a lot of things without being told. Either way, I'm glad he helped out. It would've taken us awhile to get here."

I got to my feet and brushed myself off. "I prefer modes of travel that don't make me so dizzy."

"So do I," said Connor, standing up. "But chances are we won't ever have to travel that way again."

We looked at the tranquil-seeming cottage before us. Neither of us wanted to take the first step. "Maybe they're not home." Connor sounded hopeful.

A piercing shriek came from somewhere inside the enchanter's home. "They're home," I said. "Let's go.

Chapter 49

The door to the cottage swung open before we even got up the walkway and Bruce stood in the doorway grinning at us. He was wearing a frilly apron that seemed incongruous with his status as an evil enchanter, but then again, I don't know a lot of evil enchanters. Maybe they like to wear frilly aprons when they're not out terrorizing people.

"Come in, come in," said Bruce. "You're just in time for dinner."

Connor and I exchanged an uneasy glance and Bruce laughed. "Don't worry, we're vegetarians now." He ushered us inside. "Not an easy adjustment for any of us, but it seemed the best course of action given my wife's little weakness." He led the way into the dining room where the enchanter's family was already seated. The table was set with two extra places, almost as though the enchanter had been expecting us.

Sira glanced at us but didn't say anything since she was busy trying to get Goldie to stay in her chair. Amelia and Dominicus were holding hands at the other end of the table. Amelia giggled as her husband whispered into her ear.

Bruce dished steaming vegetables onto everyone's plates. "It's my own recipe," he said proudly, and then paused. "Actually, all of my recipes are my own. I've tried to exchange ideas with the village women, but they always scream and run away." He sighed and then noticed that we weren't eating. "Go on, try it," he said.

I picked up a fork and stabbed it into a potato wedge. With more than a little trepidation, I bit into it. A delicious, spicy flavor filled my mouth. "Wow," I said. "This is really good!"

Connor shot a quick look at me and then took a bite. His expression changed from apprehension to surprised pleasure. "Yes, it is," he said in a tone of unmistakable relief.

Bruce grinned. "I'm so glad that you like it." He glanced at his distracted family. "They don't often notice what the food tastes like."

"That's a shame because this is delicious," I said. "I'm glad that we came by."

"So am I," said Bruce. "But perhaps you should tell me *why* you came by."

"Oh yeah," I said. "We, uh…need your help."

"Obviously." Bruce nodded. "People don't usually visit an evil enchanter unless they need help."

"Good point. Anyway, the thing of it is--"

Connor hiccupped. I glanced at him and my mouth fell open.

"What?" he asked.

"You're...you're *floating*," I squeaked.

"So are you, my dear," Bruce said. "It's caused by the spices I use on my potatoes. There are a few minor side effects."

"A few?" I demanded, holding onto the table to prevent myself from drifting away.

"Well, yes. Aside from giving one a sort of weightless quality, it also enables one to hear another's thoughts as though they were spoken aloud."

I glanced at Connor, wondering if he'd been right in not wanting to come here.

"I usually am," Connor said.

"I didn't say anything!" I yelped.

"There's no need to panic," said the enchanter soothingly. "Your new abilities won't last forever; only a few weeks at the most. As for your reason for coming, I would be delighted to assist you. I feel rather in your debt, since if it had not been for the two of you, I would never have discovered that I have this dear little granddaughter." He gestured to Goldie's chair but she'd just escaped through one of the dining room windows and could be seen running up the hill behind the house.

Connor and I didn't answer. We were busy trying not to float away.

"I confess that I already know what you need from me," continued Bruce. "I'll go and get the item you seek. It's a good idea." He left the room, leaving behind him the oddest silence that I have ever experienced given that, while no one was actually talking, I could hear exactly what everyone was thinking. Sira was contemplating different ways to make her granddaughter disappear, terrible thoughts that made me shudder. The two lovebirds at the end of the table weren't technically thinking: they were more in this muddle of sappiness which caused a nauseating assault on all of the senses since they were also giggling and gazing into each other's eyes. Was this how all people acted when they were in love? I certainly hoped not.

I felt Connor's eyes on me. I glanced at him and he looked quickly away. Though his lips didn't move, his thoughts were clearly audible, "Don't think, don't think, don't think, don't think."

"I hear you not thinking," I said, amused. "What is it that you're afraid I'll hear?"

He kept his eyes on his hands as they gripped the table. "Don't answer, don't answer, don't answer, don't answer.... Don't look at her, don't look at her, don't--"

I reached over to grab his chin and *make* him look at me, by golly, but I'd forgotten about my new floating ability. As soon as one hand left the table the resulting uplift of my body took me so off guard that I lost my grip with the other hand. I flew into the air, banging my head on the ceiling. "Ow!"

"Max!" Connor let go of the table as though to grab at me, but by letting go he also shot upwards. His skull cracked against the ceiling.

I looked at him reproachfully as we drifted along at the top of the room. "Don't curse," I said.

"I didn't!" he growled, clutching his head.

"I heard your thoughts quite clearly. If my old nursemaid were here, and she could read minds and float too, she'd wash your mouth out with soap for sure." I began to laugh.

Connor scowled at me. "Doesn't she know that this is no time for laughing?" he thought.

"But you have to admit it's pretty funny," I snickered.

"Stop listening to my thoughts!" he ordered.

"I can't help it," I said, wiping my streaming eyes. "You can listen to mine if you want."

"It is a pointless offer." He floated crankily. "You share all of your thoughts the minute you think them."

I twirled in the air. "Are you saying I'm air-headed?"

"Hardly. You're one of the smartest girls I know."

I couldn't tell if he'd thought this or said it out loud since I'd been turned away from him when he spoke, so I answered anyway. "Thank you."

"I didn't *say* anything," he growled. "Aaargh! Get me down!" He made dog-paddling motions in an attempt to propel himself to the wall.

"Try it this way," I suggested, gliding through the air. Connor tried it and moved only a few inches. I floated back and towed him to the wall. Using the wall as his base of support, he tried to push himself down, but only bobbed up again like a cork in water.

Bruce came back into the room carrying a small red glass bottle. "Trouble?"

"We don't know how to get down," I said.

"Ah. It does take practice." He floated up beside us. "You just sort of let yourself *feel* heavy," he said, demonstrating. He sank slowly down and I followed his lead, landing lightly beside him on the floor. "Now you," said Bruce, looking up at where Connor was still scrabbling at the wall. "Just concentrate on yourself as an object of weight."

There was a long pause and then Connor dropped like a stone and lay in a jumbled heap on the floor. He groaned.

"Oh dear," said Bruce. "You'll need some practice."

Connor got to his feet. Immediately his body began to drift towards the ceiling. With an expression of concentration he descended to a few feet, then a few inches and then his feet touched the floor. He looked up triumphantly.

"Good work," exclaimed Bruce. "Very good indeed. You're not a natural like Rosie here, but you show great self-control."

"You have no idea how much self-control I have," said Connor.

I glanced at him, wondering what he was talking about.

"Don't think, don't think, don't think," he thought.

"You know," said Bruce, "I have a feeling you're not going to like having Rosie being able to read your thoughts. But if anyone can handle it, you can." They nodded at each other in some kind of silent communication. Apparently guys don't have to think to understand other guys.

Bruce handed me the little red bottle. "This should work for what you want," he said. "You're lucky that you came to me; not many enchanters have a potion like this one."

"Thank you," I said. "What do I owe you?"

He waved his hand. "Don't worry about it," he said. "I'm glad I could be of assistance. Now come finish eating. You've got to keep up your strength for all that's ahead."

After we finished eating, Bruce instructed us on how to properly administer the potion so it would work in the way that we needed it to. We thanked him with varying levels of sincerity (Connor was thinking bitter thoughts about the spiked vegetables at the time) and left.

"Do you know where they are?" I asked Connor.

"Yes. But it will take us awhile to get there."

"If we were walking or riding it would," I said. "You seem to have forgotten about our new ability." I pushed off the ground and hovered a few feet in the air.

He groaned. "Please, let's just take the bike. I don't like flying."

"How do you know? You've hardly tried it."

"I was flying over the shoulder of the enchanter not too long ago, if you will recall," he said. "I didn't like it then and I can guarantee that I won't like it any better now. In fact, I'm surprised that you even want to, given your fear of heights."

"It's different when I can actually fly," I said. "Heights are wonderful when you don't have to worry about falling." I somersaulted in the air.

"She's going to get hurt," he thought.

"No, I won't," I said.

"I really wish that you would stop responding to my thoughts."

"Come on up, Connor. The weather's fine." I grinned down at him.

He sighed and floated up beside me. "Fine. But if something bad happens, it's your fault."

We started out. It was a little tricky at first trying to work out how to propel forward, but once we got the hang of it, it was exhilarating. I began to wonder about the spices that the enchanter had used on his potatoes.

"No," said Connor.

"What?" I asked as innocently as I could manage.

He just looked at me.

"Don't you like flying?" I asked.

"I'd rather walk, thank you. Or ride the motorcycle. Don't you like your motorcycle anymore?"

"I love my motorcycle. But it turns out that I also love flying."

He rolled his eyes. "We're getting close," he said. "We might want to wait until it gets dark--" An arrow whizzed by my face. Connor grabbed me around the waist and shot up into the sky until the clouds covered us. "Are you alright?" he asked, pushing me away and scanning me with his eyes. "Did you get hit?"

"I'm fine," I said. "But was that an arrow from--"

"The soldiers of Treagal? Yes, it was."

Chapter 50

Connor led the way through the clouds until we were a safe distance away. Then we flew down and landed. Creeping through the brush, we came up to the camp, which was still in an uproar over the strange "birds" that had been sighted.

Connor and I hid ourselves in a small stand of bushes and trees nearby to wait for the cover of darkness. We could hear the men in camp, and I realized that I was starting to be able to tell the difference in sound between the spoken word and thoughts. There was a faint reverberation in thinking that wasn't there when people spoke.

After awhile a group of soldiers gathered near our hiding place, and it was not their thoughts that we listened to but their actual words. "We have heard that the true prince of Treagal is at the castle of King Charles," one said. "Many are traveling that way and we plan to follow tonight."

"I'll go with you," said another soldier and several others murmured their assent.

Then a single thought drifted to my ears. "I will report these men to Prince Torstein. He will reward me well for this information."

"It's alright, Max," whispered Connor after they had gone. Even though I could hear his thoughts I'd noticed that he preferred to speak to me aloud if he could. "We'll be able to tell who is for me or against me soon enough."

I gave him a weak smile and tried to keep myself from worrying about what we would do if my plan didn't work.

We settled back and made ourselves as comfortable as possible as the sun slowly began to sink into the horizon. We didn't talk much and since our thinking was also open to each other's minds, we both tried to keep our thoughts to a minimum. I was dozing against Connor's shoulder when he woke me. "It's time," he whispered. I hurriedly straightened my clothes and re-braided my hair. My heart was thumping in nervous anticipation of the role I would be obliged to perform soon.

Under the cover of darkness we flew over the large pot that the camp cook was busily stirring. As soon as the cook turned away to chop some onions, I landed and poured most of the contents of the little red bottle into the bubbling liquid, hoping that the added flavoring wouldn't be noticeable.

Our next stop was the imposter prince's tent. This was easy to find; all we had to do was look for the nicest tents in camp and assume that they belonged to my aunt and the false Prince Torstein. Connor flew down first and cut a long slit in the fabric of the first tent. He looked in and then gestured for me to join him. A small lamp burned in the interior of the tent, illuminating Alexander Dublin, alias Prince Torstein, sitting at a small table studying a map.

I slipped through the slit in the tent and cleared my throat. "Hello, Prince Torstein," I said.

Alex jumped at the sound of my voice. His eyes widened when he saw me and he got quickly to his feet. "Princess Maxine? Where did you come from? How did you get in here?"

"Hardly a matter of interest," said Connor, stepping in behind me. "The point is, we're here."

Alex eyes narrowed. "You again," he said. "It amazes me that you would be so stupid as to put yourself into my hands. Guards!"

Instantly a swarm of soldiers poured into the tent, surrounding us. Connor and I were restrained with ropes around our wrists in impressive time. Alex pointed at one of the soldiers. "You. Get Captain Ketzner."

The soldier left just as Aunt Regina slipped in. "Torstein, when are we going to-" She stopped when she saw Connor and me. I noticed that her nose was slightly crooked and bruised-looking. Evidently it had yet to recover from its encounter with my fist. I couldn't help but smirk a little.

Connor glanced at me. "You punched her?" he thought.

"She was about to put a spell on me," I answered in the same way. "It was the only thing I could think of."

"I'd like to hear that story sometime."

I noticed that Alex was looking between the two of us suspiciously. It was time. I dropped to my knees, which was a little awkward given that I had my hands tied behind me. "Prince Torstein," I said, looking up at him plaintively, "I have come seeking your forgiveness. It was a terrible thing when I fled from you the way I did. I wasn't thinking clearly. I have realized that it is my true desire to become your wife and join you in the building of your empire." I swallowed. Now for the hard part. "I have traveled far, facing many dangers, to bring you this man as your prisoner. In this way I show my acceptance of the true Prince of Treagal, may he reign in peace and prosperity for many years." I bowed my head.

"No!" Connor tried to come towards me but the soldiers prevented him. "Max, what are you saying? This isn't what we planned!"

I avoided his gaze. "I'm sorry," I said. "This was the only way I could think of to get you here." I looked at Alex. "I've thought about what you said, and I'm willing to do whatever it takes to assist you."

Alex watched me with narrowed eyes. "Pardon me for having a hard time trusting you, Princess," he said. "But how do I know that this isn't just an act?"

"I suppose there is no way for you to know," I said. "All I can do is put myself into your hands. What you do then is up to you."

Regina spoke up. "Maxine, perhaps I should tell you that I have devised a counter-effect to your little whistling spell. Do not think that you may leave us all immobile while you escape again."

"All the better," I said. "There is no need for you to worry about my motives if you see that the only power I have is no longer effective. I am here, Prince Torstein. Surely that alone speaks for itself."

Just then the captain of the guards entered the tent. He was a grizzled older man with a strength about him that seemed to be of both body and character. He saluted Alex, his face expressionless. "You requested my presence, Prince Torstein?"

"Captain Ketzner," said Alex, "This man is a kidnapper and would-be assassin. Keep him under heavy guard until further notice."

My heart was pounding as I watched Captain Ketzner lead Connor away. Then Alex turned to me. "I shall allow you to share this evening's meal with me, but expect to spend a good portion of your day tomorrow explaining to me exactly what you have been up to." He leaned close and his blue eyes were cold. "I warn you, Maxine. I will not to be made a fool of again."

Chapter 51

A table had been set up in front of Alex's tent with additional tables nearby for Captain Ketzner and his officers. The soldiers were seated on the ground around the tables in a sort of semi-circle while torches placed here and there illuminated the scene. We sat down at the head table with Alex on one side of me and Aunt Regina on the other. A servant began to ladle the soup into our bowls.

"Prince Torstein?" I asked.

"Yes?" He picked up his spoon without looking at me.

"Aren't you going to give a speech before we eat?"

"A speech? What for? My soup would get cold."

"But it is customary for a ruler to give a speech before the battle in order to encourage his men," I said. "They will expect it."

Alex glanced at Aunt Regina and she shrugged impassively. "It is not uncommon," she said.

He sighed, pushed his chair back and stood up. "Soldiers of Treagal," he began. The hum of conversation died away quickly and Alex cleared his throat. "I've decided to give a, uh, speech, and tell you some things to encourage you before we go into our first battle." He looked at me and I nodded reassuringly. "As many of you know," he continued, "I was fortunate enough to be taught by the excellent Chancellor Dublin after my parent's death. Chancellor Dublin taught me many things about being a king and I assure you that I have every intention of following his guidance closely." This caused some muttering among the men but Alex didn't seem to notice as he continued praising the late, great Chancellor Dublin.

As Alex talked, I reached into my sleeve and pulled out the little red bottle. All eyes were on the future tyrant as he warmed to his topic, punching his hand into his fist for emphasis. I darted a quick glance at Aunt Regina in time to catch her stifling a yawn behind one hand. She turned to address a servant and that instant was all the chance I needed. Moving as quickly and discreetly as possible, I uncorked the bottle and poured the rest of the contents into Alex's and Regina's bowls of soup. It was particularly important that they get their fair share of the potion. I slipped the bottle back into my pocket just as Regina turned to face Alex again.

"So you see," Alex was saying, "when people lack a proper governing force, they become incapable of taking care of themselves. They are like little children who must be told when to eat, when to sleep, when to work and when to play. I will become, in essence, their father. I will be kind and wise, and when necessary, and I will punish those who misbehave."

No wonder rulers usually had other people write their speeches for them. It no doubt helped prevent a lot of assassinations. It was clear that none of the soldiers had heard Alex's views before. They were staring at him, their food forgotten. Aunt Regina leaned forward so she could see around me and hissed, "Torstein, wrap it up."

He ignored her. "Now I shall tell you about the different punishments that I will employ against those who disobey my laws."

"*Prince Torstein,*" Aunt Regina's voice sounded deadly. "*Stop talking now.*"

He glanced at her and then dropped abruptly into his chair. "What's wrong?" he asked, suddenly looking unsure. I kept forgetting that Alex was only seventeen because he usually seemed so confident and in control.

"You were saying too much," Regina snapped.

Alex sat with his shoulders slightly hunched for a moment as he stared ahead. Then his eyes narrowed and he straightened up. "This is what you and I have often discussed. Surely the men understand the necessity for proper rule."

"I'm sure they do," Aunt Regina said coldly. "But why don't you wait until *after* we have created our empire before you explain all of the tedious details to them?"

A defiant look passed over Alex's face as he picked up his utensil. "I plan to give a lot more speeches where that came from," he said. He slurped from his spoon and then added, "I'll tell them what they need to hear when I think they need to hear it."

Regina took a deep breath and held it as though she were trying the old counting-to-ten-to-not-lose-her-temper trick. Apparently she wasn't aware that this only works for people who have an inkling of patience to begin with. "That is one of the stupidest things that I have ever heard," she said, her voice quivering with suppressed anger. "You don't tell people what they *need* to hear, you tell them what they *want* to hear."

Alex shook his head. "I will do as I see fit," he said.

"I cannot wait to destroy you," she growled. Alex didn't even react. I stared at Aunt Regina with a shocked expression.

"What?" she snapped, glaring at me.

"I...you..."

"I shall kill you first, I think." Her lips didn't move and I realized with a jolt that I was hearing her thoughts. I'd completely forgotten about this new ability. There was possibly some significance in the fact that I'd hardly heard a peep out of Alex's head all night.

"Why are you staring at me like that?" Aunt Regina demanded out loud, scooping a tiny amount of soup into her spoon.

"No reason," I said, distracted from her murderous thoughts by the meager first bite she was doling out for herself. Bruce hadn't specified how much a person had to eat to be affected by the potion, but I was pretty sure that a thimble-full wouldn't be enough. "Aren't you hungry?" I asked.

"No, I am not." Her stomach growled. At any other time I would have laughed at the perfect timing but I was too busy worrying. Why wasn't she eating? Did she suspect that there was something wrong with the food? I listened carefully to her thoughts but all that followed were her detailed plans on how, exactly, she was going to kill me. It wasn't what I would call pleasant to hear my own death planned with so much relish, but I was too troubled to care.

"Is the meal to your liking, Princess Maxine?" Alex's voice interrupted my thoughts.

"Oh, yes, it's delicious," I said, giving him a quick smile as I hurriedly took a bite. I glanced back at Regina in time to see her spoon leave her mouth. Had she actually swallowed any? I peeked in her bowl but it appeared untouched. If she'd eaten something it was barely enough to fill the mouth of a flea. A tiny flea. The *baby* of a tiny flea.

She slammed her spoon down and turned to face me so suddenly that I jumped. "Do you have a problem?" she demanded.

"What? No! No, I was just..." I scooped up a huge, meaty spoonful and stuffed it into my mouth in a desperate attempt to get out of having to answer her.

Aunt Regina watched me with narrowed eyes. "Listen, you little brat, you can stop mocking me anytime," she growled.

"Mocking you?" I echoed through the mouthful of food.

"Just because I have to watch what I eat does not mean that I also have to put up with disrespectful, rude, nasty little nieces."

She wasn't eating because she was on a diet! I stared unseeingly into my bowl as I contemplated with growing dismay what this meant. My plan *required* eating to be successful. It just goes to show that you can't count on the cooperation of women when the consumption of food is involved.

"Hey, Max," said Connor's voice in my mind.

I started and then smiled innocently when Alex glanced at me in surprise. After he returned his focus on his meal, I scanned the crowd of soldiers for Connor. "Where are you?" I thought.

"Right behind you." I started to turn around and he practically shouted the thought: "Don't look! The last thing I need is for you to draw attention to me."

"Well, how did it go? Did Ketzner believe you?"

"I let him see my true face. He said that I'm the spitting image of my father!" Connor's excitement came at me in waves. "He's arranged for a few of his most trusted men to assist us when the moment comes, and everyone, and I mean *everyone*, is eating tonight. Even me. So if I'm affected I know I'm in trouble."

He sounded so happy I didn't want to mention the unexpected problem to him. I bit my lip.

"Max? You keep forgetting that I'm already in your head. What's this about an unexpected problem?"

Oh, yeah. "Um, Regina is on a diet. She barely ate one bite."

"Dragon's breath! I was counting on having her out of the way."

"So was I."

"We'll just have to deal with her when the time comes," Connor thought. "In the meantime, let's wait for the potion to work on everyone else."

"Princess Maxine, you haven't heard a word I've said." Alex leaned so close that his warm breath tickled my ear.

I shivered.

"Are you cold?" He put his hand on my shoulder. His eyes were unexpectedly kind when he smiled—it made it hard to remember he was actually a bad guy.

A faint growling sound came from behind me. Whoops. I'd forgotten about Connor for a second. The growling sound grew louder and I wasn't sure if I was only hearing it in my mind until Alex turned around. "Guard, you are excused from duty." Alex turned back to me as Connor stomped away. "These men are little more than animals," he said. "That fellow was so anxious for his food that he was *growling*. Did you hear him?"

Before I could answer one of the officers seated nearby shouted and jumped up, knocking his chair to the ground.

"What in the world?" Alex looked irritated.

The officer was peering at the ground while the other officers crowded around, murmuring in urgent undertones. Then a group of soldiers under a nearby tree scrambled to their feet in alarm. They gathered in a small circle, pointing at something and yelling at each other. Similar chaos spread down the line of men like wildfire on dry grass and in seconds the whole camp was in an uproar with soldiers hollering, knocking over tables, and running back and forth.

The cacophony of the smashing dishes and yelling was music to my ears—it meant that the plan was working. Grinning happily, I looked over at Alex. My smile faded when I saw that, aside from a red face as he shouted angrily at one of his chief officers, he appeared to be unaffected by the potion. How was that possible?

A group of men knocked into our table and I jumped back to avoid getting trampled. Alex turned and pushed me none too gently in the direction of his tent. "Princess Maxine, take cover," he ordered. Then he drew his sword and dashed into the crowds of milling soldiers.

Yeah, right. Like I was really going to go hide in a tent when there were so much to see. I found a tree to lean against, well out of the way of the running soldiers.

There's nothing so satisfying as viewing the successful results of your schemes. And the good news was that, while there were definitely fewer men now, it wasn't as drastic of a reduction as I had feared. The chaos was beginning to resolve itself into ordered activity as the men who remained darted after small objects. Small, *hopping* objects. Captain Ketzner was directing the scene by having the men place their captives into empty potato sacks.

"What did you do?" an accusing voice demanded in my ear. I'd been so interested in watching the action that I had completely forgotten about my evil aunt.

I turned to face her. "Isn't it great?" I asked. "Those whose hearts were disloyal to the *true* prince of Treagal are now frogs." I smiled into her glaring face. "Just think: your diet is the only thing that saved you from finding out what it's like to be *literally* cold-blooded."

A small vein pulsed in the side of her forehead and her mouth worked soundlessly until finally she managed to find the words she wanted. "I have had it with you, you interfering, snide, obnoxious little pest," she shrieked. "I wanted to squash you when you were a child, but Philip wouldn't let me. He said that it would get him into too much hot water with your father." She lifted her hands. "I don't think that matters now."

Chapter 52

"Now, now, Regina. This really won't do." We both jumped at the sound of the newcomer's voice.

Aunt Regina whirled to face the man who stood leaning casually against a tree in the shadows. "What are *you* doing here?" she demanded.

"I'm here for the show," said Bruce, grinning. "It promised to be vastly more entertaining than anything I've seen in ages."

Regina's face twisted into a mask of hatred. "*Go away.* I have work to do."

"Now Reggie--"

"Don't call me that!"

"Fine. *Regina.* You always were uptight, even when we were kids." Bruce winked at me. "Regina's my bossy big sister."

"It's none of her business how we're related. For the last time, go away."

He studied the fingernails on one hand. "Listen, Reggie, if you want to have it out with her, I suggest that you do it the old-fashioned way. It's only fair."

"Nonsense. The old-fashioned way takes too long."

I felt it would be in my best interest to intervene at this moment. "Why don't we all just get along?" I suggested. "That way nobody gets hurt."

They both looked at me like I was crazy. *"Get along?"* Regina asked. "With you? You've been a thorn in my side for years. Freezing my guests, making my poor son cry…"

"Weldon cried all of the time anyway," I said. "You can't blame that entirely on me."

She glared at me. "Not only that, but I know that it was you who destroyed my lovely monsters. Do you have any idea how much work it was to get them to the stage that they were at? Hours and hours of training, ruined by some pesky little red-headed misfit who should never have been a princess in the first place."

Her words hit a sore spot. "Who's the misfit here?" I demanded. "You're the one with plans to steal the throne from her own husband."

Her eyes widened. "How did you know about that?"

Before I could answer Alex returned, panting and disheveled. "Princess Maxine, what are you doing out here? I thought I told you to go into the tent."

Bruce pulled up a chair from one of the nearby tables. "Just watch the show, Mr. Dublin," he said, sitting down with the air of a man about to be amused.

Alex looked at him. "Who are you? And why did you just call me 'Mr. Dublin?'"

"Inconsequential questions." Bruce waved his hand dismissively. "We'll sort it out in a minute. Maxine, I would highly advise you to draw your sword. Now."

I hastily obeyed him. "Here, Reggie, use this." Bruce snapped his fingers and Alex's sword flew into Regina's hands.

She looked down at the sword and made a considering sound. "The old-fashioned way might not be so bad after all."

"Are you trying to get me killed?" I asked Bruce.

"I'm trying to give you a chance," he said. "You can't win by magic. The old-fashioned way is your only hope."

My mind frantically scrambled for an excuse. "But it's too dark to have a swordfight."

He waved his arm and the nearby torches suddenly flared with a brilliant blue-white light, effectively ruining my attempt to stay alive. Bruce leaned back in his chair. "Don't worry, I'll make sure she doesn't cheat."

When Connor and I were younger, we practiced swordplay for hours. I was pretty good and won nearly as often as I lost. Then Connor grew bigger and stronger and even though I tried to hold my own it was a losing battle. Finally one day Connor announced that he wasn't going to duel with me anymore. To say that I was out of practice was putting it mildly.

"Max! What are you doing?" Connor strode into view, followed by Ketzner and a few of his officers.

"Hush. She needs to concentrate," said Bruce.

"Concentrate? Are you crazy?" Connor started towards me as though to take my sword when I saw a flash of silver out of the corner of my eye.

"Watch out!" yelled Bruce. I whirled to deflect a blow from Regina that would have severed my arm if I hadn't turned when I did. In the next few minutes I did all I could to defend myself, losing ground as she launched a furious, murderous assault. Sweat stung my eyes as I gripped the hilt of my sword with both hands and tried to stay alive.

Then Regina smiled, one of those irritating smirks that evil people are so good at—the kind where one eyebrow raises slightly, the eyes narrow, and the mouth lifts up in a sneering grin of triumph. It was really aggravating because I could tell she thought she'd already won.

A burning anger rose inside of me as I looked at her smug face. I had dealt with this woman's cruelty ever since I could remember. For years she had bullied and mocked and tormented me while my family pretended nothing was wrong. A surge of determination filled me and in that moment something changed: I was no longer fighting to stay alive—I was fighting to win.

I began to match her blow for blow until soon she was the one backing away. Her hair grew damp with perspiration and she started gasping for breath. I pressed forward, feeling a grim pleasure in her growing desperation. Then I feinted, leaving myself open and vulnerable to her attack. Panting, she swung her sword into my trap. I twisted my blade around hers and snapped my wrists. Her sword flew away, landing with its point quivering in the earth several yards away.

Breathing hard, I lifted my sword, ready to deliver the killing blow. I smiled at her then, my own wicked smile, and her eyes filled with terror. All around us no one moved. It was still and silent; not a word or thought interrupted my concentration.

 It was within my rights as a princess to demand the life of one who had sought mine, but it turns out that I'm not bloodthirsty like my great, great, great grandfather Maximilian the Menace. I lowered my sword. "You were right. The old-fashioned way turned out to be pretty fun."

Realizing that I was not going to kill her, Regina slumped down onto her knees. Loud cheers filled the air. I looked around and realized that the remaining army of Treagal had gathered to watch our sword fight.

Connor stood close by, holding a drawn sword as though he'd been waiting for an opportunity to jump in. His face was pale and beaded with sweat, and even though his thoughts were jumbled, his lingering sensations of helplessness and terror swirled through my mind. I sheathed my sword and was about to walk to him when his eyes widened in alarm.

Which brings me to an *extremely important point*: never turn your back on the nefarious sister of the most evil enchanter in history, even if you did just show her mercy by leaving her alive after a sword fight. *Especially* if you just showed her mercy by leaving her alive after a sword fight that everyone watched her lose.

"Max!" Connor yelled. Something slammed into my shoulder, sending me sprawling to the ground. As I lay there trying to catch my breath, Connor threw himself at my side, frantically looking me over for damage. "Max, are you alright?"

"I think so," I gasped. "What happened?"

"Regina threw a spell at you but Bruce knocked you out of the way just in time."

"Oh." I sat up stiffly. Bruce was standing over Regina looking pleased with himself. She lay on the ground with thick ropes wound around her from neck to foot. Literally. "Thank you, Bruce," I managed shakily.

"No problem. I was waiting for her to do something like that."

Chapter 53

Alex stepped forward to assume control over the situation. "As the future emperor over everyone here, I decree that from now on, no one shall be allowed to use magic without my permission."

Bruce scowled. "Now just a minute--"

"Allow me," said Connor. He stood up and turned to Alex. "I don't think you realize what's going on around here, but perhaps you will recall that a few minutes ago there were a lot of frogs hopping around?"

Alex glared at him. "Of course I do. What is your point?"

"My point is that we put a potion in your food to reveal the loyalties of your army. Those men who were supportive of you as an impostor and usurper of the throne of Treagal are now amphibians."

Alex stared at Connor for a moment and as far as I could tell, there weren't a lot of thoughts going on behind that handsome face. Then he turned to Captain Ketzner. "Captain, this man is conspiring to commit treason. Shoot him."

Ketzner kept a steady gaze on Connor's face and ignored Alex entirely.

"Captain Ketzner! Kill this man or join him in his punishment."

"Captain Ketzner no longer takes his orders from you," said Connor. A strange flicker passed over Connor's features and I realized that he was letting Alex see him without his mask.

Alex stepped back, his eyes growing wide. "What—what just happened to your face?"

"I am the true Prince of Treagal," said Connor, "and you are under arrest for impersonating royalty and for conspiring to overtake the peaceful kingdoms of this land."

Captain Ketzner signaled to his men and they stepped forward with their swords and arrows ready.

Alex's face twisted into a terrible expression. "You are going to regret this," he hissed. "Just because you've turned a few of my men into frogs doesn't mean that I don't have supporters elsewhere. I have many who are loyal to--" He choked and then started coughing. He put one finger up and everyone waited, shifting uncomfortably. Finally Alex cleared his throat and opened his mouth to continue. "Ribbit," he said. The soldiers stared at him as he tried again. "Ribbit!" He clutched his throat, his eyes wide with panic.

Bruce looked amused. "Sounds like he has a frog in his throat."

"Ribbit, ribbit, ribbit!"

"C'mon, that was a funny joke," said Bruce. "Why isn't anyone laughing?"

"What's wrong with him?" I asked.

Bruce sighed. "Did he eat any of the potion?"

"Yes, quite a lot of it. I was surprised that he didn't turn into a frog with the rest of them. You know, since if anyone is disloyal to the true prince of Treagal, it would be him."

"He must have an unusually slow digestive process," said Bruce.

There was an odd popping sound and Alex Dublin was no longer the suave future tyrant of nations: he was a gangly green frog. Ketzner stepped forward and picked up the newest amphibian by one leg.

"Put that one in his own bag, I think," said Connor. "We'll take them all back to Treagal to be questioned and tried."

"I just had a great idea," Bruce exclaimed, his eyes sparkling.

"No," said Connor. "No more great ideas. I have learned from recent experience that great ideas tend to be really bad ideas when they're coming from evil enchanters."

Bruce looked offended. "I'll have you know," he said, "that I am a *reformed* evil enchanter. Now watch this." He turned to where Regina still lay in her uncomfortable-looking cocoon of ropes.

She stared up at him in alarm. "What are you doing, you wretched idiot? Don't you come near me!"

He raised his hands and wiggled his fingers as though he were warming them up.

"If you so much as *fleck* even a *spark* of magic at me," she shrieked.

"I don't know, Reggie," her brother replied. "It's hard to resist." Before she could say another word a streak of white light flew from Bruce's raised fingertips, hitting her right on her bruised nose. In the next instant, Regina's form shrunk in on itself to become a chubby brownish-green frog. It sprawled out on the mound of ropes, a dazed looked glazing its eyes.

Bruce brushed his hands together with an air of satisfaction. "There you go," he said, beaming at us. "Let me know if you need anything else. I'm really loving this whole good guy thing." There was a crackling noise and he was gone.

"That was bizarre," I said, after it became apparent that everyone else was speechless. "Nice of him, I suppose, but definitely bizarre." I stepped forward and picked Regina up. "Wow, Reggie, you're the heaviest frog I've ever run across.

We'll have to work on that diet of yours. Don't worry, I'll find out how fattening flies are."

That snapped her out of it. She squirmed frantically, trying to break free. I tightened my grip. "Can I get another sack for this one?" I asked.

"Of course, Princess Maxine," said Ketzner, signaling to one of his men. I dropped Regina into the bag and tied it shut. It was amazing how much it flopped around. She could really kick.

I handed the bag to one of the soldiers and breathed a sigh of relief. It was done. My plan had worked and now Connor would be safe; he could go home to Treagal and be reunited with his people.

My quest had been successful in more ways than I ever could have expected, but as I stood there in the flickering lights of the torches, a feeling of sheer exhaustion washed over me. I would never admit it to anyone, but I hadn't entirely recovered from my last big showdown with Aunt Regina's monsters. I needed to get some rest before I humiliated myself by collapsing. "Excuse me, Connor?" I asked. Connor and Captain Ketzner both turned in time to see me swaying. Connor hurried to my side and put his arm around my waist.

"Max, are you alright?"

I waved my hand. "I'm fine," I said. "Just a little tired."

Before I could resist, Connor scooped me up into his arms. "Captain Ketzner, Princess Maxine is just recovering from an illness. Do you have a place where she could lie down for the night?"

"Of course, Your Highness. Follow me."

"I can walk, Connor," I said.

He ignored me and followed Ketzner to Aunt Regina's tent. It was a very lavish place for a tent, which meant I would definitely spend a comfortable night. I convinced Connor that I could manage on my own, and he reluctantly left after making me promise I would send for him if I needed anything.

I stretched out on Regina's soft goose down bedding, every muscle in my body aching, and was about to fall asleep when I heard Connor and Captain Ketzner enter Alex's tent next door.

"Prince Torstein, I believe I speak on behalf of all of the people of Treagal in welcoming you back."

"Thank you, Captain," said Connor. "I can't tell you how relieved I am to find the army of Treagal so receptive to my return. I admit that when we employed the use of that potion I was half-expecting the entire army to turn into frogs."

There was a smile in Ketzner's voice as he replied, "I wasn't. Many families in Treagal have suffered under Dublin's twisted notions of justice. We've kept alive the hope that you would return, preferably before he began his campaign for an empire."

"In which case, we should thank Princess Maxine. She insisted that we come here to try her idea before the first battle."

"It was a brilliant move. She seems like a wonderfully intelligent and captivating young lady."

I put my arms behind my head. Intelligent *and* captivating. I liked this Captain Ketzner. He was a discerning guy.

"Yes, she is. Now, if I could meet with you and the other officers in fifteen minutes, we will discuss our plans for tomorrow."

"Yes, sir. I'll let everyone know." Ketzner stepped out of the tent.

"Maxine?" Connor's voice came to me in the clear, hollow-sounding way that indicated that he had just spoken to me in his thoughts. I kept forgetting that we had this ability.

"Um. Yes, Connor?"

"I would appreciate it if you would get some rest. I know you derive inordinate amounts of pleasure from eavesdropping on private conversations, but you forget that I can hear your thoughts. You were just admitting to yourself that you're still weak from the poison of those monsters. I heard you."

Crud-in-the-butter. I couldn't wait for this mind-reading business to fade away.

"The feeling is entirely mutual. Now will you please go to sleep?"

"But I want to know what's going to happen."

"Max. You have just singlehandedly averted a war. I trust you with my life. And I will trust you with every single dull, dry, boring detail regarding our plans for the return to Denitri. *Tomorrow*. Now go to sleep."

For once in my life, I obeyed.

Chapter 54

Early the next morning I was jolted awake by the sound of hammering and sawing. I forgot that I was wearing one of Regina's nightgowns until I moved to get up. Its long, silky folds tangled around my feet and I stumbled and fell. "Dragon's breath," I muttered, pulling my feet free.

"Are you all right?" It was Connor. What was he doing lurking right outside my tent?

"I've been out here all night," he answered.

I got up and pushed aside the tent flap. "Why?"

He blinked at the sight of me in my aunt's nightgown. It was a bit more revealing than what I ordinarily wear. I lifted the tent flap so that only my face was visible. "Why?" I repeated.

He looked sheepish. "I just..." His voice trailed off but his thoughts continued, "Didn't want anything to happen to you."

That was so sweet.

He scowled and it took me a second to realize that he was scowling because I thought that he was sweet. His scowl deepened.

"What?" I asked. "I think it's sweet. Is there something wrong with that?"

He rubbed his face with both hands. "I don't know. No. It's just hard to take being called sweet this early."

I grinned but restrained myself from saying (or thinking) anything else on the subject. Several men walked by carrying pieces of lumber. "What's going on?" I asked.

"They're building crates to carry all of the frogs in. Once we get them back to Treagal, we're going to have them restored to their human forms and then we'll see about proper trials and all that." Connor stood up from the makeshift desk that he'd set up at my door. "If you'll excuse me." He gathered up some papers and walked away.

I had noticed that I could only read the thoughts of others if they were in range for me to hear their spoken words. This being the case, I decided that Connor needed some time alone in his brain. Well, so did I.

While it was a relief to me that I was no longer going to have to worry about marrying the man previously known as the Prince of Treagal, I found myself wondering how the true Prince of Treagal felt about things. Last night, when he had thought I was going to be killed, there was no mistaking how he felt about me. The advantage to hearing someone's thoughts was that it left little doubt as to what they were feeling. I knew that Connor loved me, but that was not a guarantee of what he would choose to do about it. I wanted to have a chance to talk to him about things, but I suspected that with his newly assumed responsibilities as the soon-to-be-king of Treagal, he was going to be pretty busy.

My suspicions were soon confirmed. Over the course of the next several days, I hardly saw Connor except at mealtimes. The affairs of the army took up a significant amount of his time, and Connor was kept busy with Captain Ketzner and the other chief officers in discussing the state of the kingdom of Treagal. In addition to all of this, we needed to return to the kingdom of Denitri to reunite with King Charles and Ron.

Connor sent a messenger ahead with the good news regarding the vanquishing of Alex Dublin and Aunt Regina, and we received word back as to their happiness at the peaceful resolution of things.

Traveling with an army is significantly slower than traveling by flight or motorcycle. After I retrieved my bike from the base of the switchbacks, the only thing that kept me from revving it up and leaving the army plodding in the dust was the promise that I'd made to Connor to not do that very thing.

Over the course of the next few days, my ability to read minds faded along with my ability to fly. I can't tell you how disappointed I was when I went to soar into the sky one morning and instead lifted only a few feet from the ground. The temptation to pay another visit to Bruce was prevented by Connor, who still seemed to know what I was thinking even though he had lost the power to literally do so. I suppose my longing to fly was pretty transparent.

Once we arrived at Denitri, all sorts of official, royal protocol had to be addressed. This involved things like signing proclamations and sending them out to the neighboring kingdoms regarding the re-establishment of peace, and other matters of extremely dull royal business. King Charles was delighted that the war had been averted so neatly while Aunt Marge alternately hugged and yelled at me, depending on her mood.

Once it was firmly established in everyone's minds that there was going to be no war and no empire, there was a sort of confusion about what to do next. When men have spent months planning to fight, it's hard to convince them to just go home and plow fields. With all of the restless energy causing spontaneous outbreaks of contention among the men, Connor came up with the idea to invite everyone to Treagal to celebrate his return. The plan was received with enthusiasm and we were soon underway.

It took a few days of travel to arrive in Connor's homeland. It was a beautiful, ancient kingdom with towering oak forests on one end, stretches of green, grassy meadows through the middle, and a border of white sandy beaches with an ocean of aquamarine blue on the other end.

The people of Treagal received their long-lost prince with a jubilant welcome, gathering along the highways and streets in every village and city we passed through, their faces streaked with tears of happiness as we rode by. Connor was visibly overwhelmed by his reception. His expression betrayed an odd mingling of joy to be home and sorrow for all that had passed since he was last in his homeland.

The first order of business involved putting the large collection of hopping amphibians into a special room that had been set up for them as a substitute for the dungeons. Since Connor was already so busy, it was decided that they would just leave the frogs in their current form until things had settled down a little.

Ron and Cinderella were pretty much useless during this time. They wandered around in a haze of love-stricken bliss—it was enough to make a person ill. All that gazing into each other's eyes, holding hands and giggling...

Alright, I admit that I was a jealous. Connor had taken to avoiding me and I had no idea why. Catching up on almost two decades of royal matters could keep a guy pretty busy, but I had noticed that if I came around when he was sitting alone reading through documents, he always had some pressing engagement arise right then. He was perfectly courteous towards me, but that was part of the problem. His constant, "Good morning, Princess Maxine, Lovely day, Princess Maxine, Sleep well, Princess Maxine," was enough to drive Princess Maxine up the wall.

After several weeks of being ignored by Connor and overlooked by everyone else, I couldn't take it anymore. I needed a breath of fresh air, preferably via motorcycle. Early one morning I slipped past the guards and was soon on my way.

It was obvious that Connor was having second thoughts about me. Even as busy as he was, he had made no effort to do

316

more than give a hurried greeting if I happened to see him, which lately hadn't been very often.

I stopped my bike at the top of a hill, overlooking a pretty little valley. It was time for me to return to Veiland. I would inform my parents that the betrothal was over and spend my life mapping distant countries.

The rumbling of thunder filled the air and I looked up. Dark clouds had rolled in without my noticing. I sighed and turned the bike towards the castle.

The rain started softly and at first I thought I might make it back without a problem, but in a matter of minutes the rain was pouring down like one enormous waterfall. I rode into a stand of trees to wait out the storm.

I got off my bike and leaned against a tree, occasionally wiping water from my eyes. As I stood there shivering, a feeling of unease began to creep over me. The dark clouds and thick vegetation made my surroundings seem ominous and forbidding.

This is what comes of too many adventures: I was imagining danger around every corner. I just needed to relax.

"How fortuitous this storm is," said a voice right in my ear. "We've been following you for some time now."

I whirled around. With the plethora of bad guys that I'd been dealing with, I had completely forgotten about Prince Jaspien. The last few weeks had not been kind to him. His too-long hair was slicked down on his forehead from the rain while smudges under his eyes testified to too many sleepless nights. His face was gaunt, and his clothing was dirty and torn. The men lurking behind him looked just as unkempt. They eyed me malevolently and I shivered again, this time for an entirely different reason. Taking a step back, I pursed my lips and whistled as loudly as I could.

Jaspien smirked. "Sorry to disappoint you, Princess," he said, pointing at his ears. He had something stuffed into them, effectively plugging them against my whistle. He gestured to one of his men and a burly fellow stepped up and wound a rope around me, binding my arms to my sides. Another guy tied a foul-smelling cloth around my mouth. As soon as my lips were effectively sealed, Jaspien and his men removed the plugs from their ears.

"Much better," he said. "Now I want you to answer me by a simple nod for yes or shake of your head for no. Is my brother being held in the castle?"

I didn't respond.

His eyes flashed. "Are you not taking me seriously?" He pulled out a wicked-looking dagger. "Would you take me seriously if I severed your hand and sent it to your fiancé?" He stepped towards me with a terrible smile on his face. "Yes. I think that is rather a good idea," he muttered, more to himself than to me. "It would certainly get their attention to receive such a dainty little package."

Jaspien placed his dagger against my wrist. "The pity, of course, is that you aren't likely to survive this little operation," he said. "But I will make sure that you get the proper credit for your sacrifice."

Tears streamed down my cheeks as a feeling of terror filled me. I had never felt so helpless or alone in my life. When the piercing sound of a whistle filled the air, I hardly noticed. It was only when I felt the frantic beating of my heart slow to a stop that it occurred to me that Jaspien's face had frozen into a look of dismay.

Chapter 55

"Maxine, you wretched girl, what were you thinking to leave without telling anyone?'

I opened my eyes. Wait, they were already open. But for one terrifying second, I couldn't see. It wasn't blackness, it was just *blank*, like there was nothing to see. I blinked, and my eyes burned and then focused blearily on the woman standing in front of me.

Aunt Marge? What was she doing here?

I tried to turn my head, but my neck was oddly stiff. In fact, my whole body felt stiff, and I realized that I could barely move. My eyes widened in panic. What was happening?

"I froze everyone," said Aunt Marge, pulling the cloth away from my face. "He was about to cut your hand off and it was the only thing I could think of to do. I didn't have time to warn you. Anyway, it will take you a minute to return to full mobility."

She wasn't kidding. Slowly the movement came back into my muscles, a creeping, almost sludgy sensation, as though my blood was the consistency of mud and my muscles only slightly softer than rocks.

Aunt Marge was working on sawing the ropes from around my waist with a dainty little knife. With that kind of tool it was going to take her forever. "So this is what it feels like to be put into the whistling spell?" I asked thickly.

"I forgot that you've never experienced it personally," she said. "But yes, that's how it feels. Awful, isn't it?"

If my body were mobile enough to shudder I would have, but I was still defrosting; not from cold but from something a little worse. "No wonder Connor threatened me if it ever happened to him again," I said.

"Oh dear. Did he?" Aunt Marge glanced over my shoulder and I stiffly followed her gaze to where Connor was sitting immobile on his horse, a pained expression on his face.

Jaspien lay on the ground at my feet, looking like a statue that had been tipped over, his arms and legs sprawled out awkwardly. The dagger was still clutched in his hand.

"What happened?" I asked.

Aunt Marge looked down at Jaspien and scowled. "I pushed him over. I hope he's bruised and sore when he comes out of it, too."

"No, I mean, how did you guys know where to find me? And did you say *you* froze everyone? I didn't know that you had the whistling gift as well."

Marge squinted down at her tiny knife and kept sawing.

"Aunt Marge? What's going on?"

She sighed. "Fine. I'll tell you. First, Connor knew where to find you because he always knows where to find you. He keeps a very close eye on you, whether or not you realize it."

"Are you kidding me?" I demanded. "Connor hasn't noticed my existence for the past two weeks. I could have dropped off the face of the earth and he wouldn't have noticed."

This statement seemed to amuse her but before she could answer, Connor's voice intervened. "Marge, I love you to death. I really do. But please, please, give me some kind of warning the next time you do that. It was even worse than when Maxine whistles."

"I didn't have time," she protested. "He was about to cut her hand off."

A look went over Connor's face that I have never seen there before and hope to never see again. He turned to me. "Give me your hands," he ordered.

"What? Why?"

He grabbed my hands but he couldn't pull them up very far since my arms were still tied to my torso. He turned my wrists over and pushed up my sleeves and I realized that he was looking for damage.

"Aunt Marge whistled just in time," I said.

"Max!" Ron stumbled our way. "Was it you that whistled just now? You must be getting better at it; it was much worse this time."

Marge looked sheepish. "That was me," she admitted.

"You?" asked Ron. "You whistle too?"

"Well...yes. Actually, Maxine gets it from me."

"What?" I stared at her. "Do you mean that *you're*--"

She nodded. "Yes. I'm your fairy godmother *and* your aunt. There's a bit of magic on your father's side, you see."

It made sense. Aunt Marge always seemed to have things work out for her a little too perfectly to not have a bit of magic in the mix. I had a few immediate questions. "Why does the whistling trick not work on the people I most want it to work on?" I asked. "I can't tell you how many times I tried to freeze Aunt Regina and she didn't pause even for a second."

"It won't work on those whose magic is stronger than yours unless their guard is down. You'll need to practice to get to the point where you can freeze enchanters."

"No!" The exclamation came from both Ron and Connor. "No practicing," added Ron.

"At least while we're in hearing distance," said Connor, grinning at me.

I felt a sudden swelling of gratitude as I stood surrounded by the people I loved most in the world. I was still wet from the rain, still tied up, and still recovering from the emotional trauma of almost losing one of my favorite hands, but a warm, sweet feeling rose up inside of me as I realized how fortunate I was to have these good friends in my life. My eyes filled with tears.

Connor's expression of alarm, which had never really gone away, now deepened into something similar to panic. He put his arm around me and peered into my face. "Max! Why are you crying, sweetheart?"

The endearment, the first one he'd ever spoken to me, was my undoing. I began to sob unrestrainedly, but I was smiling through my tears.

"She's cracked," pronounced Ron, shaking his head as though it were a shame to lose a perfectly good sister.

"No, she hasn't," said Aunt Marge. "She's been through a lot in the last few minutes—no, the last few *weeks*. It's no wonder that she's upset."

"No," I sobbed. "I'm crying because I'm happy."

They all glanced at one another. Aunt Marge's ineffective sawing at the ropes slowed as she seemed to consider the possibility that I had cracked after all. Connor made an irritated noise and pulled a knife from his boot, severing the last strand of rope with one quick swipe.

"Prince Treagal, may I ask for your assistance?" One of the Treagal soldiers stood nearby, waiting for Connor's attention. I watched Connor, hoping that he would...I stopped the thought before it finished itself. He was the ruler of a kingdom now. If one of his men needed him, it was not my place to prevent it. I looked down.

Then I heard Connor say, "Ron, would you mind taking care of that for me?"

"Not at all," said Ron. He went to talk to the soldier.

Aunt Marge put her hands on her hips. "Maxine, now do you see why it's important for you to always travel with guards-"

Connor interrupted her. "Marge, I would like to speak to Maxine alone, please."

"But--"

Connor didn't say anything. He raised his eyebrows at his former guardian and waited.

"Of course," she said, looking slightly abashed. It was an unusual expression to see on my aunt's face.

"Thank you." He waited until she walked away before turning back to me. "We need to talk."

Typical. I'd wanted to talk for the last few weeks, but he chose the moment where I was wet and tear-stained, and there was no telling what my hair looked like. If I was Cinderella, I would still be glowingly beautiful and Connor would be staring at me with unconcealed adoration instead of ... Why was he grinning? Was there something *funny* about my state of dishevelment? I turned around and stomped away, stumbling a little due to residual stiffness from the whistling spell.

"Hey! Where are you going?"

I didn't answer. I reached my bike and was about to get on when he grabbed my arm from behind and whirled me around to face him. "Maxine, what're you doing? I wanted to talk to you." He glared at me.

I put my hands on my hips and glared back. "And the only way to get you to talk to me is by getting myself kidnapped and in peril of having various limbs chopped off? No thanks. It's not worth the trouble."

His expression grew thoughtful. "I see."

"I doubt it."

He turned. "Marge?"

She hadn't gone far. I suspected that she was eavesdropping, the little devil. "Yes?"

"We're going to head back to the castle. We'll see you there."

"Alone? Are you sure that's wise?"

He glanced down at me. "Positive. Will you come with me, Max?" he asked.

"On one condition." I folded my arms. "I'm driving."

Chapter 56

We made it back to the castle without any further mishaps and entered through a little-used side door. Connor took some towels from a linen closet and handed one to me. He rubbed at his face and hair vigorously and emerged from his towel looking as handsome and debonair as ever. It was so unfair. I patted my sodden hair with my towel, glad that I didn't have a mirror to tell me what I was sure would be an unpleasant story.

Connor abruptly took my hands and pulled me around so that I was facing him. He gazed down at me. "I need to talk to you, Max," he said in a gentle voice that I'd never heard him use before. "Will you talk to me?"

I nodded, suddenly nervous.

He took a deep breath and I realized that he was nervous as well. "You must be wondering why I've been avoiding you."

"You've been acting like you can't stand the sight of me."

"Is that what you thought?" He sounded surprised.

I nodded. "What else could I think? Ever since we were left Alex's camp you've been acting differently. I thought..." I stopped.

"Thought what?"

"I thought that now that you're going to be a king, you wanted someone a little more...conventional." I could feel the spread of color over my face and neck. "It's not like I was going to hold you to a betrothal that neither of us had any choice about, but—"

"Max, how could you think that?"

I just looked at him and his face turned as red as mine. "Never mind. I guess I can see why." He sighed and ran his hands through his hair. "The reason that I was avoiding you is because I..." He hesitated. "I didn't want to ask you to marry me in case you said yes because you felt sorry for me. Also, I was worried." He looked down. "I thought that maybe you liked Alex and were disappointed when it turned out that he wasn't the guy who you were really betrothed to."

"You thought that I liked *Alex*?"

"You seemed to. That night in the forest when he came--"

"I was *pretending* to be glad to see him. I thought that it would be better for both of us if I acted that way."

"You were pretending?"

"Of course! And it was one of the hardest things that I've ever done, to leave your side and go to his."

Connor put his hands on my shoulders. "I was afraid that you were upset with me for kissing you, and that you were relieved when he showed up."

I shook my head. "I was disappointed that he showed up."

"Do you want to know something?" He continued without waiting for an answer. "I've loved you since I first met you, when you were this wild, beautiful little girl, so full of life and happiness. I'd just left a world of misery and oppression and there you were, brilliant and shining, welcoming me into your world with so much kindness that I felt like I could never be away from you for too long or I was without my sun. And then, when we grew older, I came to see that my love for you was

326

deepening into something beyond the love of a child, into something that I had no right to feel. There I was, outcast from my kingdom, in hiding, always wearing a mask from the world and totally unsure about what my future would hold. I had no right to claim you. That's why I started to push you away. I was trying to save us both from what seemed like inevitable misery."

I reached up and shyly brushed his cheek with the back of my fingers. "In a strong relationship it takes two to make the decisions."

He grabbed my hand and pressed a kiss onto my palm. "You're right. But I didn't want to present you with choices that were so biased in Alex's favor that I wouldn't stand a chance. He came swooping in, looking so handsome and behaving so charmingly that I thought that maybe it would be better if I just stepped back and let him live the life meant for me."

"I hope you know better now," I said. "How could Alex ever compare with you?"

"Good point," Connor said. Then he kissed me.

It would be easy to end this story using the cheesy line that all princesses use when they finish telling their friends how they found their prince: "And we lived happily ever after." While I do believe in happily-ever-afters, I also believe that the story never really ends as long as there's somebody around to keep telling it.

Connor and I returned to Veiland to announce to my startled parents that he and I were engaged. We had to explain Alex's deception several times before they finally realized the full scope of Connor's story. It took my mother a little longer than my father to recover from years of snobbery towards

"Marge's little ward," but once she got over that she acted as though her disdain had never existed.

My father, although a little disappointed that war had been averted after all of his preparation, had to admit that things had worked out for the best. "I've been having twinges of arthritis," he admitted to me one evening after dinner. "I'm really not sure how well I would have done swinging a sword."

Ron and Cinderella married only a week after our return to Veiland. Unfortunately that did nothing to stop the constant influx of petitions from princesses, some of whom truly were damsels in distress. A solution for how to help these girls came from an unexpected source.

After we restored Alex to his human form, we learned more about his upbringing and came to realize why he believed and acted as he did. Although we were never able to convince him that people are, on the whole, fully capable of taking care of themselves, he did settle down to the point of not wanting an empire anymore. He even turned out to be a pretty decent guy.

One day as Ron was reviewing the princess letters, Alex joined him and started to read them. He got all fired up at the idea of wicked people out there kidnapping princesses and locking them into towers, so he recruited his brother and a few other young fellows and the next thing any of us knew, we had an official rescue squad set up. And because of Alex's no-nonsense, don't-waste-my-time attitude, the number of girls arranging to be falsely abducted dropped dramatically.

As for Aunt Regina, we all decided it would be best for everyone involved if she remained in her amphibian form. She currently lives in the fountains in the gardens at her husband's castle. Uncle Philip didn't seem too upset to learn that his wife had been turned into a frog. He seems to enjoy taking care of her and he keeps her well-stocked with plenty of juicy flies to eat. The last time I visited, she was one of the biggest, fattest frogs I had ever seen.

I never did find out where Marv got all of his strange machines, including the motorcycles. When a romance was revealed between Marge and himself, they began to travel to all sorts of mysterious, far-away kingdoms, and there was no end to the strange inventions and gadgets that they brought back.

Connor and I were married on the same day that he was crowned King of Treagal. He received his true name on that day, which was Conrad Raeborne Torstein the Third. I asked him what he wanted me to call him and he said, "Just Connor." So that's the name I use, but when he's being especially ornery, I call him Jack.

The End

Acknowledgements

I want to say a big thank you to all of the good people who helped make this book happen. First, thanks to my amazing parents. Mom, you always get my jokes, even the ones I make when I'm cranky but still intend for you to laugh. And by the way, Maxine's red hair is dedicated to you. Thank you, Dad, for being willing to read a book about a princess, and, bonus, for actually liking it. Jody, your work in editing, practical business advice and encouragement has been invaluable. Christie, what would I have done without your belief in me, where you were so into my book that you ended up printing a copy before it was even good enough to be printed? Katie, your words of encouragement were life-giving water to a thirsty woman in the desert. I think you may have read my book more than almost everyone and you didn't even get sick of it. Lissa and Emma, thanks for reading my book and offering editorial advice and support. Nicki, your willingness to answer my questions about the harrowing world of self-publishing has been greatly appreciated. Nathan, your patience with me in these last few weeks of ironing out the kinks and helping me with icky stuff like formatting and other boring technical stuff has been invaluable. You are wonderful!

A special thanks to my Grandma Hazel, after whom Maxine is partially named, for always encouraging me to read and write. I used to send some pretty quirky letters full of implausible stories to Grandma, and she never once questioned my sanity. …Or if she did, at least she never said anything. And finally, to all of the amazing people who have supported me and given me feedback, advice, encouragement, and helpful criticism.

In loving memory of my good friend, Ruth Slechta,
who pestered me about my book with ruthless determination until
I finally got off my duff and did what she said.

About the Author

While Jenni Archibald *can* whistle, no one freezes, which is fortunate because she tends to whistle often. She lives with her husband and children in Arizona, where the heat drives her indoors to write, eat chocolate and read amazing books. Please visit her website at www.jenniarchibald.com.